ALMOST PATHLESS

This Foreign Universe – Book 4

A Novel by
J.S. SHERWOOD

ALMOST PATHLESS
This Foreign Universe – Book 4
Copyright © 2023 J.S. Sherwood

All rights reserved. No part of this book may be used or reproduced in any manner whatsoever, without written permission, except in the case of brief quotations embedded in articles and reviews. For more information, please contact publisher at Publisher@EvolvedPub.com.

FIRST EDITION SOFTCOVER
ISBN: 1622537491
ISBN-13: 978-1-62253-749-5

Editor: Becky Stephens
Cover Artist: Cindy Fan
Interior Designer: Lane Diamond

www.EvolvedPub.com
Evolved Publishing LLC
Butler, Wisconsin, USA

Almost Pathless is a work of fiction. All names, characters, places, and incidents are the product of the author's imagination, or are used fictitiously. Any resemblance to actual events or persons, living or dead, is entirely coincidental.

Printed in Book Antiqua font.

BOOKS BY J.S. SHERWOOD

ARC ONE: THE BATTLES THEY FOUGHT
Book 1: *Foreign Land*
Book 2: *Foreign Planet*
Book 3: *Foreign Home*

ARC TWO: THE EARTH THEY LEFT BEHIND
Book 4: *Almost Pathless*
Book 5: *Almost Homeless*
Book 6: *Almost Earthless*

ARC THREE: THE SEEDS THEY PLANTED
Book 7: *The Engineer*
Book 8: *The Explorer*
Book 9: *The Sage*

DEDICATION

*For Meaghan,
my person across all dimensions.*

PART ONE

Chapter 1

It was early morning in Ireland, the dew on the grass turning to mist as the sun warmed the ground. Ailill sat on the porch of his great-grandmother's house in Carlingford, gazing at the majestic Slieve Foy mountain, its trees a vibrant deep green. In his many decades of life, he'd traveled the world and seen every natural wonder there was to see. But nothing had ever given him the peace he felt when in the town of his youth, looking upon the beauty that could only ever be associated with the word 'home.'

His mind swam back to a warm afternoon as a young man, walking hand in hand with the love his life. His name was Matrine, an American born man who'd moved to Ireland to finish his schooling. He always had a rugged, just-got-out-of-bed look that always made Ailill feel comfortable with being exactly who he was. With bare feet, they wandered through the lush, green grass talking of their future together. They would get married, adopt a child or two and travel the world as a family, teaching their children through true life experiences. That had been the day his life really started, Ailill thought. And with his precious Matrine, they'd done even more than they'd hoped.

His daughter Leona walked out of the house with two steaming cups of coffee, her red pixie cut hair matted on one side from a good night's sleep. She handed him a cup, sat down and leaned her head on his shoulder. He smiled. The doctors had said he only had two weeks left to live, and he was exactly where he wanted to be. After those two weeks, he'd be back with his husband in whatever afterlife waited for him.

"You look good, Dad," Leona said.

He laughed. "I raised a liar."

"I learn from the best."

He sipped the coffee and burned his tongue. "Damn coffee," he said, spitting onto the porch. "I'll be dead before that heals."

Leona sat up and glared at him. "Dad, how dare you talk about my coffee that way."

Both laughed and looked out at the mountain. *Yes*, he thought. *Exactly where I want to be.* As the rising sun hit at just the right angle, the trees burst in light and color. As if on cue, flocks of birds fluttered into the air, their chirping barely audible from that distance. A dozen shadows appeared over the trees, and Ailill looked up.

An altogether different flock flew high in the sky. Dozens of black, blocky planes floated in the sky. They looked more like houses than planes. Rectangles with pointed tops with four stubby wings and a thin, pointed tail.

"Leona...."

"I see them," she said.

"Is there another war on?"

Leona shrugged and shook her head. "These days there's always war, but I've never seen planes like that. And Ireland shouldn't be on anyone's target list, as far as I know."

"Which is little, for a small town mayor from Wyoming," Ailill said, his eyes still focused above.

"Truth," she said.

A handful of hoses dropped from the bottom of each plane, dangling and fluttering in the wind. They spewed out a glowing purple powder that fell heavily, unaffected by the wind. The powder touched the tallest of the trees, and a black plume popped out, the tops of the trees fading from green to brown to gray. The purple then settled on the green grass that spread out in front of his house. Each blade followed the same pattern as the trees. Green to brown to gray.

A minute later, the purple powder was gone.

"Chair, take me off the porch." Ailill's chair beeped, turned and slowly rolled down the ramp and onto the sidewalk, just next to his now gray lawn. "Dead." He looked up at the mountain, the gray slowly traveling farther and farther down the trees. "And dying."

Leona's hand touched his shoulder. "Let's go inside, Dad."

Ailill nodded. "Chair, inside," he said, keeping his eyes focused on the dying trees as the chair slowly rolled into the house.

Leona closed the door. She opened her mouth to speak, then closed it.

Ailill felt the same way. What was there to say? He told the chair to take him to his bed, where he lay down and never woke up.

Leona told her kids that the shock of losing his childhood mountain was too much for his fragile body to take. It was just as true as any other explanation would have been.

Chapter 2

With the wind of the Fourth blowing around him, Tashon looked down at the world and the people he would most likely never see again. The goodbyes had gone better than expected, and no one asked him to stay. They were surprised that he was leaving, chasing after a distant cry for help from a source he couldn't place. Tashon was surprised too, but despite how far away the source seemed, he knew he needed to follow. Even though it was a quiet, whispering cry for help, it sunk into his soul and wouldn't let go.

He turned in the direction of the sound. Somewhere beyond the tower where the twisting being had visited him was something that needed help. And, for reasons he didn't understand, he would follow its pleas. After one last look at Aethera, he took a step. Then another, and he soon made it to the bottom of the sinking, slippery slope that led to the tower. He was tired, but nowhere near as exhausted as the last time he made this journey. Perhaps it was because he'd made the same walk before, or because he had a specific direction to follow. What he hoped, though, was that his stamina for being in the Fourth had increased.

Of course he'd considered what such a long time in the Fourth might do to him. Wondered if he could even make it to his destination, wherever that might be. He adjusted the straps on his pack, reminding himself he brought along plenty of food and water. It was odd, though, to be carrying items of sustenance through the higher dimension. From everything he'd seen, the souls there needed no food or water to live.

Rosa had asked what he'd do if he ran out of food and water. He assured her, without assuring himself, that there were habitable planets along his path to which he could descend to gather food and water. For all anyone on Aethera knew, Tashon's journey followed a safe and direct path. Tashon knew it didn't, but he was content, wholly at peace with the unknown dangers that surely lay ahead.

He dropped to his hands and knees, and made his way up the hill slowly but with no problems. At the top, he leaned against the tower, staring at the city in the distance and focusing on the plea that was quickly becoming a part of him. It wasn't coming from the city, but somewhere beyond, an unknown location.

Something banged inside the tower. The surface Tashon leaned against opened and he fell into complete darkness. The surface he lay on was cold and hard. As he tried to push himself up, the ground tilted and he slid *up* for several minutes until he grew used to the motion he almost felt as if he were lying still. But the worst part was the darkness. The farther up he went, the denser the darkness grew, becoming a cold blanket of sheer discomfort.

Nothing made sense. Motion became stillness. Darkness became light. Cold became warmth. The ground became flat again, and he slammed to a stop, the sudden end to motion a shock and a relief. Yet the darkness remained, heavy enough to pin him to the ground. He lay on his side, arm bent uncomfortably beneath him, unable to move.

A presence entered. Not visible, for the darkness still shrouded all. But Tashon was aware of it nonetheless. It moved all around him, analyzing and judging him, pieces of its presence pushing into Tashon's mind, into his very soul. For what purpose? Tashon hadn't any idea.

But he did know he wasn't afraid. It didn't occur to him to be afraid, for if he died he would still be in the Fourth. Not as a strictly physical being, but he would still exist. And he didn't feel the presence had ill intentions. Even though it lurked in the dark and the cold, Tashon never felt the presence was evil. If anything, it was an objective observer. As his arm fell asleep, he closed his eyes and anxiously waited for the presence to finish the examination.

What else could he do?

Soon, the discomfort turned to pain and he opened his eyes. He could, he realized, try to pull himself to the Third to get out of the tower. *No*, he thought. *I'm above nothing but empty space. I'd die the same way Dad did.* For a moment, the thought brought back the guilt he'd felt for inadvertently causing his dad's death when he was a child.

He was a child again, walking the corridors of the Ship of Nations, walking into his living quarter with a bottle of beer in his hand. He felt the weight of the bottle, the coolness of the glass. Something flashed and the guilt from all those years ago tried to seep back into Tashon's mind and soul. But it had nothing to latch onto. No self-hatred, doubt or fear, and a moment later the guilt disappeared.

The presence paused and the darkness loosened its hold. The sense of the examining changed, softened, turning into an empathetic search for understanding. The weight lifted and the discomfort and pain disappeared. He rolled onto his back, stretched his arms out to the sides and drifted off as he let the presence come to understand his very essence.

Then he was standing outside the tower, blinking against the brightness of the fourth-dimensional sky, feeling refreshed and invigorated. He looked up at the tower, trying to catch a glimpse or a sense of the presence, but found neither. *It must've turned off*, Tashon thought. *Turned off?* Why had he thought of it that way? He could've told himself the presence had left or disappeared, but for some reason 'turned off' felt more accurate. If it were accurate, then the presence was actually a type of machine. Which, if true, meant it was created.

Tashon shook his head. Until that moment, he'd assumed everything in the Fourth simply *was*. He'd never considered that shapes and objects and places were made by someone, or something. But it made sense. Third-dimensional beings constantly created and built. Creating was an essential component of being sentient. Why wouldn't they continue it in their next phase of existence?

Excitedly, Tashon stepped away from the tower and started toward the city. For the entire walk he was lost in grand imaginings of everything he might learn and discover of the Fourth during his journey.

He arrived at the city in parts. First, a small sphere to one side, and then a short pile of cubes on the other. The closer he got, the more shapes he passed. His stomach rumbled. He pulled his pack off and sat down on a half sphere as he pulled out a food bar. With a sigh of both contentment and exhaustion, he bit into the pseudo meat and cheese flavor blend. He would have to sleep at some point. Which meant he would have to find somewhere safe to rest. Did hotels exist in the Fourth? Did beings of the Fourth need sleep, or was that only a limitation of third-dimensional beings?

The moths flew in front of him and landed on a thin cone to his left.

"My friends." He clasped the necklace around his neck. "Thank you for your gift. It saved me."

The moths fluttered their wings in response.

"What are you? Creatures or machines?"

More fluttering. Tashon finished his food, stuffed the wrapper in his bag and continued walking, the moths close behind. The structures became larger and more frequent. A few essences flew above and around him, in and out of the structures, but they seemed not to notice his presence. He didn't pause to attempt communication—he got the feeling they were focused on important tasks. But he did notice how these beings on the outskirts of the city were all as close to gray as seemed possible, each of them the embodiment of the middle ground, the state between black and white. If there was an explanation for this, Tashon couldn't figure it out.

Ahead, in the main part of the city, stark black and crisp white forms bustled around, along with nearly every shade between, save for the middle shade at the edges. *Outcasts?* Tashon wondered. *Or by choice?* He didn't necessarily need answers, but he wanted to know how life operated in the Fourth. Was there a culture or a government? Politics and different nations? Or were those merely realities of the Third, a lower form of living that didn't exist in a higher plane?

He stepped between two massive structures, one a rotating sphere, the other a turning cube. As soon as he did, beings of varying shades and origins descended and encircled him, forcing him to stop. Each looked directly at him with more than eyes alone, and he felt almost as exposed as he did in the tower. Again, he felt no fear. No concern for his safety or the successful end of his journey.

The darkest being floated forward, hovering inches above and in front of Tashon. It was a being of a species Tashon hadn't seen before. Rectangular, thin and exuding a sense of superior arrogance.

Tashon stood as tall as he could. "Hi. I'm following a cry for help. Can you hear it?"

The reply entered Tashon's mind. *"No sound but wind."*

"Maybe only I can hear it. But it is real, and I'm following it."

"Not your time."

"I'm still a three-dimensional being, yes. But I was... given the ability to travel between the lower and higher planes."

"You. Mountain told us of you."

"Mountain?" Then Tashon remembered the being that Rosa had called a god. "Right, Mountain."

Another being floated over, silvery-gray and something between the Fourth version of a sphere and a cone with dozens of thin appendages. *"Thought Mountain insane."*

"Can you go insane in the Fourth?"

"Mind and soul exist. Insanity exist."

Tashon nodded. "Am I allowed in the city?"

A shining being almost purely white and similar to a Crawler but with three legs and three arms joined the black and silvery beings. *"Allowed or not allowed doesn't exist. Not here. Exist. Act or don't act."*

"What about law?" Tashon asked.

"Law protects from harm. Harm cannot occur in the Fourth."

"Physical harm," Tashon said. "What of emotional? Spiritual?"

"Perhaps."

Perhaps? Tashon thought. "What do you mean?"

"You're free to exist and act as you wish," the bright one said.

"Be careful," said the silvery being. *"Physical harm can befall you still."*

The mass of beings spread out, though many remained, still entirely focused on the out of place being who was now among them.

With a newly realized sense of caution, Tashon entered the city.

Chapter 3

Dr. Cylindra Gaines laughed excitedly, her red hair bouncing as she ran through what was left of the Guinea Rain Forest, her muscular legs pumping with excited adrenaline. The jungle, once over thirty-five thousand square miles, was now barely over ten thousand. But she had won. After years of research, sleuthing and court battles, she and her team had returned the forest to its protected status that had idiotically been removed decades earlier.

She arrived at her favorite spot, a small pool of clear water fed by a thin stream. She knelt down and stuck her hands in the cool water, feeling the gentle movement of the water. *This place will remain unmolested*, she thought. *Whole and complete, for at least the next few decades.*

Continuing a ritual she'd started years before, she cupped her hands, lifted the water to her mouth and drank, making sure not to swallow yet. She slowly sloshed the water from cheek to cheek, savoring the purity of the water that could be found nowhere else in the world. With a smile, she swallowed and looked to the sky.

Sparkling, purplish dust rained down, landing on leaves, bark and vines. A single speck came to rest on a leaf inches away from her face. The leaf shriveled and died before her eyes. She turned and ran, fearing the powder would do to her what it was doing to the foliage all around her. She soon realized the powder did nothing to her. She was completely unharmed.

But still, she ran. The trees, leaves and vines she'd spent years fighting for were crumbling around her, and she needed to get out. The jungle had lost so much, was so much less than it once was and now Cylindra knew that what was left of it was dying and she couldn't bare to witness it.

Her legs ached, but she forced them to keep moving, keeping her focus solely on the ground in front of her feet. She would not accept the death of the jungle. Not on the day she was supposed to be celebrating its rescue. Her foot slammed onto a fallen branch, pushing it into the ground at an angle that snapped it in two.

Cylindra collapsed, tears streaming down her. She sent an urgent message using her watch. She was forced to sit and wait for help to arrive.

She let the tears fall freely as the unthinkable happened. A parrot perched atop a blackening branch. It silently broke off from bird's weight, and the animal squawked in surprise, flying off to find another branch. It landed, only to have it break off as well. It flew from breaking branch to breaking branch, increasingly frantic. It squawked louder and louder, finally landing on the ground a few feet from Cylindra.

"I'm sorry," she said, trying to hold back the tears. "I don't... this can't...." The tears pooled over and uncontrollable sobs burst from her.

Startled, the parrot flew away.

Everything she had fought for, her entire life's work, was dying before her eyes. The soft whir of an electric engine jerked her mind back to the immediate problem: her ankle. A sleek, triangular vehicle with large tires pulled up next to her and a door flung open, revealing four empty seats. She crawled over and climbed in. The door closed behind her.

"Hello, Cylindra," a robotic voice said. "Where are we going?"

"A doctor. Quickly."

The car sped away. "You have a message from your mother. Would you like to hear it?"

"Sure."

"It says: Hey, Cyl. Call me back. It's about Grandpa."

Cylindra closed her eyes and dropped her head back into the seat. "Damn it."

Chapter 4

The place Tashon had been thinking of as a city was, in reality, nothing so systematic and organized. It didn't even seem to serve any purpose other than a place for beings to gather together. From a distance, it had appeared to be a jumble of fourth-dimensional shapes and structures, some simply black or white, while others glowed more vibrant than anything in the Third. Up close, Tashon found it truly was a mess of structures with no apparent purpose or logical placement. But it was beautiful. Each shape was in constant motion, no two rotating in the same direct or at the same pace.

Tashon approached a shape of glowing colors and stared at it, unable to determine its three-dimensional counterpart. It was a mix of flat sides, concave edges and sharp angles. After a while, Tashon realized it must be multiple shapes put together to form... whatever it was. Something hissed from inside it as a concave edge toward the top split open. A thin, rope-like being floated out and met Tashon's gaze with a dozen black diamonds that popped from its sides.

"Is this your home?" Tashon asked.

The diamonds spun, but the being made no attempt to communicate. Somehow, the entire structure continued to spin except for the edge from which the being protruded. Another hiss, and Tashon realized the sound wasn't coming from the building or any outside source, but was coming from his mind. The being was trying to communicate. But it didn't know the right language, and it couldn't send feelings the way a Singer could.

A door in its 'house' opened, revealing a warm, glowing interior. The being was inviting him in, but Tashon was unsure. The being was a deep, dark gray. Not the black darkness of Aleron's monster or of the few that had attacked him in the Fourth, but Tashon sensed something sinister in its motives. Without speaking, he turned and walked away, the creature sending a painful hiss that vibrated his skull.

He continued into the maze of shapes, beings and wind, doing his best to follow the constant plea but unable to do so in a straight line. Something moved at the edge of his vision and he whipped his head around. Half a dozen beings of varying shades and species followed him, apparently keen on observing the anomaly that was his presence in the Fourth. None of them seemed malicious in any way, though he couldn't forget the fact that his physical body could be harmed regardless what dimension he wandered through. If one of them attacked, he'd have no chance to escape his fate. So why bog his mind down with fear?

"What is this place?" he asked.

Sounds rushed into his mind in response, but none in a language he could understand. It seemed he got lucky with the few that greeted him at the outskirts. But he felt it wasn't a city, not in the way the word usually meant, at least. A city was a place with stores and homes and restaurants, all types of buildings to meet the physical needs and wants of the three-dimensional body. What, then, was the purpose of the maze of shapes? Was it natural to the Fourth, or built by someone? Or something?

He could spend his entire life looking for answers, but what then of the cry for help he journeyed to relieve? He'd settle on learning what he could while still moving forward. One of the beings sent more sounds to his mind. Tashon shook his head and shrugged, wondering if the being would even understand what those motions meant.

"Keep following if you want," he said. "Don't know where I'm going."

The next hours were spent wandering the maze of structures and staring at wonderfully unknowable structures of colors beyond that of the Third. More than once he walked into a dead end and had to turn around. His group of followers slowly grew into a crowd. His pace waned and his legs ached, and he found a nook to settle into for a rest. But he wasn't sure if he should close his eyes. His audience remained, as if waiting for him to perform some three-dimensional trick.

"If I sleep, will I be safe?"

More unintelligible sounds, but none moved closer or seemed aggressive. Tashon reasoned that if any wanted to harm him, they already would have. The beings formed a wall in front of Tashon's cranny and turned their backs to him.

What was it they saw in him? He closed his eyes and pulled himself into a meditative state, knowing that was the only way he'd be able to sleep. His thoughts calmed, his heart rate slowed. Everything faded except for the call for help, louder now that all else was washed from his mind. He fell asleep thinking about what heroic acts he might perform to save it.

His mind flashed in and out of dreams. He walked along a flat, empty world of stone. He sank into an ocean of black water. He swam through the gray, thundering clouds of a world covered in forests of blue. He danced with a seven-legged animal, its face covered by a mask of liquid. A fire burned white hot, screams radiating from deep within its swirling flames. Six birds flew in a green sky, lightning struck from white clouds, striking one on the wing. He became the injured bird, fearfully flapping his functioning wing as it plummeted to the ground.

Tashon opened his eyes. His audience was gone. No beings were in sight. Alone, he stood up and slowly stepped out of his crevice of safety. Nothing around save the maze of twisting structures. Tashon felt a flash of abandonment, but did his best to push it aside. He couldn't help but think of Rosa, and how she was with him as often as possible, both to learn from him and watch out for him.

He continued on in the same direction, trying not to settle on the realization that his journey in the Fourth was going to be a lonely one. Instead, he focused on the ever complex and dizzying structures that surrounded him. Eventually, he ended up on a lone path, finding no forks or turns for what felt like hours, but his sense of time was nearly gone. For all he knew, he could've been asleep for a minute or a year, and had been walking for an hour or twelve.

The towering shapes that lined his lone path did nothing to block out the light, and he wasn't sure if that comforted him or not. He'd grown so accustomed to, and content with, the opposites that made life in the Third, life in the Third. If he spent long enough with no darkness, would he forget what it meant to be in the light?

Yet the fact that he was still on that single path gave him a sense of hope. It felt like it was leading him somewhere. Perhaps out of the maze of shapes, to a place where the sound he followed was louder and clearer. The path opened up and he walked into a vast space filled with dozens upon dozens of different paths to choose from. Thousands of beings thronged the air and the paths.

The paths went in every conceivable direction, at every possible angle. Some curved quickly out sight. Others ascended at steep, smooth inclines or descended in shallow stairs. Each was lined by paper-thin walls, and none were marked as far as Tashon could tell. He shook his head, then scanned the mass of beings. If he was lucky, he could find the soul of a human. But in the mashup of light and dark, dull and bright, small and large, it was impossible to distinguish one form from another.

He walked as near to the center as he could get. "Any of you human?" he called.

Some looked in his direction. Most ignored him or possibly didn't hear him.

"You're not dead."

Tashon spun in a quick circle, but couldn't find the source of the words. "Where are you?"

Movement to his left, and there was a small being that was definitely human. *And,* Tashon thought, *a child.*

"You're not dead."

The child essence stopped in front of Tashon, its head level with his but its feet hanging just past his waist.

"You're not dead either," Tashon said. "Not really."

"You know my meaning."

Tashon nodded. "I do. What's your name?"

"Ishlea."

"What planet are you from, Ishlea?"

"Planet? Never saw one."

"The Ship of Nations?"

"Born. Died at seven."

Tashon didn't remember a child ever dying on the Ship of Nations. That seemed like something that would've made a big wave throughout the ship's community. Maybe Ishlea was suffering from insanity? Or Tashon might have forgotten. But the answer wouldn't impact his decisions moving forward, so he decided not to question it.

"Why are you in the Fourth?"

"I'm following a... sound. A voice asking for help."

"I don't hear anything."

"So far, I'm the only one who does."

"Are you sure it's real?"

Tashon focused in on the sound. Still quiet, yet urgent. "As sure as I can be."

"Which road do you need to take?"

Tashon shrugged and scanned the paths again, trying to determine the direction of the voice he heard as he did so. "I don't know yet."

The small human essence floated off without another word. The being had considered if Tashon were insane, and Tashon had done the same of the being. *Am I insane?* Tashon wondered. He didn't think so. Though he was aware of what he was doing, and how insane it must look to everyone else. He walked slowly in the direction of the sound and stopped in front of three paths to choose from. Straight ahead and on top a ledge lay a path that disappeared quickly in a sharp curve to the right. Up and to the left rose a set of stairs that ascended steeply out of sight. Below and to the right of the first, a smooth, steep decline that led into a hole of darkness. Of the countless roads that lay around him, he was confident one of the three would bring him closer to the end of his journey.

As he clambered onto the ledge in front of him, he felt the essences flying about turn and look. Pretending not to notice, he stuck his head into the opening and listened. The sound was quieter, though still there. He jumped down and re-examined the remaining two options. A long row of beings went into the path leading down. Then three others came down the steps and into the curving path. Before the last of the trio disappeared, it turned and shrieked something into Tashon's mind. His heart jumped and adrenaline pulsed through his veins, but nothing more happened.

Tashon turned and met the gaze of all those who watched him, wondering for a moment why some seemed so intent on his actions while others seemed oblivious to his existence.

"Does anyone else hear that cry for help?"

No answers.

Tashon nodded, turned back and started up the stairs.

Chapter 5

Avet Gaines sat at a bar in Cody, Wyoming sipping on a beer as he watched the morning news on the screen that hovered above the top shelf booze. He kept catching glimpses of his scarred face and shaggy hair in the mirror, no matter how much he hated looking at himself. To both sides of him sat other men and women, all just off their night shifts at the electrical factory. Soon, he'd walk into the bright sun, stumble home and try to find sleep before doing it all over again. If he ever left. The world outside was only getting worse, and sitting there with bottle after bottle didn't seem like the worst idea.

A new spokesperson appeared on the screen. "It's no secret that the first of these bio attacks occurred exactly twenty years after Humans for Humanity, the biggest charitable organization on Earth at that time, sent their Ship of Nations to the stars," the man said. "After which, H for H completely disappeared."

"They abandoned the rest of us," Clawman, the bartender, said, scratching his muscled chest, then his protruding gut.

"...believe that was a day of change on the Earth," the spokesman said. "H for H took who they thought were worthy, and then left the rest of us. Many have asked, if they were the best, what's that make the rest of us? Things changed after they disappeared, and to many, life here has been on a steady decline. And with this attack on the anniversary of their disappearance, the question being asked is are these attacks by Humans for Humanity, returning to get rid of those of us they considered less than the best?"

The bar erupted with shouts of both agreement and disgust.

"No arguing in my bar." The bartender turned the screen off. "Do that at your own tables."

A balding man stood up drunkenly. "But no sane person can believe that conspiracy theory shit."

"You callin' me crazy?" a man with long, curly hair said, standing up, puffing out his chest.

"Avet?" the bartender said.

"You got it, Clawman." Avet stood, walked to the two men and backhanded each across the face. "Take your shit somewhere else."

Both men looked at Avet, as if considering if they should take their fear and anger out on him. But Avet knew they wouldn't. No one would dare pick a fight with him. The last person who had ended up in the hospital for over a month. The two men left the bar without another word.

Avet sat back down.

"Like back in the war," Clawman said.

"Me taking care of your shit?" Avet smiled. "Sounds right, Clawman."

The bartender laughed and handed Avet another bottle. "On me."

"Thanks." Avet slapped a bill on the counter. "But I know you can't afford it."

Clawman laughed again and stuffed the money in his pocket.

Chapter 6

    Tashon neared another peak of the staircase. The last ten had proven to be false tops, leading flatly to another ascent. Or, with two of them, ending in a steep descent only to ascend again hundreds of steps later. He reached what he hoped was the top, but found that the stairs continued on. They went down a few steps, then rotated sideways to the left, forming a stepped corkscrew. He paused briefly, examining it. Nothing about it seemed insecure or faulty. Though, given its extra dimension, Tashon had no way of understanding exactly how it was constructed. *It had to have been constructed somehow*, Tashon thought. *Who built it, and how?* Beings of the Fourth weren't physical, so how could they build such structures? Or, Tashon realized, they *could* be natural, somehow. Even though that idea seemed impossible.

    Tashon lifted his left foot and placed it on the first angled step and gravity shifted, pulling him down and to the left. He quickly put his right foot on the step. Gravity felt natural again. With each step, the angle from which gravity pulled on him changed, and to keep from falling, he fell into a hopping jog, a man skipping as he twirled farther and farther along a multidimensional staircase. The sudden and constant changes of gravity should have left him dizzy and nauseous, but Tashon felt no ill effects. He reasoned it was because a part of his mind was of the Fourth. But even so, the physical exhaustion took its toll and he had to force himself to keep up his pace. Sweat dripped down his face, his legs burned and his heart pounded. His foot slipped, and he recovered just in time to avoid crumpling to the floor.

    Ahead, something other than stairs appeared. The simple change in scenery gave him a moral boost that pushed him to reach the end of the spiral without falling. He stepped off the last stair as gracefully as possible and sat on a flat surface, staring at a small tesseract perched on one of its points, leaning to one side. Just beyond it, the ground disappeared.

    Tashon walked past the leaning structure, and, standing at the edge, looked down. A pit with no bottom, a hole directly into the empty space of the Third. As if something had pushed from one dimension to the other. Something massive. He looked across, but couldn't see the other side.

"A dead end."

A dead end for him, at least. Could fourth-dimensional beings float across the chasm? Or would the break between dimensions somehow prevent it? To his left and right, the edge of the cliff gradually curved forward. Perhaps Tashon could follow it around and eventually get to the other side.

He sat down and closed his eyes. He'd been sure this was the right way, but now he questioned that certainty. With a sigh, he focused in on the cry, now coming from above and in front of his position. He calmed his mind and his breaths, a habit he barely had to think about anymore. Then he became completely aware of the tesseract behind him. It suddenly seemed more than what it had originally appeared. Remaining in his meditative state, he walked back to the fourth-dimensional cube.

One side glowed a warm color Tashon had never before seen. It called to him, and without words, told him that it was the way, that no matter where he wanted to go, it would take him where he needed to be.

"It's never done that before."

Tashon looked behind him. Ishlea floated near the edge of the hole, a sense of worry mingling with the glow of her essence.

"Never?"

"We've all tried to understand this place. The hole into the lower plane. Nothing like it anywhere else that we know of."

Tashon pointed at the glowing cube. "What about this?"

"Always been here. Still and dark. This is new."

Tashon nodded, turned back and reached out to the inviting glow. The side went from opaque to translucent, revealing a multi-angled interior of various colors, all exclusive to the Fourth. Again, it reached out to him, giving gentle assurances that following it was the right choice. Tashon stepped in, and Ishlea followed. The cube spun in a circle, slamming Tashon into a sitting position. The opening remained as it spun around and around, giving Tashon a dizzying view of the outside. Colors swirled by, followed by shapes and places Tashon had never seen before, though Tashon hadn't felt their vessel carry them to another place.

The opening closed, and the spinning stopped.

"You're sure this hasn't happened before?"

"Never that I've heard."

"What is it?" Tashon ran a hand along an angled surface. "It's warm. Softer than I thought. Is it a machine? Or alive?"

"Everything's alive in the Fourth."

The shape, or being, opened up again before Tashon could ask what Ishlea meant. Wind whipped around him as he stepped out to find that they were indeed somewhere new. They were at the bottom of a tall, narrow rectangular hole. Ishlea emerged from the vessel. It flashed, spun and vanished. Tashon turned in a circle, the wind that surrounded them rushing in from small holes in the walls. Every strand and color of wind traveling from one hole to another, twisting and twirling.

Tashon nodded and looked up, to the direction of the plea. The wall rose straight up, but the holes could be used for climbing. If the wind rushing out didn't knock him off.

"You still hear it." The words entered Tashon's mind as a statement.

"Yes. Coming from up there. Ishlea, could you fly to the top? See what's up there?"

Ishlea flew upward. The wind blew harder out of the holes, slamming her into the wall. The holes above her pushed more wind out and down, forcing her back to the bottom.

"I'm sorry."

"It's okay, Ishlea. I think I can climb up." He looked up, then back at his companion. "Can you climb? Can you touch the wall, the holes?"

Ishlea moved to the wall and reached out her multifaceted, fourth-dimensional appendages. Awkwardly, she began the ascent. Once Tashon was sure the wind wouldn't increase its force, he followed.

It was slow going. Each hole was a different size, and there was no way to tell how strong or warm or cold or hot the wind was without first putting a hand in its path. Tashon spent the first few minutes of the climb trying to decipher a pattern, hoping to discover that each colorful wisp of air had its own attribute. When that proved inaccurate, he tried counting every hole to see if every third one was hot, every fifth one more forceful. But no such logic was at play, and he was surprised he expected it to have a pattern.

Little else made sense since he started his journey, so why should this be any different?

Hand over hand, foot over foot. Inch by inch, foot by foot and yard by yard. Tashon's muscles ached and throbbed, but he had no choice but to keep moving. That, or fall and die at the bottom. The thought reminded him of that night alone on top of the ship, when he almost jumped and ended his life. That memory gave him more motivation to keep moving.

He may have wanted to die then, but not anymore. His newfound determination increased morale, and lent more strength to his physical body.

"*I loved rock climbing on Earth.*"

Tashon glanced at Ishlea. "You said you were never on a planet."

"*I climbed everything I could. El Capitan. The Dolomites. The Matterhorn, in Switzerland. Before it was destroyed, of course. But Colorado was my favorite. Garden of the Gods, they called it. First place I learned to climb.*"

None of the places were familiar to Tashon. He'd studied Earth history on the Ship of Nations, but what Ishlea talked about didn't seem significant on a grand scale. Or in any way reliable.

Ishlea went on. "*I once got stuck on top of a rock they called Montezuma's Tower. My rope got stuck between two thin sections of rock. Tried to get it out for hours. Didn't have enough slack to get down. Started raining on me. And....*"

Ishlea's flow of words into Tashon's mind ceased. If she had only lived on the ship, how did she have so many details of Earth? Were those details accurate, or made up? Or perhaps she never lived on the ship.

"*I fell off,*" Ishlea said. "*That's how I died. I'd forgotten that.*"

Tashon paused and let go with one hand at a time, shaking his arms out. He wiped sweat from his eyes and looked up. The top wasn't far away. "Hope it's not a false top." He paused. "You lived on Earth, Ishlea?"

"*Of course. I hiked and climbed all around Earth. How could I have done that if I didn't live there?*"

Tashon shook his head. The point wasn't worth arguing. Either she'd lived and died on Earth or on the Ship of Nations. The answer didn't impact him. He just hoped the fact that she couldn't keep it straight didn't indicate a more serious problem.

Once at the top, Tashon dragged himself over the edge and rolled onto his back, heart pounding and face soaked in sweat. Ishlea hovered nearby, showing no signs that the climb tired her. Tashon rolled to his hands and knees and crawled to the edge of the hole. He couldn't see the bottom. Just four endless, descending walls enclosing thousands of strands of billowing wind. Tashon laughed and shook his head. He shouldn't have made it. There was no way he could've made that climb, but he did. He rubbed his necklace between his fingers, wondering if it had given him the extra strength and endurance. Or if he was stronger than he gave himself credit for. *Most people are*, he thought.

With a smile and a contented sigh, he stood and turned around. Stretching out before him was a vast field of pure light and color. The ground undulated up and down with small, gentle hills. Thin, needle-like shapes stretched high into the air, waving in the wind. No two of them were exactly the same color, and some were multiple colors all at once. Wandering gracefully about were beings that Tashon hadn't yet seen in the Fourth. And it wasn't just their anatomy that was new. Something about them *felt* different. All of them flowed a calm, peaceful light, not one casting an aura of fear or darkness.

Tashon walked slowly forward, eyes focused on the dozens of new and unique beings. One caught his eye that seemed familiar. He moved closer, and his mind connected its fourth-dimensional form with what it had looked like in the Third. It was the essence of a bush creature from Aethera.

"Animal essences," Tashon said. "Animals in the Fourth."

Ishlea walked to one that in the Third, Tashon thought would've had six legs and four wings. A creature he'd read about in fictional books from Earth, and seeing that it actually existed was somehow one of the most surprising things Tashon had seen in the Fourth.

"Those were on the first colony," Ishlea said. *"We tried taking them to ride, but it never worked."*

"The first planet colony? You were there?"

"Of course. That's why I fought to get a spot on the ship. All I wanted was to see another planet."

Tashon nodded as they continued to walk. He spotted another bush creature, this one laying with a sonic bird, the kind that had killed Ballas. In the Fourth, without its survival instincts, the beast was not a beast. Tashon smiled.

Ahead, a small, tree-like structure appeared. Floating above it was a being of such strange anatomy that Tashon could scarcely comprehend it. It exuded a powerful, welcoming aura that made him feel at home. The being beckoned to Tashon and Ishlea, and they excitedly answered by moving quickly to join it.

"Welcome," the being said. *"Come, see and listen. For I have much to tell and give to those who have found and endured the path to this place above all other places."*

Tashon almost asked how he knew there were no other places above it, but decided to hold off. Perhaps the being was speaking in metaphor. And even if it weren't, it still said it had much to tell. Tashon hoped it would be answers to at least some of his questions about the Fourth.

"What names do my new guests bear?"

"Ishlea."

"Tashon."

"Welcome, Tashon and Ishlea. Tashon, what brings one so lowly, yet great, to this wonderful place?"

"What do you mean?"

"Excuse me. Lowly, because you are still one of a lower plane of existence. Yet great because, somehow, you can exist as a lower being in a higher plane."

Tashon nodded. "Right, okay."

"Why have you come?"

"Why ask me and not Ishlea?"

"It seems Ishlea is following you."

"I am," Ishlea said. "And he's following a sound."

"A sound, Tashon?"

"A plea, a cry for help."

"Something calls to you for help from across the grand cosmos?"

"No, not me. It's a plea for anyone, anything to give aid."

"You know not who or what is seeking aid?"

"No."

"How far in your journey are you, lesser-higher Tashon?"

Tashon thought for a moment, then focused on how far the sound felt. "Just beginning."

"There are many things that would be prudent for you to understand about this higher plane before you continue your journey."

"Yes."

"I will teach you."

Chapter 7

Bennet Gaines stood outside, staring at his childhood home in Cowley, Wyoming, looking at everything that should've been there but wasn't. And the fact that there was no sign of the poison that fell from the skies. Not a speck on a sidewalk, street or rooftop. Not in the entire world, as far as he knew. It'd dropped, killed and then disappeared. A warm breeze blew through his shoulder length black hair.

"The tree and swing that once were here, are now gone," he said. "Not out of necessity or desire, but out of venomous destruction." He walked across the dirt yard. "The lawn, pristine in summertime for bare feet and games of tag, vanished, and I fear it will never return." He stopped at the front door, the yellow paint faded. If he had time before his mom returned from his father's funeral in Ireland, he'd repaint it. But first he'd dust and clean the inside, just as he'd told her he would.

He tapped his watch against the handle, and the door unlocked and swung open. Lights flashed on as he stepped inside. A familiar virtual voice welcomed him by name and asked if he'd like a drink.

"Room temperature water, my virtual friend," he said as he walked to the nearest window and threw open the curtains. Natural light joined artificial as Bennet looked around. A thin layer of dust covered the leather couch and faux wood floors. "Some dust and grime. I'll give it a spit shine." He laughed to himself.

"Bennet, your water is ready in the pantry."

He walked into the kitchen, a small rectangle with a single-burner stove and concrete counters. The pantry door was a solid wood block that slid up at his command. In a square, metal cubby sat a glass of room temperature water. He took a long guzzle and set it on the counter.

"Thank you, my virtual friend."

He turned back to the pantry and pulled out a small, plastic backpack with a tube attached to it. With the press of a finger, the machine hummed and he held the tube's end over the floor. Sensors surrounding it would determine the type of floor and the amount of debris, adjusting the suction accordingly. If they sensed something more difficult to remove, the machine would beep to let the user know to pause while the machine let out bursts of steam until the spot was loose enough to be sucked into the tube.

"Not the automated, cleaning homes we were promised," Bennet said. "But I suppose advancements never happen as fast as fiction would make us believe."

As he fell into the comforting rhythm of cleaning, he decided to take the time to try to come to grips with what the world had come to. As always, he did this by talking to himself.

"They came from nowhere and dropped their poison to... what purpose? Whoever did it, to what end? It is an act of war... or so it seems. But of course it is, that's a strange thought to have. What would it be, if not an act of war? They took out nearly all of our vegetation, which will truly hurt us. It will hit the economy hard. But it also would've been a far more effective tactic a century ago."

The machine beeped and Bennet stood still as it cleaned what looked like a few spilled drops of cola.

"We have vitamins and artificial fruits and vegetables that will take care of all dietary needs... now I sound like an advertisement." He laughed. The machine beeped, and he moved on to the couch. "They obviously wanted to harm us, and Ireland, and all the other nations on which they dumped their poison. Yet no people were actually hurt. Not directly. The loss of the Earth's natural beauty is devastating, without question. Especially for Cylindra. That's right, she'll get here before Mom."

He finished the couch, quickly cleaned the hall, then made his way into his childhood room. The two twin beds where he and Avet had slept were still there, along with all of The Almost Homeless tour pictures. Their grandpa had been the front man for the popular folk band. The one who'd instilled a love of music in the entire family, and a love of words in Bennet. Though Bennet never felt he was as good with words as his grandpa had been. Or as his mother was.

Bennet quickly cleaned the room, then moved on to the rest of the house.

"It just doesn't make any logical sense," he said. "I'm glad that the attacks didn't actually hurt anyone. But what then was the point? It wasn't an act of goodwill, but it wasn't an act of outright violence."

He finished cleaning in silence. When he placed the machine back in the pantry, the answer splashed into his mind. "There will be more attacks. Different than this one."

He shook his head, walked outside and sat in the dirt. With his finger, he began to write. No matter how great he thought the words were, he never put his lyrical writing on anything permanent. Because, in truth, he never thought any of it was good enough to keep around. But he enjoyed it, nonetheless.

***

I write these words in the earth of a dying Earth.
With the next strong wind or rain, they will disappear.
But that, know that I do not fear.
What fills me with despair, with dread
Is that this very Earth may soon be dead.
It matters not to me if my words are forgotten.
(Maybe that's a lie, if I'm being honest.)
The idea that stops my heart yet runs it faster is this:
Earth and humanity die, their existence less than a whisper
On the lips of whatever life remains out in the universe.
As if none of this ever existed at all.
Earth a pointless planet, humanity a meaningless species.
Those are the fears worth losing sleep over.

***

He stood up and read the words through three times, then wiped them away with a few swipes of his shoe.

Chapter 8

"In what direction is the plea you follow?"

Tashon sat on the ground next to the the treehouse, as he now thought of it. He pointed up and to the left. "What's your name?" he asked the being.

"Name... I have had no need of a name in eons. Names are to differentiate one from another. I have been so long sequestered with just these creatures. Yet now... for convenience, refer to me as Circa. Tashon, you are certain that is the way you must journey?"

"It is," Tashon said.

"That is essentially up, left and ana, then."

"Ana?"

"More directions in this higher plane need names. That is what your language uses in their sciences to describe it in your lower plane. Ana and kata."

Tashon thought for a moment. "Okay, yeah. I kind of remember hearing that. So we have up and down, left and right, forward and backward, ana and kata."

"Yes, Tashon. It is surprising you did not already know those terms. How have you been mentally processing this plane?"

Tashon shrugged. "As best I can with my three-dimensional mind. It seems... that sometimes my mind and eyes gloss over that extra direction if I'm not focused on it."

"You'll need to be careful. In your lower plane, would it not prove disastrous if you suddenly forgot about forward and backward, or left and right?"

"It could. I'll be careful, Circa."

"Good. We will return to our previous topic. Ishlea, do you know anything of what waits on the course your friend intends to follow?"

"No, Circa."

"Tashon, you are a physical being. Have you anything with which to draw?"

Rosa had sent him off with a small stack of yellow leaf papers and a few writing utensils. He pulled them out of his bag. "What for?"

"You'll want to map it out, Tashon. The paths to follow, the paths to avoid.

Dangers and successes lie ahead for you. And to fully understand them all, you'll need to understand the histories of them all."

Tashon wondered how long the something he was chasing had before any form of help would prove ineffective. But if he charged blindly forward, he wouldn't make it at all. "Okay," he said.

"Are you aware how far your journey will take you?"

Tashon shook his head. "No."

"I'll explain all I can. The higher plane seems infinite, though none can say for certain. Perhaps I'll tell far more than you need, perhaps far less. First, you'll come to a field of floating holes. Openings in the air, going upward at various angles."

"Tunnels?" Tashon asked.

"No, Tashon. Holes is the proper term."

"Do they lead anywhere?"

"Most of them do not. But you will need to find one that does, for an impassable wall lies beyond the holes."

"You said you never saw the end of the Fourth."

"It's nothing more than a massive wall that prevents any from moving forward. There are still three other directional lines in which to move."

Tashon nodded.

"The holes are holes and not tunnels because they aren't pathways that lead from one place to another, not like the stairs you walked or wall you climbed to find me. They are holes between two places. Step through a hole by the wall, and you step into another place entirely. Some holes disappear on the other side, some do not. Some lead, for beings of a higher plane, to places thick with fear. For you, Tashon, I am certain those places would prove distinctly dangerous. The edges alone are visible. You will not be able to see what is on the other side until you step through the hole."

"That's why you want me to map them out," Tashon said.

"Here is a fact I have refrained from sharing, and it will make mapping difficult. The holes move, blown around their field by the beautiful winds of this higher plane."

Circa continued explaining the size and shape of each hole in explicit detail, along with what Tashon would find on the other side of each. The more Circa pontificated, the more Tashon realized the being's intentions were not to help Tashon, but to prove superiority. Circa wanted an audience. Tashon had been so excited to learn more of the Fourth the he hadn't even considered Circa's intentions. But now that he did, anxiety filled him. Was he certain he had enough time before the plea for help went silent?

And then he realized he didn't need Circa's help. "Wait," he said.

"*Do you need to rest before we continue?*"

"No, I can find my way on my own. Thank you, Circa. But I don't have time to sit and listen."

"*Tashon of a lower plane can find his way through this higher place?*"

"I'll follow the cry. I'll find what hole it's coming from, and follow it. The one it comes from won't be a dead end."

"*What if it leads you to dangers beyond your capability to face?*"

"I'm going to do everything I can to answer the cry for help." Tashon stood, threw his pack on and looked away. "I don't have time."

Circa's words echoed into Tashon's mind. "*You could learn the secrets of this place from me.*"

Tashon didn't respond. He knew of the wisdom that could be gained from sitting, discussing and contemplating. But there were times when one simply needed to act. Ishlea followed as he left the monologuing Circa behind.

***

There was nothing in sight. Not Circa nor his house behind them, nor any sign of holes blowing in the wind in front of them. Left and right, ana and kata were just as empty. Circa had never mentioned how far the holes were, but it occurred to Tashon that measuring distance for a Fourth being would be far different than measuring it for one of the Third. He still had to walk.

"*I think Circa thinks he's a god,*" Ishlea said.

Tashon huffed a laugh. "Mountain is more of a god than Circa."

"*Mountain is amazing, but he's not a god.*"

"I was hurt on his mountain form. Then he changed form and healed. What else would he be?"

"*In three dimensions, his species could shape-shift. A survival mechanism developed over centuries. The healing... some beings are able to do that after being in the Fourth for long enough.*"

"Progression," Tashon said.

"*Progression. We are not in a final state of complete joy or absolute misery after death, as I was taught when I was young.*"

"On Earth?"

"*Yes. As an orphan raised in a classical Catholic school. Heaven or hell, no in between. This life is the only chance to prove our goodness. Our value. Hell terrified me. The idea that my life here could lead to an eternity of misery. I tried to use that fear to be perfect. I screwed up, like everyone does. Got slapped on the wrist, sometimes worse. One time I slapped a nun after she whooped me. Almost got kicked out on the streets. And, eventually, I believed I was destined for hell. Once that belief settled in...."*

Ishlea's essence darkened and her aura twisted, expanding outward. It pushed like a physical presence, emanating a cold pressure that pushed into Tashon. Rage, anguish and fear pulsated from her form and filled Tashon. He stepped back, weeping with guilt and shaking with anger. The tears fell heavy down his cheeks, blurring his vision so all he could see was Ishlea's form, vibrating between dark and light, calm and chaotic.

"Ish... Ishlea." He forced the words out as he dropped to his knees, then all was still and silent.

Ishlea was as Tashon had always known her to be.

"What happened?"

Tashon took a deep breath. *Should I tell her?* He decided not to. *So far, she's done no real damage.* "You were telling me about your life on Earth, at the orphanage."

"I... was never on Earth."

"Right... you said you were born and died on the Ship of Nations, right?"

"No. I died on the first colony."

The words came forcefully into Tashon's mind, and he knew it would do no good to ask more questions. He looked down at the Third, still nothing but a sea of black. Nothing for him to go down to it he needed to get out of the Fourth. Or wanted to, as he did in that moment. All he wanted was to be with others of his own dimension, whose anatomy was easily discernible, whose logic was similar to his own. Really, he wanted to sit with Rosa. Ask her what she thought of Ishlea, if he had made the right choice walking away from Circa. *No*, he thought. *Staying or leaving wasn't right versus wrong. Neither choice was evil. I just did what I thought best.* He nodded and stood up.

"Why did you choose to follow me?" Tashon asked as he resumed walking.

For a few minutes Ishlea didn't respond. Tashon thought that, maybe, she couldn't remember the reason herself. Which one was she, when she'd made that choice? The one who had died on the ship, or the Catholic school orphan? Or the rock climber, maybe the one who made it to the first colony? Or one Tashon hadn't even talked to yet.

"I'm not sure why." Her sudden words in his mind made Tashon jump, and she laughed. A pure and innocent giggle. *"I'm sorry. I followed*

because... I wanted to see where you were going. You were – you are – so convinced this call for help is real. A call no other has heard. You're going to answer it, no matter what. That's the type of faith most Catholics only pretended to have."

"You followed because I have blind faith in my goal?" Tashon smiled.

Ishlea laughed. *"Maybe. But I see it in your eyes. You hear, or believe you do. Strongly. I've seen so few with that form a conviction in anything, that I couldn't help but follow."*

Tashon nodded, and left it at that. The words seemed wise and observant, and Tashon had to wonder yet again: was this an Ishlea he'd talked to before, or another version?

Chapter 9

Bennet held his mom's hand with a firm, loving grip. His sister sat on his other side, head on his shoulder. Avet, thin and brooding, paced back and forth behind the couch. They all stared at the projection on the wall, still trying to make sense of the world.

The woman on the screen told of how the unmarked planes had flown over every nation on Earth, dropped their poison, and then disappeared. "No nation or group has taken credit for the attacks," she said. "And exactly twenty-five percent of every nation's greenery was left untouched. There's no way to determine who the culprits might be. Now, to share his thoughts on the subject, we—"

Leona turned the TV off.

Avet stopped pacing. "Mom, the hell?"

"Language," she said. "They don't know anything more than we do."

Cylindra wiped her eyes. "*Why*? Why would anyone do it?"

Avet mumbled profanities under his breath.

"I haven't any idea," Bennet said. "And the question I keep coming to is this: what do we do now?"

"Do they even *understand* what they've done? Entire species are going to be extinct within *weeks*."

"The economy's going to die," Avet said.

Cylindra pulled at her hair. "And then it's going to get worse from there. Higher up the food chain, dying and dying until the Earth herself is dead."

"Itself," Avet said.

Cylindra screamed and threw a pillow at Avet. He caught it, laughing, and threw it back.

"Damn it. Please stop," Bennet calmly told his brother.

Cylindra slumped off the couch and onto the floor, quietly weeping. Bennet sat down next to her and pulled her into him.

Leona stood up. "Grab us some drinks."

Avet threw his hand in the air. "No comment on his language?"

"You deserved it."

Bennet smiled. "That you did, brother."

"You've always been her favorite."

"No, Cylindra's the favorite."

Avet dropped onto the couch. "That's true. And she deserves it." He rubbed her hair. "Sorry, Cyl."

"It's all right," she said. "None of us are okay right now."

Avet nodded. "Truth."

Bennet nodded but said nothing. He was far from all right, but it'd been far too long since the four of them had been together. He hated that it took their grandpa's death and the largest biological attack in history, but at least they were together.

Mom walked out of the kitchen. "Outta drinks. Head to Cub's Den?"

The three siblings jumped to their feet, and the family walked out the front door.

"It's depressing walking through town," Cylindra said.

"It's a sh — poop show," Avet said.

"The entire world is," Bennet said. "Our home is dying."

"Is anyone going to do anything about it?" Abet asked.

"Avet, you were in the Army. What could they do to fight this? What can anyone?"

"I planted some seeds in the yard," Cylindra said. "I think the soil's dead, but we can try."

Bennet nodded. He was usually the optimistic one of the family, but it was difficult to find a silver lining. "At least we're together, right?" he said.

Avet and Cylindra laughed.

"Truth, brother," Avet said. "But cliché and cheesy as hell."

"Language," Leona said.

"You're both right," Cylindra said. "Honesty is cheesy sometimes."

They turned a corner, walking down another street void of plant life. Bare lot after bare lot. The houses that remained seemed old and weathered, though little about them had changed besides the lack of trees, bushes and grass. They walked the rest of the way to Cub's Den in silence.

The only restaurant in Cowley, centered on Main Street, had been around for decades. It'd gone through multiple owners and names, but it had always been a favorite gathering place for the Gaines and many others in the town. Some preferred to drive the six miles to Lovell for more options, but for Bennet and his family, there was nothing like Cub's Den for an afternoon drink.

They walked in to shouted greetings from nearly all in the restaurant.

"Mayor Gaines!" the hostess called as she ran to meet them, her short blonde hair bouncing with each step.

"Afternoon, Gella," Leona said. "Ran outta drinks at home."

"Not just here for the good company?" Gella looked at Bennet and winked.

Bennet blushed. "That too, of course, Gella."

Cylindra elbowed him and he shrugged.

Avet ignored the entire exchange, or perhaps didn't notice at all.

"Sit at any open table," Gella said. "Start you each off with a bottle of Thinka's?"

"You know us well," Leona said.

They passed a few tables, everyone greeting Mayor Leona Gaines on the way. They settled into a round table beside a square window.

Avet laughed softly and shook his head. "Gotta tell you the truth, Mom. Almost forgot you're mayor."

"Me, too," Leona said. "How I like it. The town runs itself."

"But when the town needs you, they know you'll be there," Bennet said.

"It's why they elected you," Cylindra said.

Avet lifted a hand in the air. "Wait. Bennet, you mean *if* the town needs her."

Gella appeared with four bottles and set them down. "Anything else?" She placed a warm hand on Bennet's shoulder.

"No, thank you, Gella," Bennet said. "I would think later, though."

Gella smiled warmly at him, nodded at the other three and walked away. His family knew about his... budding relationship with Gella, but also knew he wasn't ready to talk about it. He was grateful they chose to respect it.

"Bennet," Avet said. "Why *when* and not *if*?"

Bennet looked out the window at the blue sky, trying to imagine what he might do if the black planes reappeared. "Do we really think the poison drop was it? Avet, you were in the military. You understand tactics and strategy. Someone obviously wanted to hurt us, but would they really just leave it as is?"

Avet shrugged and looked down at his hands.

"Brother, I know you don't like talking about the war. But think about it. There has to be more coming."

Avet looked up, his face set firm and focused. "It's possible. Very possible. But first we need to look at what we know about who launched the attack, which is nothing."

"We could make educated guesses," Cylindra said.

"How?" Avet took a sip from his bottle. "Everything we know has been discussed to death, then on to complete decomposition. We don't have enough facts to make an educated guess. No crashed plane. The powder disintegrated into nothing. No one's taken responsibility and every damn nation was hit." He stopped and glanced at his mom.

"Fair time to swear," she said. "And good points. But, Bennet, it isn't a bad idea to be prepared if another attack comes. Avet, from your tactical experience, what kind of attack might come next?"

"There's never been an attack like this before. That's what I'm saying. *I don't know.*" He took a long draft from the bottle, then slammed it down. "It could be anything. And *why* was every nation hit?"

Cylindra ran a finger around the rim of the bottle. "It could be to confuse everyone."

"What government would care so little for their own people that they'd attack their own nation just to throw everyone off their scent?" Leona asked.

"There's at least one I know of," Avet said.

For a moment, no one responded. Bennet knew how Avet felt about his country after being in the military, but his brother had never divulged the reason.

"Maybe a nation did it, then." Cylindra said. "But still *why*? What's the goal?"

"It wasn't a nation," Bennet said. "It's couldn't be. The nation would weaken itself as much as everyone else. How would they wage a war in that state? Our nation couldn't."

"Then who, Ben?" Leona asked.

"A corporation, Mom," Bennet said. "One with its hands in artificial vegetation and lab-created nutrients. Most of us still prefer real salads to the imitation lettuce. Make that impossible, and their profits skyrocket."

"Someone did this to get even richer?" his mom asked.

"A theory, Mom."

Cylindra half smiled. "A good theory."

"I'd think the experts are already looking into it."

Avet sighed and shook his head. "Unless the experts got paid off. Or killed."

The family went silent. It seemed all too possible. That one percent had only grown more and more rich, and few seemed prone to share their wealth with the less fortunate ninety-nine. But were they really greedy enough to threaten the very planet they lived on just to make more than the entire town of Cowley would see in a thousand lifetimes?

"Oxygen," Avet said.

"Huh?" Leona said.

"Gonna get harder to breathe. Bottled oxygen."

"But if it became a need to survive, those companies will make more than they'll ever need," Leona said. "And the rest will be even worse off than they are now."

"But that doesn't make sense," Cylindra said. "Over half of Earth's oxygen is produced by our oceans."

"Really?" Avet said.

Cylindra nodded. "We're still out a lot of oxygen. But I don't think it's a company ploy. There's no way to know how long it will take for the lack of oxygen to impact us. Maybe it'll just feel like everyone's living at a higher altitude."

Bennet tilted his bottle back and finished it off in one large gulp. He slammed it down. "But a company doing it for profit still doesn't seem like an insane theory. And I hate that."

Chapter 10

Tashon saw the holes long before he was certain that's what they were. At first, he thought they were the moths fluttering in the wind. Small specks in the air swirling and hovering. The moths turned into small rips in the air that grew bigger the closer they got. But his thoughts remained on the moths. They came and went with no apparent reason, other than to offer him comfort. And, at once, a gift of protection. *But isn't that reason enough?* he thought. *I'm walking across the universe to answer a cry for help just because I believe I should help. Maybe the moths are similar.*

He looked down at his necklace. "Ishlea, have you seen anything like this before?"

"The necklace? I... maybe. Where did you find it?"

"Moths that seem to exist in both dimensions at once. Or *can* exist in both at once. They gave it to me."

"I've heard of creatures like that. Not moths. Some type of biped reptile. I've heard legends about it ever since I found my way to the Fourth."

"Legends?"

"It's a long story."

Tashon looked at the distant holes. "We have time."

Ishlea shifted and twisted, then settled into a new position in which to float along. Her voice deepened, as if she had suddenly aged. *"Long ago, before intelligent life existed anywhere in the universe, there lived a species on a single planet that we would consider* **almost** *intelligent. Similar to the more intelligent primates of Earth, but of reptilian origin. And like primates, they had their own social order.*

"They were in constant battle with the weather and other beasts of their world. Their survival skills evolved in a way no one really understands. Some say it was natural hallucinogens in their diet or water supply. Others say it was pure accident. Some say they must've been more intelligent than they're given credit for. But most, as with any legend, chalk it up to entertaining untruths.

"But it's said that their leader, their alpha, found or created – depending who you ask – a tear between dimensions. The first time her mind was not capable of grasping what she saw, and it nearly killed her. But

something kept calling her back. And each time she went through, it hurt her less and less. She ended up in the fourth dimension while she was pregnant, and gave birth while on the other side of that tear. A child of the Third, born in the Fourth. They found that this child simultaneously existed in both, and from then on all births took place through the tear, in the other world they knew so little about."

"When was the last time someone saw them? Still alive in both the Third and the Fourth?"

"No one that I've talked to has seen them. Just a legend as far as I know. But most legends come from somewhere."

Tashon nodded. "It's a good story. If they do exist I'd love to meet them someday. Any other legends you can tell me?"

"No. Most of the time here is spent figuring out what's going on, trying to come to grips with the fact that there is an afterlife, and it's not like most religions or sages said it would be. Before you came, what did you think would await you after death?"

"I didn't think about it much. I hoped that there was something. My parents died when I was young. I lost my sister when the Ship of Nations went down. But it wasn't something I truly thought about until I got my first glimpse of the Fourth outside of the ship. Whatever I thought it was, it wasn't anything like this. But what it is, is more wonderful than I ever thought."

Ishlea didn't respond. She floated along as Tashon plodded on, step after step, ever closer to the holes he hoped would lead him where he needed to go. And what would he find when he arrived? A person or sentient calling for help, alone on a planet or ship fearing the worst would come but hoping for the best? Or was it something larger, something more unknowable? There was no way to know. And then, the other question that lingered at the back of his mind: what if he got there only to find there was nothing he could do? He gently shook his head. Let his mind wander in those waters for too long, and he would certainly give up on his journey before completing it.

In time, they arrived at a small precipice that looked down on a field of swaying shapes. Above them floated thousands of holes, not a single one perfectly circular or of any particular shape. Each one seemed to have been cut with a jagged knife, and Tashon wondered how the holes had been made. The imperfections in them made them seem more natural than any of the other shapes he'd seen in the Fourth.

"Will you really be able to find your way among all these paths?"

"I will. The call is louder here. We're getting closer."

Closer, but still farther than Tashon was certain he could walk. He wished that while he was in the Fourth, his physical body was somehow made stronger and more resilient, but he could feel himself weakening. He rubbed exhaustion from his eyes, then followed the sound to a cluster of a few dozen holes. Through one he saw nothing but air and a few wisps of wind, through another darkness interrupted by soft speckles of light, as if he were looking at the night sky back on Aethera. Others had various settings on the other side, from masses of beings to cluster of structures to wandering creatures more bizarre than those he had already seen. Yet none of them were the source of the sound. He sat down and closed and his eyes, focusing all his energy and attention on the sound. Ishlea said something to him, but he tuned it out.

In his mind, he saw the sound as a straight line leaving his ears. He opened his eyes, letting all of his senses trace it to the exact hole from which it came. He stood up, continuing to focus all his energy finding the hole that would lead him closer to his destination. He found it hovering above him what would have been a few dozen feet in the third dimension. It was more of a slit than a hole, a half-closed eye staring down at Tashon and his companion.

"That one," Tashon said, pointing.

"That one?"

Tashon shrugged and ran a hand through his hair. "Fourth-dimensional beings have made contact with me a few times. Do you think you could carry me up there?"

"Maybe. Yes. You should rest. Let me see what's on the other side."

Tashon sat down and sipped from his bottle of water as he watched Ishlea float up. She paused to peek in the hole, then disappeared on the other side. Tashon sat alone, feeling the wind on his face, listening to the cry for help that had been his constant companion since he left Rosa and the others behind. He thought of the legend Ishlea had told him and couldn't help but consider what legends might be told of him to future generations. He knew Rosa already saw him as some type of prophet. But how would history look at him? Would they see a delusional human who'd simply disappeared? Or say he sought to bring peace and understanding through the people of Aethera? And if it was the second one, would they say that his leaving was abandonment? Or would they understand that he followed the sound because it would not let him stay in his home and place of comfort? Because it would not allow him to remain knowing that something out there was hurting and dying? Did it really even matter what history would say of him? He decided it didn't.

He was doing what he thought was right, though he did like the idea of being talked about as a legend, discussed over meals and at parties. Either way, he knew he was on a legendary journey, one that no other human had ever before been on, and perhaps never would again.

Ishlea returned, obvious dismay emanating from her. Tashon felt it was a different Ishlea than the one that had went into the hole, but couldn't be sure.

"It's a war zone."

"A war zone?"

"A place like where you found me, but everything is torn and blown apart. Beings and essences rallying, fighting and punishing one another. For reasons I don't understand."

"War? I think I saw a battle my first time in the Fourth. Beings of light and darkness, and in between, rushing each other, slamming into each other and hurting each other. Or maybe not hurting each other. Back then I didn't understand what they were exactly. What good does war do in this higher dimension? You cannot harm or kill each other, so what's the point?"

Her aura shifted again, becoming something heavier and more jaded.

"I've seen my fair share of battles and wars, here and during my time on Earth. Mostly for the same idiotic reasons wars have always been fought. Over differences of opinion. Differences that could be discussed civilly. Differences for which both sides could come to understanding of the other, if they were willing. It is true that this life is better than the life before. But it's not perfect, and I don't think perfect exists in the universe, regardless of dimension. As far as harm, we can feel pain. On an emotional or spiritual level."

"Spiritual pain?"

"It's only happened to me once. I don't know quite how to explain it. It was when I first came to the place where you found me. I came across a large, angled being with a small trembling form tangled in its jagged arms. It reminded me of being a child, the angry man that was my dad staring down at me. Full of rage and violence. I tried to intervene, to help the trapped soul, but got trapped myself. It seeped its darkness into me and drained me of my conviction, of everything I believed about what was right and wrong, true and false. It was a slow process, and I could feel myself slowly disappearing, becoming an empty shell. Finally, it let go, and I hovered in the air motionless, barely aware that I existed or had any idea of who I was or what was going on around me. It took me a long time to return to my normal self."

Tashon blew out a breath. "That sounds worse than a physical attack. But I still don't understand why. Why the war and the fighting? Nothing comes of it, not even truly killing the opponent."

"It is not a physical death, you're right. But it still hinders the enemy, slows them down. And in some cases, if you are drained for a long enough time, you never recover. We remain a confused and lost soul, never remembering where we truly once were or who we truly are."

Tashon thought for a moment, deciding that Ishlea must be one of those souls that had been attacked and was now confused and lost. It was the only way to explain the conflicting stories she had of her life.

"Yes," Tashon said. "I could see how that's a kind of death. But I still don't understand the reason for the war. There are no governments here. No nations, or freedoms to fight for. Is it truly just opinions and ideas that they're fighting over? And what's the reasoning?"

"The reasoning only makes sense to those who fight the wars, and not even to them, sometimes. As far as I can tell, at least. It seems that groups who share ideas and opinions of how this afterlife should or could be want to stick together, want to have control of their area, pushing all else aside. It's like they're trying to create some semblance of the world before, to find some sort of comfort in deciding how their afterlife will go, and ordering it exactly how they see fit."

Tashon shook his head. "Just more meaningless violence, pain and hurt because of our inability to accept and understand those around us. This dimension is truly larger than I can comprehend, and if a group should want to live alone among themselves they could find a place. It saddens me to find that this still happens in the Fourth. That any soul or being could get so angry about things of such little consequence, ignoring the wonders and beauties and majesty of this higher plane."

Ishlea didn't respond.

Tashon sighed. War, here? It made even less sense than the needless wars that were fought all across the third-dimensional galaxies. Less sense than the wars that nearly destroyed Earth. He realized that if he brooded over the darkness, denying and ignoring the beauty around him, he was little better than those actively perpetuating the darkness and pain. He closed his eyes and lay down, overcome with a sudden urge to sleep.

"Mom, I found a friend," Ishlea said.

Tashon opened his eyes, briefly squinting at her.

A sense of naïve innocence flowed from her as Tashon fell asleep.

***

The halls of the Ship of Nations were calm and quiet. Almost everyone still slept, the day cycle just beginning. Tashon sat alone in the farming sector, a soft smile on his face as he watched a leaf turn into two, then turn into a fully grown and blooming tree within seconds. A girl sat on its lower branch, humming tunelessly, her black hair touching her waist.

"Ishlea," Tashon said.

She pulled two purple spheres of fruit from the tree and hopped down. Continuing to hum, she sat next to him and handed him one of the fruits.

Tashon took a bite, juice squirting out and dripping down his chin. "Thank you." He took another bite.

She nodded and smiled, all the while humming and eating.

He stood on the top floor of the ship, looking down the large opening that ran through each floor. Ishlea stood next to him, thirty years his senior. She had a long rope hanging from one shoulder.

"You sure about this?" Tashon asked.

She smirked. "It's been too long since I've been on a cliff. It's not El Capitan, but it'll do." She clipped to a harness around her waist, climbed over the edge and jumped.

They were on Aethera, fighting off a horde of Crawlers. Ishlea, the same age as Tashon, brandished two knives and jumped onto a Crawler's back, cackling as she slit its throat, collapsing to the ground with the bleeding corpse. She ripped the head off completely and lifted it into the air triumphantly.

Then she was a little girl again. She dropped the head and collapsed to the ground, weeping.

***

"*Tashon? Tashon?*"

He opened his eyes. Ishlea hovered next to him, lying on her back as if she, too, had been asleep.

"*You're awake!*" Her voice squealed into his mind. "*Now we can play! Momma has put together the most amazingly realistic game of war. You'll love it.*"

She scooped him up and shot up and through the hole.

Chaos surrounded him. Structures erupted, shards and beings careening through the air. Souls hung limp and lifeless in the air, empty shells. Some sped around, avoiding the attacks of others. Some weren't so lucky, the appendages of their enemies wrapped tightly around them. Tashon wondered how any of them could tell friend from foe. All were shades of gray or darker. It wasn't an obvious battle of light versus darkness, but something more complex. More sinister. A sense of hatred and unbridled rage constantly erupted from every being. As if their sole purpose were to extend that anger to others who saw the universe differently than they did.

The necklace vibrated around his neck. A single moth appeared, flew an intricate pattern and disappeared.

"Isn't it wonderful, Tashon? Momma worked very hard on this. And it's so real! I've never been in a simulation that felt so real."

"Ishlea, it's not a—"

She shot off to the center of the destruction, still holding Tashon in her arms.

Chapter 11

Bennet sat in the dirt of Gella's front yard waiting for her to get off work, the full moon glowing in a clear sky. She lived in a small, well-maintained cottage-style home. Her two horses, Coop and Olive, neighed softly from the backyard as a cool breeze drifted by. Stars sparkled down on him, and he couldn't help but wonder what had happened to the Ship of Nations. Did humanity begin anew on other planets as they'd planned? Would they turn out any better than here on Earth? He let out a small grunt, placed his finger on the ground and wrote.

***

Is this the end of Earth?
Or the start of something new?
We have the potential to turn this around,
Make something better than what we had.
~~~
*Will we?*
*?*
*Maybe.*
~~~
Wars abound, more are bound to come.
War, unavoidable.
As is the death of Earth.
Maybe.

***

Someone coughed behind him. "You write poetry?"

Bennet quickly wiped the words away and stood up. "Gella. How was work?"

She shrugged. "Seems a bit pointless lately. What you wrote was good."

Now Bennet shrugged. "Just something to get the thoughts out. The last one was better."

"Can I read it?" she asked.

He shook his head. "Wiped it away as soon as I finished it."

She tilted her to one side, pursing her lips. Then she shrugged. "You ready?"

"Yeah, Gella," he said, smiling.

The two walked around the house to a small backyard. A small shed sat just outside a circular metal fence that held two beautiful horses. Olive had coarse, white hair speckled with brown; Coop a deep, consistent shade of brown. Both neighed, and Bennet slowed his steps.

Gella laughed. "I thought you were messin' when you told me you're scared of horses."

"Yeah, yeah, Gella." Bennet stopped a few feet shy of the fence.

"Okay, why're you scared of horses?"

"You remember my other sister?"

"Not Cyl?" Gella asked.

Bennet shook his head. "No, Hil came after Cyl. One day... I was young, carrying on around Old Betty's place, when she still had a few animals. Wasn't paying attention and walked too close behind a horse. Spooked it, I guess. It kicked its back leg out, straight into Hil's head. She... right in my arms, Gella. Limp, lifeless." He looked at the ground.

"Shit, Ben, that's... that's...."

Bennet laughed. "A bold-faced lie." He smiled and jumped back as she reached out to smack him.

"Damn it, Ben," she yelled. "Something's wrong with you."

"Yeah, yeah, Gella."

She shook her head and laughed once. "And they say Avet's the mean one."

"He is."

"Think he'll ever find someone?" Gella asked.

Bennet nodded. "He's got a boyfriend in Cody. Bar owner. Clawman."

"Clawman?"

"A Marine nickname. They met in the war."

"Which war?"

"The Sandwich War," Bennet said.

"What?" Gella asked, eyebrow raised.

"The Sandwich War, Gella. Against Canada and most of South America."

"You mean the Immigration Wars. When we gave sanctuary to their supposed political criminals."

Bennet nodded. "Right. We were sandwiched between our enemies."

Gella laughed. "Never heard that one."

"Don't lie, Gella."

"You're the only one who's lied tonight." She bumped him with her shoulder and smiled.

"Truth," he said.

"Where'd Avet fight?" she asked. "He doesn't talk about it. None of you do, really."

Bennet shrugged. "He doesn't like talking about it, and we respect that. I mean, he's talked to therapists and the others, but it's not something he wants to remember." He paused, wondering whether he should tell more or not. "He was in Los Angeles and San Diego," he said, deciding he trusted her.

She looked at the ground. "Shit," she said. "Wait. You're not messing with me again?"

Bennet shook his head. "Wish I was."

"Was he there... when...?"

Bennet nodded and sighed. "He was."

"How'd he get out? They leveled both cities and everything in between." Her eyes were wide as she spoke, her voice a mix of confusion and awe.

"He won't give any details. He got separated from his regimen. Clawman went back for him, which was specifically against his orders. But they were the only two of the regimen to make it out."

Gella shook her head. "The radiation alone... How is he still alive?"

"Don't know completely. But they were part of the lucky twenty percent of American soldiers the government actually gave protective gear too. Advanced, tactical hazmat suits. It's what Avet called them. That, and they know how to kill their way through a city. That's all Avet's ever said."

Silence fell between them. Words for a new poem started taking shape in Bennet's mind. A poem questioning the bravery of violence, the heroics of war. Perhaps Avet was a hero, but Bennet knew better than to tell his brother that.

Gella cleared her throat. "How'd Cowley get so lucky? How'd our entire *state* get so lucky?"

Bennet laughed once. "We have more cows than people in Wyoming. Even if everyone here owns a gun, which they don't. That's stereotype. But if they did, we still don't pose much of a threat."

"Our unimportance saved us," she said.

"Being important isn't all it's said to be."

Gella smiled. "So how's it you never learned to ride?"

"Just never did. Never needed to. No one's needed to in centuries."

"But now you might need to," she said.

"Truth." He walked to the fence and rested his arms on the cool metal. "Who're these two? They're beautiful."

"The white one with brown speckles is Olive. The other one is Coop."

"Who am I riding first?"

"You gotta get on before you can ride," she said. "Which one you want to ride?"

Olive neighed softly.

"Olive says she wants me." Bennet smiled.

"That makes one of us," Gella said, walking to the shed.

Bennet laughed and followed her, holding the door as she pulled out two engineered leather saddles. He took one from her and they walked into the corral. Coop and Olive walked straight to Gella, nuzzling their noses into her free hand.

"All right, my friends," she said. "Let's saddle up."

She walked around to Coop's side, lifted the saddle up and set it on his back. She touched a circular indent etched into its side. The saddle cracked quietly as it cinched tight around Coop's sides and belly. Gella put her right hand on the saddle horn, her right foot in the stirrup and effortlessly swung herself up and onto the horse, sliding her left foot into the other stirrup in the same motion. Bennet smiled as he saw the glint in her eyes, the joy she felt just sitting on her horse.

She smiled back. "Your turn."

He walked to Olive's side and lifted the saddle up, but as he went to turn it level with the horse's back, lost his grip and the saddle fell to the dirt.

"That's vintage," Gella said, stifling a laugh.

The only reply Bennet could think of was 'you're vintage,' so he picked the saddle and kept his mouth shut. He got it on easily on the second attempt, Olive offering a congratulatory neigh.

"Thanks, girl," he said.

"Anytime," Gella said.

"I was talking to Olive."

Gella rolled her eyes. "Put your hand on the horn first, then your foot. Right hand, right foot."

Bennet put his left hand on the horn. "I'm left handed. It seems easier."

He put his foot in the stirrup. Awkwardly and without grace, he clambered onto the horse, making it into the saddle without falling.

"Well done," Gella said.

"Thanks, Gella."

"I was talking to Olive," she said with a smile.

Bennet laughed. "Now what?"

Gella clicked her tongue and walked Coop to Olive's side. "Click your tongue and give a soft squeeze with your legs."

Bennet did and walked forward slowly.

"Pull the reigns back and say 'Woe.'"

Bennet did, and Olive stopped. "Seems easy enough. I could've watched an old Western and learned this."

"So you could rob a bank and gallop off into the mountains without falling off?"

Bennet pursed his lips in thought. "I'd never rob a bank."

"Whatever," she said with a smile. "Choke up on the reigns. Closer to her, not the ends. Yeah, like that. Turn her to the left. Good, now right. Good."

Bennet shook his head. "This seems easier than it should be."

"Because these are the two best horses in the state." She stroked Coop's neck.

Bennet considered making a cheesy comment like 'and the prettiest riding teacher,' but decided against it.

"Ride in a slow circle, clockwise."

Bennet clicked his tongue and guided Olive to the left. "What're you feeding them?"

"My parents left a cellar full of survival food. Horse feed bars, food bars, MREs. One bar gives them each all they need for a day."

Her parents had both died the day after high school graduation, leaving the house and land to Gella. She had siblings but no other blood family. But the town has supported her, helped her get a job. And Bennet thought she seemed happy.

"They always thought ahead," he said.

Gella nodded. "I heard you talking at the Cub. You really think another attack is coming?"

Bennet pulled Olive to a stop. "I do. This feels like the start of something."

"The beginning of the end," Gella said, looking up at the moon.

"Maybe. There's just no way to know what's coming next, or when."

"Avet have any ideas? He see anything like this in the war?"

Bennet shook his head. "The attack is unprecedented. The idea out there is that it wasn't anyone on Earth."

"We've all thought it. It's possible. We found alien tech in the ocean. We sent humans into the fourth dimension."

"It's possible. It could've been some sadistic dictator, or a terrorist group not associated with any nation. I'm tired of speculating, though." He squeezed his legs and clicked his tongue. Olive walked forward.

"Yeah. The speculation seems pointless, too," Gella said. "Turn her around, go clockwise."

Bennet turned his steed in a sharp left until they faced the other way, then went back to circling along the fence.

"You look comfortable up there," she said. "You sure you've never ridden?"

"Yeah," Bennet said. "I've always liked animals, though."

After another thirty minutes of riding around the corral in casual conversation, the two dismounted and went inside.

"Coffee?" Gella pulled out two mugs.

"Have any tea?"

She looked at him as if he were insane. "Tea?"

"Hey, I like tea, Gella."

"I think I have some of my mom's left." She opened a cabinet above the fridge and pulled out a dusty, torn box of tea packets. "Does tea expire?"

"No. It just won't be as strong if it's old. What kind is it?"

"Green tea with ginger. Gross."

"What? One of my favorites. Although I prefer loose leaf." Bennet stood up. "I'll make us some. Tea kettle?"

"We have boiling water on tap. The red faucet."

Bennet rolled his eyes. "Tea making is a lost art."

She shook her head and put a mug under the faucet, holding two buttons to release the water. "It's not like tea's hard to make."

"Woah, just trying to be helpful."

He grabbed the mug from her and they locked eyes, for longer than Bennet would normally be comfortable. But it felt safe, right. She put a hand on his face. He leaned in, his heart beating faster, and kissed her soft, warm lips. He held her for a moment then pulled back. They smiled at each other, and then talked until the sun came up.

ALMOST PATHLESS

***

From Avet's War Journal, Audio Recording
click

Just got back after leave. They're sending us south. L.A. then to San Diego. Thought we'd given up on Southern California. Kick the enemy out, take back the city. Secure the southern border. They talk like just saying it's gonna make it happen. It could happen, but really I don't give a shit either way right now. As long as Claw and I make it back alive.

sigh

They're splitting the troops now, too. Claw and something like half the others are going in on the ground. We're diving in from the skies. Don't know which way I'd prefer, really. At least I'll get an aerial view of what the city's like now before I get there. Don't even know where in the city I'm dropping. They won't tell us. Don't want it to somehow get to the enemy and give them a chance to prepare.

cough *spit*

We're somewhere between Fresno and L.A. now. Got the planes and tents all in a field. Some Mexicans came for help. Citizens, not soldiers. Asked for food and water. Sergeant turned them away.

'Can't be helpin' none o' the enemy,' he said.

I told him it was just a man and his kid, not the enemy. You would've thought I got his teenage daughter pregnant, the way he yelled at me. Pure rage and racism, the prick. Think he would've shot the kid if he found any reason. Yeah, he sent the two off. I thought about chasing after them. Giving them some food. But —

sniff

— need my strength for L.A.

Don't think he likes that me and Claw are together, either. Doesn't like that we can talk about it now. But we're not the only couple, not even in our troop. If he said it outright, he'd lose his authority. Damn, he almost lost with some of us already. The prick. But he doesn't want us dead, and he wants to help win the war. There's some good in him, at least. I think.

"Meal time, soldiers!"

sigh

Finally.

click

Chapter 12

Ishlea laughed excitedly as she evaded another being's sharp appendage. She spun haphazardly away, the end narrowly missing her head. Tashon hid behind the glittering shrapnel of an exploded structure, cautiously looking around the war zone to decipher a path to relative safety. The difficult part was convincing Ishlea she needed to find shelter. For her, it was just a simulation created by her mother. Tashon had spent the smallest moment wondering on the balance within a 'real simulation,' but was pulled out of his mind by a flaming hunk of shrapnel flying past his face.

Fire in the Fourth was immensely more terrifying, and mesmerizing, than fire in the Third. The added colors and directions within the fire turned each flame into a dancing, glowing diamond. The heat that it created brought sweat to Tashon's forehead within seconds, draining his body's energy and moisture. And half the battlefield seemed to be on fire. Tashon wondered again how fire was made in the Fourth. Wasn't fire a physical, inanimate thing? *'Everything's alive in the Fourth,'* Ishlea had said.

Something screeched. Ishlea sped around to Tashon and lifted him high into the air.

"*I beat it!*" she squealed. "*Let's find the next one.*" She stopped high above the destruction, scanning the battlefield for more enemies, the next stage of her war-game.

All Tashon saw was more pointless, misplaced anger. Perhaps it would be easier if he pretended it was all a game, but that was impossible.

"*See that one, Tashon? Forward and kata from us. At the top of that massive cone.*"

It was easy to spot. Not the largest being fighting, but by far the angriest. Its screeches and commands echoed all around, in and out of Tashon's mind.

"*That's our final goal. But we can't go straight for it. Gotta take out all the others along the way.*"

Hundreds of beings collided along that path, and Tashon still didn't understand which ones Ishlea saw as allies and which as enemies. Though she did tend to go after the more terrifying ones each time.

"Ishlea, this isn't a sim—"

Ishlea dive-bombed to the ground, and deposited Tashon in a crevice between two chunks of rubble. Two vaguely spherical beings held a dozen paper thin ones hostage inside them, slowly draining their resolve. Without hesitation, Ishlea leaped on top of one, shooting glowing gray tendrils from her arms. Two pierced each enemy, the result a meaning so dense that it knocked the air from Tashon's lungs. Gasping, he watched as wind spewed from one of the spheres, sending Ishlea tumbling up and ana, toward the center of the fighting and out of sight.

Tashon was alone again. He hoped none of the combatants would see him as an enemy, but his experience told him otherwise. A part of him wanted to help Ishlea, but there was nothing he could do. Was there? He slid farther back into the crevice and closed his eyes, trying to tune out the sounds of higher dimensional warfare and determine what direction he needed to go. Luckily, or not, it was the same direction Ishlea had been thrown. He opened his eyes and squeezed his necklace. A moth appeared in front of him and flew out of the crevice. After a deep breath, Tashon ran after it.

The spheres and their victims gone, the area was eerily still. The moth stayed in front of him at arm's length as the two sped closer to the heart of the battle. They took a hard right around a blazing fire. The moth swerved left. Tashon followed, but not quick enough. Blunt shrapnel stuck his shoulder, flipping him around. He lost his balance and fell onto his back, head slapping the ground.

His shoulder ached. He looked at it. Swollen, but no blood. He rolled onto his hands and knees, then stood up. The moth was waiting for him. Tashon touched the back of his head. Again, no blood, but a bump half the size of his fist had already formed.

"Okay," he said to the moth, and on they went.

Shrapnel and rubble rained down on them, but Tashon moved quicker now. The moth stopped, he stopped. It darted right, Tashon followed. Up, around, kata and ana they dodged explosions, shrapnel and the occasional ball of fire. Sweat poured down Tashon's face and his muscles burned, but he refused to stop until he knew it was safe.

He clambered over a large pile of rumble and into a massacre. A single being, not much bigger than Ishlea with an egg-shaped form spun fiercely around and around, black strings spooling out from a white body and latching onto every living thing in sight. Beings large and small, all of different shades, were trapped within its grip. It reached for the moth, but it gracefully maneuvered out of the way. Tashon jumped over one that went for his legs. When he landed, his right foot slipped out from under him and he heard a loud snap. He rolled down the pile, along the ground and stopped directly at the bottom of the spinning egg. A large triangle that seemed like an eye moved down, examining Tashon. It slowed its spinning, then came to a stop, its strings rolling back into its form. Those it had been latched to hung unmoving in the air.

It spoke something into Tashon's mind.

"I don't understand," he said, wincing from the pain in his ankle.

More words, or maybe just noises, came into his mind.

Tashon shook his head. "I'm sorry."

It moved closer, its eye focusing on his ankle.

"Broken," Tashon said.

The egg slowly sent out two strings, these thicker and less aggressive. They scooped him up and floated off. The moth disappeared.

They moved along the path of the egg's massacre. Dozens of what Tashon could only describe as 'corpses.' Empty shells just as Ishlea had described, their essences drained. Would they really recover? And if they didn't, was there something waiting for them in the fifth dimension? Could progression be infinite, eternal?

One of the beings was an emptied human. It moved slightly, its eyes tracking Tashon as he walked.

"Get away from it," it said weakly. *"It wants—"*

A string exploded through the human soul's center, sending wisps of dust of yet another new color. *The human color*, Tashon thought. The wind twisted back together, reforming its original shape, but it was now entirely empty.

"Moth?" Tashon whispered.

No response. He grasped his necklace tightly, soaking in the warmth and comfort it provided. It boosted his morale, but offered no insight or direction. They moved into a low but wide trapezoidal structure, passing a row of guards that paid them no attention. There was no roof to the structure, and the walls were lined with thousands of other beings, with at least a few hundred different species represented. Humans and other bipeds intermixed with every shape and size beings imaginable and beyond comprehension. They were all mixes of black, gray and white. The egg being, though mostly bright white, felt darker to Tashon than some of those that were deeper black. Tashon questioned how he'd viewed the beings he'd come across. The snake-like one who'd opened a door for him, though black, did not seem sinister in Tashon's memory. Then Circa, though bright, proved to be pompous and arrogant. *Are they able to hide their inner essence?* he wondered. *Or are my eyes becoming more in tune with the Fourth? Or less?*

They stared at the emptiness of the open sky. The egg being moved away from the entrance and settled into a corner.

"Tashon!" a familiar voice called into his mind.

It wasn't Ishlea, but he knew the voice. He scanned the crowd, looking for an essence that felt familiar. Nothing. Then a being dropped in front of him, its entire essence beaming like a grand smile.

Tashon laughed. "Jonstin!" Tashon kept smiling, seeing Jonstin's middle essence a mix of dark gray and yellow white. Yet the familiarity of it was warm and comforting. *Maybe the Fourth is like the Third,* he thought. *You never really know one's intentions.*

"Tashon, Tashon," Jonstin said. "*I heard there was a three-dimensional human up here, but no idea it was you. What's happening on Aethera? How are you here? Why are you here?"*

"That's... a lot to tell. What's happening here? What's this war about?"

"Also a lot to tell. Here, we're waiting."

"For what?"

"You'll see. That's why your guide brought you here."

Tashon looked at the egg. "Guide? It killed at least a few dozen essences out there."

"No, not killed."

"Or drained their essence, their conviction."

"That's... one way of looking at it. But not completely accurate."

"Then what is it?"

"It doesn't hurt them. It leaves them... stunned, if they don't accept what we're offering them."

Tashon raised his eyebrows. "What're you offering them?"

"The chance to move on. The Fourth is an afterlife, in a sense. But there is much more."

"How are you giving them that chance?"

"A lot of them are stuck here, in their old ways. Lower ways of living, of perceiving reality."

"Is that why the war's happening?"

"Yes. Really, there's three sides. The two actually fighting, then us, trying to stop it."

"Why're they fighting?"

"This is the oldest place in the Fourth. So it's said, at least. The cone is the creation point. The war is but another one of opposing beliefs. Those who believe

the cone is the point from which God created their universe. The others believe it was something more like a Big Bang, and they want control of the area to study it in order to replicate it themselves. Make gods of themselves."

"Which would be blasphemous to their enemies." Tashon twisted in the egg's grip and the bones in his ankle shifted. "Ah! Damn it."

"You okay?"

"Broken ankle."

"Physical pain. Best part of being done with the Third is not dealing with physical pain."

"Can you ask my *guide* to set me down? I need to splint it."

Jonstin turned to the egg, and after a moment it placed Tashon gently on the ground. He shrugged off his pack and unzipped it. Then, silently and without warning, the pyramids stood in front of him. The pyramids to which he'd lost Evalee and Laos.

"Here it is, Tashon," Jonstin said.

"The pyramids," Tashon said quietly, the pain in his leg moving to the back of his mind.

Tashon examined every facet of the structure. Pyramids sunk and twisted into pyramids. Not one of them stood exactly upright, nor a single one independent of another. The pyramids had a presence about them, as if they were aware of the souls surrounding it as individuals. Just by looking at it, Tashon felt known in a more complete way than he ever had. He wasn't sure he liked it, for it seemed the pyramids understood things about himself that he didn't. But he couldn't quite grasp the idea of what any of those things were.

They glowed brighter and brighter until a hole of brilliant golden-yellow opened up, stretching across multiple pyramids. Hundreds of beings in the crowd lifted as one into the air, a wave of souls rising and moving into the hole. As the crowd pouring in thinned, the hole slowly shrunk until it closed completely after the last being disappeared. It spun, lifted into the air and then vanished.

"Many moved on today," Jonstin said.

Tashon nodded. "What does that mean, really? And how'd you end up being a part of it?" Tashon wasn't entirely sure Jonstin was helping those souls or not, but he would refrain from judgment until he understood what was happening.

"That's a long and complex story," Jonstin said.

Tashon looked at his ankle. "I've got at least a few weeks until I can walk. I have time." Tashon grabbed his pack and pulled a thick rod out of each shoulder strap. A survival tool designed into every colonist's pack. "I'll splint it up while you start." He ripped two lengths of cord from the edges of the straps, and went to work.

"I'll start at the beginning, then. Or the end, you could say. Aleron's monster connected to me, and I thought that was the end. I was aware of my existence, but nothing. My movements were not my own, nor were my thoughts. Then the engine shot us back into the Fourth. All of us were still connected to Aleron. I was still a physical body, like you are. But I couldn't get away. None of us could.

"We stayed attached to it as it wandered all over, slowly dying of hunger and thirst. All I knew was hunger, thirst and exhaustion. Pain, too. My mind always on fire. We all died in our own time. I was one of the last to go, and when I did, I was free. My spirit or soul – I'm still not sure what to call it – split from my physical body. I was relieved to know dead wasn't dead.

"But I had no idea where I was, or where to go. I'd always imagined the afterlife to be more ordered and accessible, but why would it be? Life isn't. The universe isn't. It shouldn't have surprised me this was any different, but it did."

Tashon tied the last knot on his splint and leaned back into the corner.

"I wandered all over, looking for answers. For heaven or hell or something reminiscent of what humanity always said the afterlife would be. But then I heard of this place, this cone and this never-ending war. I hate that there's war here. That there's war anywhere, really. But the idea that the point of creation could be visited was too powerful to ignore, so I asked around.

"And in my asking, I came across the pyramids and those that... follow them, I think that's the best way to say it. The pyramids are a conduit that help those who desire to progress do so. It isn't necessary, in any way. But it can aid in continuing on."

Tashon cleared his throat. "When someone's done in the pyramids, do they physically move on to another dimension? What happens to them?"

"They come back into the Fourth, changed. Usually for the better, but not always. But I believe that, eventually, we'll all end up in the Fifth, then the Sixth, and so on. A controversial opinion."

"Really?" Tashon asked, adjusting his leg. "It seems logical, knowing what we know now."

"To some, yes. But never-ending infinity is a difficult concept to grasp. Many think it has to end at some point. Many want it to. But that controversy has not turned to violence, thankfully.

"So, in my searching, I heard about the pyramids, and found that coming here was the easiest way to find them. Show up, and wait. No one told me it was a war zone, but the first fighter I came across was merciful. There are those with mercy on both sides, and ones that'll act before speaking a single word.

"But she was kind and understanding. She asked who I fought for, and when she saw my confusion she explained the war to me. I told her I still did not wish to fight, that I came looking for the pyramids. She directed me, and I found the group that you've seen here."

Tashon nodded slightly. "But what exactly do you do? I don't think I understand."

Another being, this one three-legged with a triangular body, approached and drew Jonstin's attention. The two looked at each other, presumably communicating though Tashon heard no words. Jonstin seemed just as important to this group as he had been to the Ship of Nations. *But what do they do?* Tashon wondered again, trying to dispel the feeling that something wasn't right.

"Tashon, I need to go. I'll explain more later."

Tashon waved his hand. "I'll be here, resting." He pulled a bottle out and took a long drink of water. "Should've packed some pain pills," he whispered, wincing as he gently touched his splint.

Chapter 13

As Avet leaned on the kitchen counter, he held the phone to his ear, pushing it hard into his cheek. He fought back rage and tears. "Who were they?"

Clawman answered on the other side, his swollen lip giving his speech a thick lisp. "Doth'nt matter, Av. They're gone. Tho'th the bar. The beating, I could take that. But all the cath. All the booze. Drank, thtolen or burned up. Thit'th gettin' worthe, and fatht. Thtoreth getting ranthacked all over, people lothin' jobth. Damn, Av. I never eat my fruitth and veggieth, but now they're all gone and it'th killing everything. People are going crathy."

Avet nodded. He didn't care about all the other shit. He just wanted to know that Claw was safe. "What'd the EMTs say?"

Silence.

"You stitched yourself up?"

"Alwayth did in Than Diego," Claw said casually.

"Because you were the only medic we had," Abet said firmly.

"And thtill the betht medic anywhere," Claw said. "You told me that."

"Damn it, Claw. Can you drive? Get the hell to a hospital."

"They thole the car. Ripped the key right from my pocket. Hothpital'th a meth, anyway."

Avet nodded. It was true. Nationwide, the hospitals had been going downhill. Lack of funding, lack of doctors. Clawman would be lucky to be seen within a day, even in the state he was in.

"Damn drunk rednecks," Avet said. "How'd you get home?"

"Legth're fine. Ith waist up that ain't workin' tho great. And it wath a group of lawyerth, I think. Not redneckth."

Avet sighed. "Good thing you live close. You get a few of 'em, at least?"

"Didn't have my clawth on me, but knocked a few down. Too many of 'em, and they thnuck up on me. Didn't have a chanth, Av."

"What'd the cops say?"

"They're looking into it. But all the thecurity footage was lotht in the fire. And they didn't believe me when I told 'em it was grown men in thuits."

"Suits?" Avet asked.

"Thuits," Claw said.

"I'm coming to get you. Things aren't so bad here. Not yet."

"Didn't even have to athk," Claw said. "An hour?"

Avet smiled. "I'll make it in forty minutes. Love you, Lonce." The use of his boyfriend's real name felt strange, but if any time was the right time to use it, it was then.

"Av, love you."

Avet hung up and dropped the phone in his pocket. "Mom?"

She walked into the kitchen from the living room. "I heard, son. We got a full charge in the Chevy. It'll get you there and back without stopping. And don't stop. For anything but Claw. Then bring him back."

Avet wrapped his mom in a tight hug. "Thanks, Mom. You seen Ben? I want him with me."

She smiled. "At Gella's."

"See ya soon, Mom." He ran into the garage, hopped in the car and sped off, tires squealing as he turned off his childhood street.

He skidded into Gella's yard, tossing dirt everywhere and honked the horn. Bennet and Gella ran outside as Avet rolled down the window.

"Get in. We're going to Cody. Claw's place got torched. They beat the shit out of him, too."

Bennet gave Gella a quick hug and jumped in the car without any hesitation. *That's a brother*, Avet thought.

"What happened?" Bennet asked as Avet floored it back onto the road.

"They drank and stole all the booze, beat him half dead and torched it."

Bennet looked across the car, his eyes cold and heavy. "Avet, we're getting Claw and coming back. Nothing else. No crusades, right?"

Avet kept his eyes on the road. "Not making any promises."

***

Leona's phone rang minutes after Avet left, the high-pitched tone making her jump.

She answered, heart pounding. "Yeah, Deputy Meerf?"

"Mayor Gaines, uh, well... the war or whatever it is that's happening out there... it's found Cowley, I think."

"Where?"

"We're, ah, out on the 789. West two miles."

"Right. You need me there?"

"Ah, no, no. Meet us at the station. Just... be ready for... a surprise."

"Will Sheriff Ling be there?"

"Yeah. He... ah, would've called you but he's dealing with these... people."

"Visitors?" Leona asked.

"Sure, sure... visitors."

Leona hung up. She'd walk to the station, then. They'd probably beat her there, but that was fine. Maybe it'd give Meerf a chance to get his head on straight. She walked to the back bedroom and opened the door, where Cylindra lay on a bed, softly crying.

"Hey, Cyl. I'm heading to the station. You want to come?"

She wiped her nose and shook her head. "I can't bear being outside right now."

Leona sighed and sat on the foot of the bed. "Cyl, I know. You've done so much work for the environment. Rest for now, but you'll need to come out eventually."

"Come out to what?" She lifted her head up and looked at Leona. "It's all going to be gone soon, anyway."

"Come be with your family." Leona stood and kissed her daughter's head. "When you're ready."

Cylindra nodded and closed her eyes.

Leona left quietly, wishing she could do more for her daughter. But Cylindra was strong. She'd come around. Leona left the house and made her way to the station, doing her best to ignore the absence of green as she walked. The town had always been slow to catch up to the world, slow to catch the diseases the world had to offer. But not this time. It hit everywhere at once, no prejudice or bias.

The occasional walker greeted her with a smile and a greeting, as if nothing was wrong. And, in many ways, nothing was. Her town was still alive, and there was still enough food and water to go around. The problem was when the food started to run out. Sure, there was artificial versions of every grain, vegetable, fruit and meat imaginable. But with all of the real versions in short supply, the demand for artificial would only grow. Shortages were coming, of that she was certain. *I need to call a town meeting about rationing,* she thought. *After I figure out what the hell Meerf's talking about.*

Deputy Meerf stood at the front door of the station, brown hair slicked back and uniform in perfect shape. He bounced up and down on his knees nervously, his thumbs looped through his belt loops.

"Miss Gaines, Mayor Gaines," he said, the words tumbling out far quicker than was natural. "Ahem. I mean, come in. Welcome." He opened the door. "Goat in... I mean, go in."

"Thanks, Deputy."

She walked through the door into what should've felt like the station she'd been in dozens of time before. The three desks lined in a row, three cells line against the left wall and the sheriff's office tucked in the back right corner. It looked the same as ever, but felt different. It felt almost... silly. *That's an odd word*, she thought.

Sheriff Ling sat in a rickety office chair, staring at the cells. His typically smooth black hair was matted in section, sticking straight out in others.

Each of the three cells held a single prisoner. Two women and one man, each in full combat military gear, but again, something about the design of the uniforms didn't seem right. One of the women, blonde hair braided to one side of her head, stood stone-faced, hands clasped behind her back. The man had a strong, sharp jaw and his head was shaved cleanly on one side, splotchy on the other. He sat on his cot wailing wordlessly, tears and snot pouring down his face and pooling on the yellow linoleum flooring. The last woman was completely bald, her scalp and face covered in scars, old and new. She lay on her back, arms and legs spread wide, laughing hysterically, her eyes and lips bright with the joy of it.

"Where're they from?" she asked.

Sheriff Ling started, oblivious to her presence until she spoke. "I have no earthly idea, Miss Mayor. None at all. They appear to be soldiers, but I don't think that's the reality of it."

"What were they doing? Why'd you lock them up?"

"Deputy Meerf didn't tell you?"

"No." She shook her head. "Just that we had visitors, and I should come see."

The sheriff rolled his eyes. "Yes, visitors. We found them on the side of the road around a campfire, cooking up pieces of one of Patty Lynn's cows."

"They killed it?"

Sheriff Ling nodded. "They came fairly willingly with me and the deputy. But as soon as we locked them up, this started."

"Have they said anything?"

Ling shook his head.

Leona walked over, stopping in front of the motionless woman. Her uniform looked real, but it wasn't right. She'd seen Avet's combat uniform dozens of times, cleaned it herself half that many. The patch of the American flag on the woman's uniform was on the wrong shoulder, the buttons of her jacket left of center. The shades of green were off, and the boots had no laces. A copy, a mimic.

"Where're you from?" Leona asked.

The still woman broke out into laughter.

The man instantly switched from crying to giggling.

The other woman laughed louder.

"I'm a comedian, Ling," she said.

Ling rolled the chair to her side. "Where're you from?"

All three wailed, tears streaming down their faces.

"And I'm a regular Shakespeare," Ling said.

"He wrote comedies, too," Leona said.

Ling shrugged and nodded. "I need to relieve the bowels." He stood and walked through a door on the opposite wall.

The three so-called soldiers went silent. Leona kept her eyes trained on the woman in front of her. The woman, without moving, was instantly facing away from Leona. *But she didn't move,* Leona thought. One second she was facing Leona, and the next nanosecond, her back turned to her. The soldier's form buzzed and vibrated, then she was standing two feet to the left of where she had been. A heaviness descended on Leona, dark and muddled. The world was going wrong, but Leona was now convinced something far worse than any could conceive wasn't coming, but was already there.

She looked to the other two. The man still sat and the woman still sat on the cot, both silent.

A door opened. "You say something to make her mad?"

Leona blinked her eyes. How long had she been standing there? It felt like hours. "I didn't say anything."

Ling opened a bakery box on his desk. "Croissant?"

"Not hungry."

She walked to the next cell, where the man sat. The flag sewn to his shoulder was different. It was still American, or, a child's interpretation of what an American flag looked like. A few stripes of alternating red and white, with a blue square in the top left corner filled with hastily drawn stars. Leona looked at the first soldier, whose flag matched the man's. *It was right a minute ago, wasn't it?*

"Their flags are wrong," she said.

"Yes, I saw that. No name patches or dog tags, either. They have no form of identification."

Leona shook her head and walked to the bald woman's cell. "What's your name, soldier?"

The woman rose to her feet, a kind and genuine smile on her face. "I'm Hilary Clinton reincarnated." She laughed. "The queen president herself!" Her voice bounced off the walls, echoing all around.

Ling laughed. "Now *she's* the comedian."

A patch with the name 'Clinton' appeared on the soldier's jacket, trembled, then disappeared.

"Cow farts in a skillet," Ling said. "What was that?"

The soldiers laughed once in unison, then lay down on their cots and closed their eyes.

Chapter 14

The pain refused to let Tashon sleep. It shot from his ankle, up the side of his leg and stopped in his lower back, pulsing. *Worse than I hoped,* he thought, trying to adjust the splint. But it was no use. He'd have to lay as still as possible until it healed.

"Damn it," he whispered.

The plea for help ceaselessly called on, and for the time, he couldn't do anything to answer it. He was stuck in the Fourth with limited food and limited water. *I wonder how close the nearest planet is.* Expanding his field of vision, he found there were none within his sight.

"Yeah, damn."

He was the only one in the massive walled area, had been soon after Jonstin left. With the pyramids coming, the place lost its popularity. And Jonstin had been gone for... hours? A day? How long since he'd had anything to eat? His stomach grumbled, but he pushed the hunger aside with a small sip of water. Three beings entered, Jonstin among them. They hovered for a few minutes, discussing some aspect of the Fourth Tashon didn't know. They split apart, and Jonstin rejoined Tashon.

"Sorry, I had to take care of something."

Tashon twitched against a surge of pain. "It's okay. What was it?"

"One of our own was attacked. Left an empty shell."

"Didn't you say that's not what happens?"

"It's not when we do it. But those fighting the war drain each other of everything that makes a soul a soul. What we do is... try to quiet their old selves so they can see what their new selves can become."

Tashon nodded, hoping what Jonstin said was true, though could be they were doing the same thing but explaining it in different ways.

"You have more questions?"

"Yeah, but...." He winced and swore. "My ankle is bad. Just... go on with your story. It'll distract me. Hopefully."

"I found this place, but it was different than it is now. Far less souls here. A small band, trying to end the endless war, one soul at a time. But when I first came, it was for none of that. I wanted to see the cone, the point of creation. I

didn't know, or care that much, whether it was where a creator stood or the spot from which some Big Bang occurred, spreading out. I just wanted to see it, to feel it for myself. The point of creation? Who wouldn't want to see it?

"The soul that greeted me was like a branch, twisting and turning. Calm, kind. They — I don't know the gender, don't want to call they 'it' — took me to the top of the cone, let me stand there on the point all alone. Tashon, the grandeur of it is difficult to explain. It's a place of pure and utter serenity and joy. I closed my eyes and laughed. I laughed for days, it seemed.

"But when I opened my eyes I saw the chaos of war. Of those fighting for control of this place, as if any of them deserve it. They make a mockery of it, Tashon. Whatever created the universe — something natural or a higher being — none of it and none of us were meant for war and violence."

Tashon nodded. "That I agree with. Many on Aethera do now, too."

"They do?"

"I'll tell the whole story, but finish yours first." He gritted his teeth against another twinge of pain. "How do you help stop the war? Help them move on?"

"I lamented to them, the branch-like one. Lamented on the pointless war and violence. They told me of their purpose, the goal of all that they worked with. To convince and show those violent ones the harm and futility of war.

"And, Tashon, there was my path. The only real good I ever did in my life was helping Abe survive. I saw my chance to make the universe a better place. I jumped on it. I've helped many move on from war and violence."

"I still don't understand the how, though. Ugh." A spasm of pain set his leg to trembling. "You attached yourselves to them, like Aleron did to you and the others?"

Jonstin seemed hurt by that comparison. "No, not like that at all, Tashon. Outwardly, it might look the same, but the internal struggle is far different, and far more personal."

Tashon nodded slowly. Something about what Jonstin was doing felt wrong, but he wasn't sure what. "But what exactly happens? I'm trying to understand, because there were those on Aethera who were bent on war. Beyond convincing."

"It's an... emotional process. Each being I connect to is a different experience."

"What happened with the most recent one?"

"I found a being, small and lithe, stalking a group of its enemies. I didn't know what side she fought for, but she was a soldier. That I could tell from her aura. I sent out a string, what we thought of as tentacles with Aleron. I connected with her easily.

"When I connect to something... it's not to harm them. It's to connect to their essence, their core, to see why they are how they are. The key moments of their life in the Third."

Tashon felt that was a stark invasion of privacy, but kept the thought to himself for the time being.

"Good memories and bad. See, when we enter the Fourth, we still have the mindset we had when we died. Same beliefs, same habits. Though the physical habits and urges can't be fulfilled here. Some have gone insane simply from withdrawal.

"But back to this being. She came from a planet of numerous small continents, populated with people much smaller than humans. They walked on three legs. A very spiritual people with a tribe-based culture. The being was born to a family of multiple parents. The custom, there. Dozens of siblings. This was when I learned she was a she.

"Then I saw flashes of key life moments. Never the entire memory, but I feel the emotional impact of each. I saw her lose much of her family and tribe to something — I don't know what. A disease? A rival tribe? But the impact was that she learned she was a survivor. After the initial heartache, she chose to turn her grief into strength. Noble, perhaps, but not always.

"War broke out, the reason unclear to me. She fought out of necessity, and fought well. Victories piled up, with few losses. A day came when she faced enemies she was almost certain would overpower her small band. But she was a survivor, she told herself. Her tribe's priest tried to pray with her, to tell her she was too arrogant. She needed to put more faith in their god, and less in herself.

"She didn't listen. She went into the fight, fighting and killing to survive. She did, but was the only one left of her tribe. She saw the dark side of surviving. Her belief moved closer to trusting in that god she had been forgetting. Eventually, she convinced herself the priest had been right. She set out on a crusade, killing as many heathens and nonbelievers as she could until her life was taken.

"Of course, I felt dozens of other memories, but those were the main instances of her life. After reminding her of her life experiences, my work started. I showed her her memories, all of the key moments. Showed her different versions of them, showing her the way she had been determined on so many small variables. Showing her what she was is not what she has to be. Then I showed her glimpses of the peace I've found in the Fourth, the same peace that could be hers. When I disconnected from her, she was calm and quiet. She followed me here, and went into the pyramid. I, of course, explained to her beforehand that the pyramids could progress her, move on, become better."

Tashon shook his head. Did Jonstin truly see no wrong in what he was doing? Tampering with the core of someone, there was no way it would be painless. And even if it was, what gave this group the right to change someone like that? Another surge of pain stabbed his ankle.

"Damn it."

"Are you all right?"

"No, Jonstin." The words came out harsher than he intended, and he took a deep breath to calm himself. "I know you're trying to do the right thing by getting these souls to stop fighting. But... is it truly painless?"

"I've always thought some pain was involved. Change is never completely painless. But no true harm is done, Tashon. I thought you would appreciate what we're doing here, Tashon."

"I appreciate that you're trying to bring peace. But your methods are an invasion of privacy."

"There were laws about that on Earth and the Ship of Nations. It doesn't mean those laws apply here. And even if there were, we're doing it for the greater good."

"Governments have said that for years, but that doesn't make it right. And...." He paused, gritting his teeth against another ripple of pain. "Damn it. I'm not talking about laws. I'm talking about right and wrong. Changing who a person inherently is? Messing with their personal experiences that make them who they are?"

Jonstin didn't respond. *Maybe he sees my point,* Tashon though. *I thought he would. He's smart.* But Jonstin's silence went on far longer than made Tashon comfortable. What was Jonstin thinking?

"Jonstin."

"I needed to calm down. Tashon, I've devoted almost my entire life here to stopping this war. Why are you questioning that?"

"Bringing peace is good, Jonstin. I just... I get the feeling what you're doing isn't actually bringing peace." More pain, and Tashon swore under his breath. "Has any being done to you what you do to the others?"

"No."

"And have you talked to any of them after you do it? What are they like after you... change them?"

"They're quiet... contemplating their past and their future."

"You *know* that?" Tashon asked.

"I've been told that."

Tashon took a deep breath. He didn't want to shatter the purpose Jonstin had found in the Fourth, but he also didn't like the idea of Jonstin unknowingly causing harm and anguish.

"Who told you? The ones you do it to, or the others trying to end the war?"

Jonstin's aura vibrated. *"No. Tashon, no. You're not a part of this place. You don't understand. Violence and war do not belong here."*

Tashon sighed. "It shouldn't be here, I agree. But something about this feels wrong, somehow. I feel that whatever you're doing to them isn't harmless."

"Don't you need war to bring peace?"

"That sounds like the thought process of a lower plane," Tashon said. "Did it ever work on Earth?"

Jonstin shifted and stayed quiet.

Ishlea floated toward them, stopping at Jonstin's side.

"Ishlea, you're all right," Tashon said.

"Of course I am," Ishlea said. *"It's only a game, remember?"*

Tashon nodded, not wanting to argue the point. "Jonstin, this is my new friend, Ishlea."

Jonstin silently nodded to Ishlea.

Tashon winced again and tightened the splint. He could sense Jonstin processing, considering the implications of what Tashon said. If Tashon was right, he knew it would be hard on Jonstin. Learning that the good you thought you were doing is, in fact, causing harm isn't easy for anyone.

Without a word, Jonstin left.

"What's wrong with him?" Ishlea asked.

"I wish I knew, Ishlea. I wish I knew."

Chapter 15

The sun was blocked by clouds, the air outside chill as Bennet and Avet came to a rolled semi truck just outside Cody. Bottled water and food bars were scattered across the road. They had two choices: drive around it and keep going, or stop and see if they could help.

"Avet, Claw can wait a few minutes," Bennet said. "Let's just check on the driver."

"Just call 9-1-1 and report it," Avet said. "I'm not stopping."

Bennet sighed and pulled out his phone. He knew there was no changing Avet's mind. His brother was loyal to those he loved, no matter what. But just as Bennet looked down to dial, Avet swore and slammed on the brakes. The phone flew out of Bennet's hand and disappeared on the floorboard. He looked up.

Two men in suits, blue shirts and ties stood in the middle of the street. One held a shotgun, the other an AK-47.

"Suits," Avet said.

"What?"

"They're wearing suits," Avet said. "So were the ones who attacked Claw."

"Control," Bennet said. "Stay calm, Avet."

Avet nodded, but Bennet wasn't convinced. Avet reached under his seat, pulled out a sawed off shotgun and laid it on his lap, then put both hands on the wheel.

"Avet, that's against your parole," Bennet whispered.

"This is Mom's car, not mine. Her guns. Glovebox."

He opened the glovebox and found a vintage Ruger Single-Six revolver. "Dad's," Bennet whispered.

Avet nodded. "Keep it out of sight and shut up. Only shoot if you have to."

Avet inched the car forward and rolled down both windows. "Nice score there," he said as the one with the shotgun walked over. "But we don't want any." He slid his weapon between his seat and the center storage unit.

Bennet's mouth went dry, his palms sweating. He hadn't shot a gun since before their dad died, and never at something living.

The suit leaned down and put his masked face right up to Avet's. "Ours," he whispered.

"Yes, yours," Avet said. "Just let us pass."

The suit pulled his face back an inch or two, tilting his head in consideration.

Movement in the side mirror drew Bennet's attention. Another figure, a woman in a suit, snuck around the far side of the downed truck. She held a knife in one hand, a pistol in the other. Bennet sneezed.

Avet twitched his nose, indicating he understood.

Their childhood paintball strategies were proving useful. Now Bennet just had to wait for Avet to make the first move. Time slowed. Blood pounded through Bennet's head. He briefly realized the situation would impact his brother's PTSD, but there was no avoiding it now. In the mirror, the woman lifted her pistol.

Bennet coughed.

Avet's hand shot up, grabbed the mask and slammed the man's face down into the door. He pulled up the shotgun, jamming the butt into the man's face. Bone crushed beneath the mask, and man slumped unconscious to the ground.

Bennet swung his door open, stood, turned and fired. His shot missed. The woman pulled the trigger, her gun vibrated, but no bullet came. Bennet took a breath and fired again, hitting her shoulder. Again, and he hit her chest. She collapsed, and Bennet hoped he hadn't hit her heart.

Then he remembered the AK. He dove back into the car a second before a spray of bullets shattered the glass. The man was slow, or Bennet was fast. Or maybe, like Bennet, he'd never shot at a person before. At that thought, Bennet had a pang of sympathy for the three shooting at him. *Couldn't we just talk it out?*

"Hold on," Avet said.

The car sped forward, bullets thunking into metal, leather and plastic. Then they hit the man and he let out a shriek, sliding across the hood, through the broken windshield and into Bennet's lap. Avet slammed the shotgun into his temple, and the man went limp, blood leaking out of his mouth onto Bennet's pants. Bennet coughed, then vomited uncontrollably all over his clothes, the body and the dashboard.

Avet stopped the car. As Bennet sat motionless and in shock, Avet got out of the car, walked to the front of the car. He grabbed the man's legs, pulled him off the hood and rolled him out of the car's path. Then he jogged to the foodstuffs and water, carrying armfuls to the trunk. Bennet saw all of this, but picked up none of its meaning. All he knew was that he was alive, and he might've just killed a human being.

Then Avet was back in the car, and on they rolled. "You did good, brother." Avet gripped his shoulder.

Bennet nodded, staring at the blood on his pants. Someone else's blood. He would've preferred it to be his. Then reality flooded back, every detail crashing into his mind. He pulled out his phone.

"Calling 9-1-1," he mumbled.

"What?"

"Don't want those people to die," he said. "And we're going to get pulled over with the car like this. Better to tell them what happened."

Avet sighed. "You're right. Better call Claw and tell him we're gonna be late."

Bennet nodded. "Wonder how long the phones will work."

***

The two brothers sat in a square room of the Cody, Wyoming sheriff's station, the vomit and blood now dry on Bennet's clothes. Both of their guns sat on a table between them and a hulking police officer, her black hair styled in tight dreadlocks.

"You two lucky we're in Wyoming," she said. "Only state this shotgun won't get you at least five years in prison." She eyed both of them and they nodded.

"Also one of the only states with traditional police force," Avet said.

"You sayin' that's a bad thing?" She glared at Avet.

Avet held up his hands. "Not at all," he said. "If it weren't for the law, I'd never have met you." He winked at her.

"He's a funny one," she said to Bennet.

"He thinks so," Bennet said.

She smiled and nodded. "Good thing I know your momma, too."

"You know us, too, Ms. Pole," Avet said.

"*Sheriff* Pole, Mr. Gaines," she said. "Sheriff. And I know you from your drunken brawls at Claw's place. And Bennet, I haven't seen you since you were crappin' in diapers."

"I was probably covered in puke then, too," Bennet said.

The sheriff laughed loudly at that, a hearty, booming sound. "But really, you said they were wearing suits?"

"Yeah," Avet said. "Like the ones who torched Claw's place."

Pole nodded. "We'll see. They're headin' there now."

"Who used the revolver?" she asked, picking up the gun.

"Uh...I did, Sheriff," Bennet said.

She placed the gun on the table, picked up the shotgun and looked at Avet. "Didn't fire this?"

Avet shook his head. "That'd be against my parole, Sheriff."

"Holding it is against your parole, technically." She examined the gun. "There's blood on the butt."

"Still had to defend myself, Sheriff."

"Huh. We'll see what they find," she said. "Guess nothin' to do but wait and see if they find what you say they will. How's your momma?"

"All right," Bennet said. "Her dad died. She just got back from the funeral in Ireland."

"I didn't know. I'll call her later. Actually, I'll call her now."

Avet clicked his tongue. "Uh, you don't have to do that."

"But I want to." She pulled a phone out of her pocket, dialed and put it on speaker.

Leona answered on the second ring. "Sheriff, don't tell me you have my boys."

"I got 'em, Mayor. But they didn't do any wrong, don't think. Just self defense."

"Are they all right?"

"We're okay, Mom," Bennet said.

"That one is covered in puke, though," Pole said. "It's disgusting."

"What happened?"

The sheriff nodded to Avet.

"Some people on the 120 took out a semi. They were ransacking it, had guns. We tried to pass without getting shot at. Didn't work."

"Glad you're okay," she said. "We've had, uh—"

Pole's phone started buzzing. "Got another call, Mayor. Bye."

"Thanks, Sheriff."

Pole pressed two buttons, answering the new call and turning off speaker. "What'd you find?" She listened, eyebrows low. Then she hung up. "They found your suits."

"Are they alive?" The question jumped from Bennet. He hadn't realized how much he needed the answer.

"They are. The woman will make it, no question. The other two... maybe."

Bennet blew out a long breath. "Okay. Okay."

"They didn't find a car, though," Pole said.

"We never said anything about a car," Bennet said.

The sheriff nodded. "Right. How'd they get there, then? Did they just walk down the 120, guns out for everyone to see?"

Bennet and Avet glanced at each other.

"You sure you only saw three?" Pole asked.

Both nodded.

Pole sighed and shook her head. "Doesn't make sense. They took out a semi with no means of escape. And the woman's gun wasn't loaded. I had them check that, Bennet, 'cause you said her gun didn't fire. Who takes out a semi with no car and a woman who doesn't know how to reload her gun?"

Bennet raised his eyebrows. "And... what about the driver? I didn't see anyone in the truck. Didn't think to look 'til now."

"Damn it. I shoulda thought of that too," Pole said and picked up her phone. "Deputy. Did you see the trucker anywhere?" She nodded and hung up the phone. "Driver's dead. From the crash, they think." She looked at Bennet. "Dead before you got there. Nothin' anyone could do to help."

Bennet nodded. "Can't believe it's this bad already."

Avet huffed and shrugged. "Shit's been getting worse for decades, brother. These planes... they're just speeding up the decline."

"Damn people," Pole said. "Everyone's strugglin', gonna be strugglin' more and more. And these suits think they can take a truckload of supplies for themselves."

"With no car to put it in," Bennet said.

"Bet they were planning to take the truck," Avet said. "But that went bad."

Pole shrugged. "Yeah, maybe. You two need to get back to your momma. We got a shower. Go get cleaned up, Bennet. I'll give Avet some clothes for you."

***

Bennet stood under the cold spray, water and tears dripping down his cheeks and off his chin. Tears of relief that the woman survived. Tears of fear and hopelessness, too. Yes, the world had been going downhill faster and faster. But before today, he'd still seen a life kind and well-lived. But he'd almost died, and now he felt that he could die any minute.

And he knew, too, that he could be the one to cause death if it came down to it. If he needed to defend those he cared for most, he'd do what he had to do and live with the consequences.

But wasn't that what his brother tried to do? *And look at him now,* Bennet thought. But he knew that wasn't fair to Avet, knew he couldn't judge his brother. He couldn't help Avet, either. Not when he never spoke of what actually happened in Canada. What guilt or fear plagued him day and night.

"Got a towel and some clothes out here for you," Avet said. "Move quicker. Gotta get Claw still, and we need to be home before dark."

Bennet turned off the water and flung the curtain open.

Avet shielded his eyes. "Bennet, damn, you're skinny. Cover all that up."

Laughing, Bennet dried himself off quickly and pulled on a worn pair of jeans covered in holes and tears. Then he grabbed the shirt, and paused. The text on it read, 'I'm with stupid.' Bennet smiled. "Well, that's accurate."

Avet laughed. "Shut up. Let's go."

***

From Avet's War Journal, Audio Recording
click

Three weeks. Three damn weeks and we're still stuck in this field. The higher-ups haven't sent the command yet. Damn idiots.

sigh

We've already buried five of our own. The enemy's already coming north. A dozen of them snuck up on us the other night. Killed five before we had a chance to take them out. Five of us is on the ground while we sit here because some idiots up top can't sign some damn papers.

The world's run by arrogant idiots. That's why it's going to shit. Arrogant idiots grabbing whatever they can for themselves. And the rest of us suffer. Yeah, what kinda patriotic talk is this for a soldier? Ha. Yeah, I know.

But I fight to protect the people here. My family's here. This country is my home. Maybe one day we can bring it to greatness again, after the idiots kill themselves off.

And as long as more idiots don't take their place.

cough

Three. Weeks. Just for them to sign some papers to get us more supplies. They say supplies cost money. Damn right, they do. And the idiots have more than they know what to do with. They just know they don't want to give it to the soldiers. To those protecting their damn lives.

I'm not fighting for them. I'm fighting for my family. If Wyoming had its own military, I'd be keeping that border. But this is the best I can do. Too dumb for anything else.

Claw says I shouldn't say that. He says I'm smart. About tactics and strategy and killing, yeah. I wouldn't call that smart, though. Not the kinda smart that gets you a safe job with a good salary.

Not many of those exist anymore. Unless you're working for the idiots. My family got lucky, there. Money from the musicians in the family. Now they're nice and safe in their small town. We'll make sure it stays that way.
click

Chapter 16

Jonstin hovered at the point of the cone, hoping to find a clear understanding of the role he was playing in the war, and whether it was the part he should be playing. But understanding always hovers somewhere between translucent and opaque. One just has to find the truth as best they can, and find the clearest path. Until Tashon questioned him, Jonstin thought he was on the right path. Was convinced entirely of the righteousness of his cause. But now he wondered if there was such a thing as too much conviction, and not enough doubt.

A grain of doubt could cause him to see the truth to which he was previously blind. It could also lead to the unraveling of what he saw as his purpose. And where would that leave him? The cone gave no answer, and the peace he had once felt at the point of creation was gone. He dropped slowly to the bottom of the cone, contemplating how he could find the answers he saught.

It would be easy enough to get another anti-war being to connect to him so that he could experience it firsthand. Though, if Tashon was right, that would leave Jonstin's soul permanently injured. No, he'd have to observe it on the battlefield. He took off, sticking to the structures, trying to stay out of sight.

He soon saw a being he knew well. A mass of interwoven tubes intertwined to form an angular, four-legged, winged body with dozens of eyes. Jonstin referred to him as 'Vrushle.' While not completely accurate, it was the best Jonstin could do with the bizarre sounds the soul used to communicate.

Vrushle stalked a being from a species with which Jonstin wasn't familiar. Small, diamond-like, with no apparent appendages, the being's aura suggested it fought for the side that believed in a creator. Jonstin couldn't explain how he knew that, but after so long around those fighting the war, he came to realize that both sides had a uniform that could be felt rather than seen.

A part of Jonstin wanted to warn the unsuspecting diamond of Vrushle's impending attack, but if he did he would lose the opportunity to investigate Tashon's concerns. In an instant, Vrushle shot out his lone string and latched onto his prey. The diamond jolted back, then went still. Jonstin's heart pounded as he waited for the ritual to be over. Even then, without knowing for certain that Vrushle was harming the diamond, his aura darkened. How had he not seen it? It looked just like what Aleron's monster had done to him in the Third.

But was what Jonstin had been doing as bad, or worse? He was starting to think so. Had he just been so eager to do something *good* that he ended up blindly hurting dozens of souls? Souls, he knew, were only trying to do what they thought was right, just as he was.

Vrushle disconnected from the diamond, and Jonstin floated into view.

"*Human Jonstin,*" it said. "*You seem heavy.*"

Jonstin paused. If he let Vrushle know he was questioning the cause, he'd be attacked. "*Yes. I was following that one for a time, but you beat me to it.*"

Vrushle indicated understanding.

"*You continue to another target,*" Jonstin said. "*I'll take this one back.*"

Vrushle's essence lifted and brightened. "*Gracious, gracious of human Jonstin.*" Vrushle took off.

Jonstin turned to the diamond. Motionless, like he'd seen of so many other beings. Usually, he would gently guide them back to wait for the pyramids, speaking to them vaguely about peace and change and how the pyramids would help them. Sometimes, they'd indicate they heard, sometimes not. But he'd always assumed they were better off than they were before.

He moved in front of the diamond. "*Are you okay?*"

They bounced up and down once, then sunk to the ground. Something about the movement reminded Jonstin of an infant.

"*Do you understand me?*"

They made a few sounds that were either gibberish or a language Jonstin didn't understand. He sighed. He felt like he was stuck in the middle of two potential truths, with no way of knowing which was reality. Could he connect to the diamond in a way that let him sense its condition without harming it?

He thought it possible, but he would have to be careful. Would have to make sure all he did was observe, making the connection with observation his one and only intent. He needed to learn the true reality, not the reality that would make him feel the least amount of guilt and shame.

Slowly, cautiously, he sent out a single string. He had the capability to use five, and often did. But that was when his intentions were different.

"Observation and truth," he said to himself. *"Observation. Truth."*

He was falling, rising, twisting, falling again. He was the diamond, motionless in an empty vacuum of white. He couldn't move—no, didn't *want* to move. Was there a difference? Movement all around him. Shapes and light, darkness and shadow.

A memory: he was small, staring up at three others larger yet similar to him. He was excited, laughing. It disappeared.

Back in the white, now crowded with the shapes and shadows. They bumped into him, oblivious to his existence. Or willfully ignorant.

Another memory: despair seeping into every part of him. Prone and motionless forms all around him, each somehow familiar. But why he should know them was unclear, each a memory forever gone. The only evidence he had known them the image of their still bodies, lying in a greenish-orange substance, emitting a smell that stung his nose and eyes.

The memory was gone, as was the white room. He floated in a sea of green, surrounded by less shadows and more colors than in the white. Strings blowing around, all different shades than the other. He had no idea what to call them, if they were dangerous or safe, or something between. Movement came to him, slowly, almost unwillingly. Where was he going, and why? What was the *point*?

And whisked to the past again. He was grown, standing with a small group, walking down a glittering road. Tinkling laughter echoed off towering pillars and a shining wall. They were on their way to... somewhere, to do... something. It had once been important to him. Expedient, even. Necessary. But all that remained with him were the images, and none of the conviction.

Jonstin knew he wasn't the being whose memories he saw. But it was the same way his mind knew he was dreaming when asleep, yet still unable to wake up. Helpless, he bounced between obscure, colorful rooms and meaningless memories. There he was, standing at the head of a crowd shouting about... something. Then in a room of blues and pinks, shadows creeping close around him. Next, standing over a grave, the death one he knew he had mourned at the time, but now he couldn't even remember a name or a face. In a place of reds and oranges, the shadows creeping ever closer.

And all at once he was overcome with an immense sense of apathy. He had nothing to do, and didn't want any tasks. He saw no reason for struggling or persevering, for doubting or hoping. None of it mattered, and he was shocked at the idea that it had ever mattered. Purpose was exhausting, doubt was confusing and perseverance was never real. Struggles would always exist, no matter how hard you fight. So why keep fighting at all?

But something was there in Jonstin's mind, even if it was gone in the diamond's being. Desire. A desire to improve and to be better. The desire brought Jonstin back to an awareness of his purpose: observation and truth. He'd observed and found the truth. It was the truth he feared finding, but just because the truth goes against what you believe is no reason to ignore it. The truth proved to Jonstin that he'd causing far more than just physical harm to those fighting in the war. He could deny the truth, ignore it, or do something to right his wrongs. He tugged gently at the connection, hoping he wouldn't cause the diamond any more harm.

Bit by bit, he returned to himself. Slowly regaining his conviction, though that of which he was convinced had changed drastically. Returned entirely to himself, he looked at the diamond being with sadness. They had taken its purpose away. Jonstin had taken the purpose away from so many. Their purpose, he knew, had been one of violence. But he, too, had committed violence to them. Violence to their very souls.

"Is there no way to restore what we have taken from you?"

The diamond twisted back and forth. Gargled more meaningless sounds.

"*Come with me,*" Jonstin said, gently grabbing the diamond being, ensuring not to reconnect.

The diamond followed haltingly as they always did, but now Jonstin knew the real reason. Not because they were processing the new life they'd been blessed with, no. They were simply empty and lost, void of anything but apathetic confusion. *Stupid, stupid,* Jonstin thought. *I let myself be blinded by my desire to do good.*

As they neared the courtyard that intermittently housed the pyramids, Jonstin noticed the entryway was flanked by two beings. Both were large, hulking human forms. On the left, a woman stretched tall and thin. The other, also a woman, was just as tall, but three times as wide.

Jonstin had never seen the entry guarded before, and he feared he knew the reason. *Have they discerned my change so soon?* he asked himself. Then the two beings turned their attention to him, their auras heavy and firm. He had his answer, but was undeterred. Tashon was in there, helpless. Plus, he still needed answers.

He met the two at the entrance.

"*You took Vrushle's target,*" the thin one said.

"Yes," Jonstin said. *"He's always eager to get more, and I was ready to get back to my three-dimensional friend."*

"Saw you reconnect to target," the larger one said. "Why?"

"Making sure the job was complete. Vrushle can be hasty."

"And was it?" she asked.

"It was."

The thin one moved closer. "Then why connected so long?"

Jonstin held his ground. *"I got... stuck. Lost. It took me some time to disconnect."*

"Why we have rule to not connect to changed target." Now the larger woman moved closer.

Damn, Jonstin had forgotten that rule. *"You're right. I wasn't thinking clearly."*

"More than that, I think," said the thin one. "You trying to change target back. You turn against us, against peace."

Not exactly right, but Jonstin could tell that no matter what he said they wouldn't let him go quietly. So why not tell the truth? *"I was concerned with our methods. I wanted to know what we actually did to them, the targets."*

"Exactly as we've always taught." The skinny one moved closer.

Jonstin decided to make one last effort to convince them. *"No. It's not. We take their very souls. We leave them lost and conf–"*

The thin woman shot out a thick rope. Jonstin ducked, and it zoomed past his head. The other woman shot a sting out just above the ground. Jonstin grabbed the diamond and sped straight up, the two women close behind. He flew over the courtyard, looking down to see Tashon asleep in the corner, Ishlea at his side. If Jonstin was leaving, he was taking the injured Tashon with him. But, first, he needed to figure out how to escape, and where.

His pursuers split up, the thin one to the right and the other out of sight. *Not good*, Jonstin thought. He looked at the diamond being, apathetically flopping behind as if it didn't care whether they were caught or not. And most likely, they didn't. Without hope or fear, how could they?

Another being, this one nothing but a swirling tangle of strings, stopped in front of Jonstin.

Reinforcements, he thought as he darted up and ana, narrowly dodging a flurry of strings. One slid across his back, but not close enough to make any meaningful connection. *They'll send more*, he thought. He glanced down at Tashon. His three-dimensional friend lay in the same spot, but now a small form hovered next to him. Jonstin wasn't sure, but he was convinced it wasn't friendly.

Another string shot at him from below and wrapped around his fourth-dimensional leg. Not enough to make him useless, but enough to slow him down. He pulled and yanked, gaining the smallest distance but not freeing himself from the trap.

Tashon shouted something, but the words were lost in the growing winds. Another string from another being grabbed Jonstin's arm, and he was slowly pulled down. Closer to a small group that had formed in the courtyard, their auras exuding fear and anger. As if Jonstin's doubt was an act of violence against them. *No better than those in the Third*, Jonstin thought numbly, accepting defeat.

Then Tashon yelled, "Go! Pull harder!"

Jonstin did, and the small being next to Tashon shot up, strings spiraling and stabbing through Jonstin's captors. He'd never seen that before. His leg and arm were released and he spun around to thank his savior, but more were coming. Jonstin dodged and zoomed, the diamond being still lazily trailing behind, as his helper made quick work of his enemies. Each was pierced through in a matter of moments, their forms more limp than any targets they had ever acquired.

Jonstin floated to Tashon, hoping it was all over. He hoped in vain, for a horde now came through and over the entryway. Every one of his former allies, it seemed, were there to shut down his doubt before it caused any more trouble. As if it were a tumor that needed to be eradicated before it grew. *No way out,* he thought.

The pyramids filled the space. Jonstin turned in awe. They had never appeared without him being told of it beforehand. He turned back to see the horde had gone still and reverent. The pyramids grew brighter and brighter, and Jonstin remembered another rule: they must never enter the pyramids.

He picked up Tashon, grabbed hold of his new companion, the diamond being, strengthening his grip, and shot to the structure.

His enemies screeched, wailed and shouted behind him, but they did not follow.

The pyramids opened. They entered, Ishlea darting in a moment later. Just before the doors closed, the diamond being was yanked from Jonstin's grasp.

They were shrouded in darkness.

"Isn't this game the best?" Ishlea squealed.

Chapter 17

Clawman snored loudly in the back seat of the old Ford Sheriff Pole lent them. He'd fallen asleep by the time they were five miles outside of Cody, his head resting on Avet's lap. Cuts and bruises covered his face, and one eye was swollen half shut. A two-inch gash, now stitched, stretched from the middle of his left cheek to the middle of his bottom lip. The stitching was tight, clean and straight. The cleanest looking part of Clawman's face was that stitch job, and it was impossible not to admire it.

Avet reached his hand out, squeezed Bennet's shoulder and nodded at him in the mirror. Bennet smiled softly and nodded back. He'd always been close with Avet, but there was a part of Bennet that was always jealous of the camaraderie Avet had with his fellow soldiers. Now, after the most terrifying minutes of Bennet's life, it seemed that same camaraderie had formed between the two of them, but he wasn't sure he wanted it anymore.

His phone rang loudly through the car speakers and all three jumped, Clawman throwing a wild fist into the roof of the car, leaving a shallow dent.

Bennet cleared his throat and pressed a button on the steering wheel. "Hey, Mom. We're on our way back."

"You got Claw?" she asked.

"Yeah," Bennet said.

"How is he?"

"I'm jutht fine, Mayor Gainth," Clawman said as he sat up.

"You sound great," she said. "Where are you?"

"Just a few minutes outside of Cody," Bennet said.

"Okay. I want you to drive through Byron, down to Lovell then back here."

"Sure, Mom," Bennet said. "What for?"

"Recon," she said. "Stuff ain't right. The suits in Cody. Some soldiers in uniform showed up here. We need to know what's going on with our neighbors."

"Soldiers?" Avet asked. "What troop? What branch?"

Her sigh crackled through the car speakers. "I don't know. I don't think they're real soldiers. Their uniforms... you'll see when you get here. Recon first. Please."

"Copy that, Mom," Avet said.

"Yeth, ma'am," Clawman said.

"See you soon, Mom," Bennet said.

"Thanks, you three. Love you all."

"Love you," the three said simultaneously, and Bennet hung up.

"Tholdiers?" Clawman asked. "In Cowley?"

Bennet nodded, eyes straight ahead on the road. "Sounds like it. But... not real soldiers? What does that mean?"

"Fake uniforms," Avet said. "What it sounds like to me. We saw it in San Diego."

"Yeth we did," Claw said.

"Why pretend to be soldiers?" Bennet asked.

Avet shrugged. "Can't say for the ones in Cowley. But, in San Diego, they were trying to get free supplies. They'd put on something like a uniform and come to the camp at night when we were eating."

"Civilians?" Bennet asked.

"Yeah."

Bennet raised an eyebrow. "Didn't you have relief supplies for them already?"

"A few humanitarian groups did, but they ran out. Or were robbed by militant groups stockpiling for themselves. For a lot of the civilians, getting food from us was the only option." Avet looked out the window. "Some of us didn't care. We'd pretend we thought they were real soldiers and give them half a portion, at our own expense. Eventually, the less merciful ones caught on and only let certain of us dish out the food."

"Damn." Bennet shook his head. "But I don't think that's what these want. Or, maybe. I don't know. And what about the ones wearing suits?"

"Damn suits," Avet said, looking at Claw's face. "I don't know either. Some kind of gang, maybe. Shits just gotten crazy."

"And now I look like the Joker." Claw smiled.

Bennet laughed and Avet shook his head.

"Byron," Bennet said. "We're here."

He slowed down as the highway became Main Street, eyes peeled for anything out of place. But the town seemed normal, other than the lack of plant life. A few kids played in their yards, an elderly couple walked their dog down the street. A man stood on a corner juggling half a dozen bowling pins and wearing a towering white top hat. Bennet drove about a half mile past him, then pulled over.

"Wait. Did you see that?" Bennet turned around.

The man was still there, juggling three knives just as he had been only seconds earlier. *Or was it pins?* Bennet asked himself.

"I snapped a picture of him," Avet said. "Keep going."

"Shouldn't we talk to him?"

Claw shook his head. "Recon. Jutht recon."

"Right." Bennet pulled back onto the road.

"Bar seems busy," Bennet said as they drove past.

"Makes sense. I'm sure everyone's drinking more these days."

They reached the end of Main Street, and started leaving Byron behind.

"Let's check the whole town," Avet said. "Drive up and down. It's not like it's that big."

Bennet turned around and headed back east. He took a right onto Mountain View Street and they systematically combed each street in the town, but found nothing out of place. No jugglers, soldiers or suits. Just yards void of life.

"On to Mormon town, it is," Avet said.

"I like the Mormonth," Claw said. "They've alwayth been nithe to me."

"Not everyone in Lovell is a Mormon, brother."

Avet shook his head. "Close enough."

"Meemaw wath a Mormon," Claw said, turning his head away from Avet.

"I know, I know," Avet said. "I just... had bad experiences with them."

"Jutht one," Claw said.

Bennet laughed. "He's right, brother. You had one bad experience with one Mormon."

"That douche was a damn bigot," Avet said.

"But Claw's meemaw raised him," Bennet said. "No way a bigot raised your man."

"I know," Avet said, grabbing Claw's hand. "Wish I could've met her."

Claw tried to smile. "Meemaw woulda hated you."

The three laughed, and soon they were pulling onto Main Street in Lovell, Wyoming. The sun was almost behind the horizon. A large crowd was gathered in the parking lot of the large Mormon church, staring up at the steeple, all dressed in their 'Sunday best.'

"Didn't realize it was Sunday," Avet muttered. "What're they looking at?"

A little girl with flowing white hair was perched on the point of the steeple in full ballerina dress. She spread her arms out wide, the last rays of sun casting a mesmerizing glow over her form. *Like an angel*, Bennet thought. She bent her knees and jumped. The rays of light blinked on and off her as she flew through the air and over the crowd, one leg forward and one back, forming a perfectly horizontal line. She floated over the heads of the crowd slowly, as if carried along by a gentle breeze. Bennet smiled, eyes wide with wonder. All that existed for that moment was the floating girl, aglow with sunlight from the heavens.

Then gravity took over. She dropped, remaining in perfect form, and landed in the road right in front Pole's old Ford. The air erupted with screams as Bennet threw the car into park, jumped out and ran around the hood. The girl was on her feet, smiling and waving. Then she curtsied, walked to the sidewalk and sat on the curb. The crowd muttered among themselves. Bennet took a deep breath and sat down next to her as an elderly man in an oversized suit sat on her other side.

"That was something," Bennet said.

She looked at him, forced a smile, and then looked away.

"I'm John Shepherd," the man said. "What's your name?"

No answer.

"You don't know her, John Shepherd?" Bennet said.

"None of us do," John said.

Bennet turned, the shock plastered on his face. "That makes no sense, John. Where'd she come from?"

"We just came outta church, and uh... she was up there."

"When?"

John looked at his watch. "Five minutes ago."

"Avet, Claw," Bennet called.

The two walked over and stood in the street, just off the sidewalk.

"John says no one knows her."

"What, no one in Lovell?" Avet asked.

John shrugged and shook his head. "No one."

Claw crouched down, wincing at the task, and smiled at the girl. "Hi. Whath your name?"

She looked Clawman in the eye, giggled, stood, spun in a circle and sat down again.

"I thought this was just recon," Avet said.

Blue and red lights flashed and a siren bleeped once. The sheriff's car parked at an angle in front of Pole's car, blocking it in.

Avet shook his head. "Not this prick."

Claw smiled. "He ain't Mormon, though."

Avet shrugged and spat. "So much for recon."

The car door opened and a tall man with broad shoulders and a glowing white smile stepped out. His uniform was pristine, as was his cowboy hat and boots. He walked to John, who had stood up, and shook his hand.

"Bishop Shepherd, my friend, nice to see you. Would you be so wonderful as to tell me what has transpired that resulted in your call?"

Bishop Sheperd coughed. "Yes, yes, Sheriff Locke. We finished our block of meetings, our services. And this girl, she ah... was on the steeple."

Locke looked up and pointed. "That steeple, my friend?"

"That's the only steeple around," Avet muttered under his breath.

Bennet glared at him.

Avet rolled his eyes.

"Yeah... yes, Sheriff Locke," John said.

Locke looked at the crowd. "Any of my other fine friends here have a different story?"

Head shakes and soft 'no's' rippled through the crowd.

"Strange, I would say. Strange indeed." Locke took off his hat, ran a hand through silky smooth hair, and then replaced it. "What happened next?"

"She turned into an angel!" a little boy squealed.

"She jumped," a man said.

Locke turned to Bennet. "Mr. Gaines, did you see what transpired?"

"Like both said," Bennet answered. "She jumped over the parking lot. Looked like an angel in the air until she landed in front of my car. By the time I got out, she was just standing there."

Locke looked around the crowd. "Does anyone dispute the story of this fine man?"

None did.

Locke clicked his tongue, then pursed his lips. "A most strange incident, indeed." He looked down at the little girl. "Hello, little one. How is it you happened to get on top of that steeple?" he asked, pointing.

The girl raised her eyebrows and tilted her head.

"It seems she does not speak," Locke said.

Avet opened his mouth, but closed it at another glare from Bennet. No reason to piss off the sheriff.

"Truly, none of you have seen her before?" Locke asked loudly.

Again, everyone answered in the negative.

Locke crouched down and reached out a hand. "Okay, little one. Come with me. We'll find somewhere safe."

She stood up, stretched her arms out to her sides and ran down the street. With a squeal of pure joy, she leaped into the air and floated higher and higher, out of sight.

"Bye, angel," a girl yelled, waving her hand wildly.

Sheriff Locke looked at the crowd. "Does this happen to be some Mormon culty prophecy, or some similar occurrence?"

John Shepherd laughed. "No, no. But... a beautiful sight. Innocence, she is. Pure innocence."

The sun was almost completely out of sight, and Bennet thought of the suits on the highway. "We should leave. I want to get home before it gets completely dark." Bennet stood up.

Locke stepped forward, nose less than an inch from Bennet's. "No, Mr. Gaines. You were witness to—"

"To what?" Avet asked. "There was no crime... Sheriff." He added with a sneer.

Locke turned and narrowed his eyes. "A young girl appeared, perhaps from the heavens or perhaps from whoever sent the planes. If that is what happened, we need to talk to all who saw her. And"—he looked at Bennet—"all who talked to her."

Bennet rolled his eyes, but didn't speak, deciding to let Avet take care of that.

"Sheriff, what crime was committed?" Avet asked.

"A child is out, alone in the world with parents or adults to aid her if she is in need," Locke said. "And you wish to simply drive home? I thought better of you, Mr. Gaines and Mr. Gaines."

Now Claw stepped forward and John Shepherd stood up.

"Sheriff Locke," John said. "They have done nothing... at all. Nothing wrong. A girl appeared... and flew to the sky."

Claw cleared his throat. "The girl wath not human."

"Right." John nodded. "Yes. Why, uh, she obviously doesn't need help."

"She got away from you just fine, huh, Sheriff?" Avet laughed softly, as did others in the crowd.

Locke's face tightened, then he blew out a breath. "Depart, then, if you wish. Everyone go home, and keep a keen eye for the girl. Or anything else that might be strange or angelic, or even seemingly innocent. Mr. Gaines, please make your exit hasty, will you?"

Avet shrugged. "Once you move your vehicle out of the way, Mister Sheriff, sir."

Locke looked at his car, as if only then realizing he'd blocked another car in. "Yes, I will need to do that." He took one last look at the crowd. "Go home now, my friends. Go home." He got in the car and drove off.

Bennet looked at John. "Thank you, John Shepherd."

The man waved the words off with a wrinkled hand. "Just told the truth. Good night. Safe drive, huh?"

Bennet waited a moment, looking at the crowd, trying to determine what they might be feeling and thinking. Did they see the girl as a sign of hope for the future? Or did any feel like he did, that all the hope the Earth had flown into the heavens with her?

"Hey, brother, let's go."

Bennet turned. Claw and Avet were already in the back seat of the car. He got in, started the engine and headed north, back to Cowley. Within minutes, the sun was gone completely, and a part of Bennet felt certain it would never rise again.

Chapter 18

As soon as the pyramids closed, the three were left in complete darkness. Tashon still rested in Jonstin's grip, the pain in his leg flaring, calming and flaring again, an unending pattern of discomfort.

"Momma," Ishlea said. *"I think the simulation is broken."*

Tashon sighed, tired of Ishlea's constant comments about them being in a simulation. It was real. The grumbling in his stomach, the dryness in his throat and the aching of his leg convinced him of that fact.

"How long have we been in here, Jonstin?"

"Don't know. Time isn't measured here, not really. Time tells you when you need to eat or rest, or get somewhere. None of that is needed here."

Tashon nodded once then closed his eyes, though it made no difference. He could see nothing from any viewpoint. "Do you see anything, Jonstin?"

Jonstin spun in a circle, twirling Tashon around with him. *"No. Wait... A few faint lines of light. Maybe a door?"*

"Yes, I see it," Ishlea said. *"The game continues."*

"Wait," Tashon said. "Jonstin, what supposedly happens in here, to the ones you send in?"

"Not that it can be taken as truth, but they say it changes you by encouraging you to be the best version of yourself. The strange thing is I have no idea how it works."

"Evalee came to the pyramids, I think," Tashon said. "Of her own volition."

"They say those are the best ones, who do it with no... outside pressure. They say the only better are us, the ones who change and... encourage those unwilling to enter. But that's not what we were doing, after all." Jonstin's form emanated a heaviness that was palpable, and Tashon felt his guilt.

"Jonstin, maybe what you were doing was wrong, but I don't think sending them to this place was. If Evalee came here, it must be good. Let's find an exit."

"Yeah! On we go," Ishlea yelled.

A light breeze moved across Tashon's face and Jonstin moved through the darkness. Soon, the door Jonstin had seen was visible to

Tashon, as well. Though it seemed more of an entryway, far off in the distance. It was a small cube, tilted slightly to the right, a soft reddish-blue light glowing from whatever was on the other side.

"*That's the only way out?*" Ishlea asked.

"*The only one I see,*" Jonstin said.

"*It's not right. The color is.... Are we really going that way?*" Ishlea's voice trembled, sending quivers through Tashon's mind.

She's changed again, Tashon thought. "Ishlea, is this a simulation?"

"*Simulation? No, this is... real, all too real. I wish it weren't.*"

"*I don't see anything wrong with the door,*" Jonstin said.

No response. They went on, the cube slowly growing as they neared. Tashon examined the entryway, trying to discern if there was something wrong with it. But as far as he could tell, it was just another fourth-dimensional structure, and the light that came from it was a welcome sight amidst all the darkness.

But there was *something* there, in the center of the light. Though there was no way for Tashon to know what it was, or whether it was good. It was a shapeless spot, nearly in the exact center of the light. And it was dark, darker than the blackness that surrounded the door.

Tashon thought for a moment, then remembered. "Fuligin," he said. "Blacker than black." He'd read it in the library on the Ship of Nations, though he always considered it a fictional color.

Yet there it was, at the center of the door. They soon at arrived at it, and Tashon realized that the fuligin was not a part of the color radiating from the door. No, a fuligin figure stood far off in the distance on other side of the entryway, across a vast area dense with the red-blue light and filled with shapes that moved with the wind. Something was different about those shapes just across the threshold, something that made them different than the other structures Tashon had seen in the Fourth. He couldn't figure out *what* the difference was, though. Not from the other side of the threshold.

"Are we going?" he asked.

"*It's the only way out,*" Jonstin said. "*Ishlea? Are you okay?*"

Dimly lit by the light streaming into the darkness, Tashon saw Ishlea shake and vibrate, then become completely still. "*The... only way. Then it must be... the right way. But wrong, too. What to do when the* right *way is the* wrong *way?*"

Interesting question, Tashon thought.

"*It's the only way,*" Jonstin said again.

"*It is,*" Ishlea said. "*I'll go first.*"

She floated into the red-blue light, Jonstin close behind, Tashon still in his arms. It was warm, almost hot, and the wind carried a smell that seemed to embody life itself. Tashon didn't relish being carted around by Jonstin, but a perk of being this incapacitated was that he could focus all his energy on observation. Behind them, the entryway and the pyramids were gone, and Tashon felt certain the pyramids had left him and his companions exactly where they wanted him. But was that a good thing, or not?

Small specks of dust floated along in the wind, dots of infinite colors. One landed on Tashon's leg. He pressed his fingertip against it and lifted it to his nose. As he thought, the specks were the source of the scent of life. Ishlea moved intently, focused on whatever it was that she thought might be a threat to them. But as far as Tashon could tell, it was one of the most calm and beautiful places he'd ever been. He examined the shapes that moved with the wind. Some were tall and thin, like the field near Circa. Others were short and round, while some were towering tubes with multi-faceted arms sticking out of them. Dozens of other shapes were mixed in, creating a mesmerizing forest.

"Forest," Tashon said quietly. "These are plants."

Jonstin laughed softly. *"I forget how strange it must be to see all of this with three-dimensional eyes."*

"It... makes sense that they'd be here. They're alive in the Third, so why wouldn't they ascended to the Fourth at death too?" He paused, smiled, and then frowned. "Smith and Rosa would love this."

"Tashon, you still haven't told me what happened after I died."

Tashon smiled and shook his head. "I think it's more unbelievable than your story, Jonstin."

"Doubt it, but let's hear it."

"I need to eat," Tashon said. "Set me down somewhere. I'll tell you while we take a break."

***

"Maybe just as unbelievable as my story," Jonstin said. *"Wish I could've seen it. History being made, Sage Tashon at the center of it all."*

Tashon shook his head. "Maybe. Everything I did just... felt like the things to do."

"The right *things, I think,"* Jonstin said.

"I hope so." Tashon stuffed an empty food wrapper into his pack, and looked at the surrounding forest. The souls of small creatures wandered along the ground, up and down the trees. Some fluttered in the air from branch to branch. For those, it seemed life in the Fourth was much as it had been in the Third, without the needs and worries of physical existence. From all Tashon could see, they brought no biases from the Third to hinder their existence in the Fourth. They simply lived, and let live. In the distance, the fuligin shape remained, fluttering in and out view, still a shapeless, blacker than black jumble. Ishlea was focused on it, oblivious to anything else. Tashon called her name, but she didn't move.

"Let's get going," Tashon said.

Jonstin picked him up. *"Which way is the sound?"*

Tashon pointed. Not exactly the direction of the fuligin form, but not away from it, either. If it decided to intercept them, it would have no problem doing so. "Ishlea, are you coming with us?"

"I... just... yes, I am. Not right here, though. Not right." She moved cautiously forward. *"I'll keep in front, keep an eye out."* She floated in the direction Tashon indicated, her form tense and trembling slightly.

As they moved forward, weaving in and out of the plants, soaking in the warmth of the light, Tashon tried to bring back the peace he'd felt upon first entering the forest, but Ishlea made that impossible. She said nothing, but fear dripped from her essence, pooling around her and draining Tashon's desire to observe every detail of the forest. Though he tried. For a few seconds he would get lost watching a spiky cylinder blowing through the wind, or the essence of something like a monkey bouncing between the branches, only to be drawn back into the terror by a twitch or quiver from Ishlea.

They progressed in as close to a straight line as possible, Tashon telling Ishlea to adjust this direction or that as the sound moved. The dark figure remained in roughly the same area in which it had been when he first saw it, and it was soon more to the right than in front of them.

"Jonstin," Tashon whispered. "Why is she so afraid of the fuligin?"

"Fuligin?"

"It's... a color, darker than black. The dark form. Why is she so afraid of it?"

"I don't know. But it makes me think we should be scared, too."

"Are you?"

"A little, yeah. But I don't think it's dangerous. Just Ishlea's fear rubbing off on me. Are you scared?"

Tashon looked at the being, partially visible through the trees. Still shapeless, from this distance. "Its... unnerving, seeing something that dark. And... yeah, I am scared a bit. But I think I've been scared since I left Aethera." Tashon hadn't recognized that fear before then, but as he said it he knew it was true. "I'm a paper man in a world of flesh and bone."

Jonstin laughed softly. *"How's your ankle?"*

"It's actually feeling somewhat better." He wiggled his toes. It hurt, but didn't force a wince out of him. "Getting there. In the Third, it would've been days before it felt this good."

"Days? It all feels like my first day, still."

Tashon nodded. If he hadn't taken his few breaks for sleep, healing and eating, he would've felt the same way. Days only mattered to the physical.

Ishlea stopped moving. *"That darkness... is closer."*

Tashon jerked his head to the right. The fuligin was there, at most half as far than it had been. Tashon looked at it closely, and concluded that it hadn't moved closer to them, but they had moved closer to it. It stood by the same three plants it always had, a triangle of vegetation that looked more like tall blades of grass than trees.

"Ishlea, we're the ones that've advanced on it, not the other way," Tashon said.

"Darkness... draws us in," Ishlea said.

Tashon realized immediately that she was right. They'd been going steadily straight, and Tashon had constantly told them to angle more to the left. Evidently, it hadn't helped. Would they really end up at the fuligin, regardless what direction they chose?

"Ishlea, what *is* the darkness?" Tashon asked.

"Not certain. Darkness is not right. Just... something wrong here." A severe tension surrounded her.

"Then maybe we should go the other way, and get back in the right direction once we're out of its reach," Tashon said.

"Try. Might work...or not."

They turned from the fuligin form, as if pretending it didn't exist, and walked away. Tashon watched it grow farther away. A colored speck floated and he sneezed, forcing his eyes shut for a less than a moment. When he opened them, the scene behind them had changed. The fuligin was gone, as was the trio of plants. He turned his head around and yelped. The being was to their right, not more than ten strides away, half of it hidden behind a plant. Even up close, Tashon could make no sense of the mass. Something like a large, torn piece of fabric that seemed as light as a feather and as heavy as a stone, all at once.

"Jonstin," Tashon whispered. "Ishlea."

Jonstin stopped and trembled, softly shaking Tashon's body. Ishlea's form drooped, the fear seeming as though it would drag her down completely. But the sage, for no reason he understood, was calm and free of fear.

"Hello," he said.

The form moved into full view, but still Tashon could make no sense of it. The fuligin bulged in some places and shrunk in others, but didn't advance.

Tashon took that as a good sign. "We're travelers here. Who are you?" *Or what?* he thought, still unsure if it was a being or not.

It twisted and rose slightly into the air, then rotated and focused entirely on Tashon. Though how Tashon knew it was focused on him, he couldn't say. But he knew the fuligin wanted him.

"Jonstin, bring me closer," he said.

"Tashon, I...."

Frustration flushed into Tashon. "Jonstin, take me closer or I will walk."

"Darkness draws us in," Ishlea said, though Tashon barely heard it.

Jonstin placed Tashon on the ground. *"Let me,"* he said.

Tashon protested and tried to stand, but collapsed as his ankle gave way underneath him. He swore and helplessly watched as Jonstin inched forward.

"Darkness draws us in. Draws us in."

The fuligin's attention shifted to Jonstin. Something gray flashed at the edge of the shape. Tashon crawled forward to see it, but the fuligin bulged again, covering whatever had been there, and Tashon got the feeling it only wanted them to think it was entirely fuligin. Or was that a trick to make Tashon think it wasn't dangerous? He looked at Ishlea.

"...draws us in. Darkness...."

Jonstin stopped three strides away from the fuligin, his essence giving no indication whether or not he was afraid. The fuligin bulged again, and a line of white flashed out then back again. *A sheep in wolf's clothing?* Tashon asked himself. Jonstin made another move forward, shortening the distance.

"Darkness draws us...."

Tashon knew that shade alone wouldn't tell him the intent of a being in the Fourth, though he wished it would. Ishlea's fear pooled off of her, strings rising from the puddle beneath her like steam. If he trusted her fear, he would yell at Jonstin to turn and flee.

"Darkness... darkness... darkness...."

"Fuligin, not darkness," he whispered. At least not the evil, fear-mongering darkness Ishlea thought it was. *That's the difference*, he thought. *Real darkness can be seen and felt. There is black and fuligin, then there is darkness. They are not the same.* How had he not seen it before?

Jonstin was now close enough to touch the mass. The fuligin bulged toward him.

Tashon's heart jumped. Maybe he'd been wrong.

"*Draws us. Draws us....*"

The bulge stretched out in all directions, nearly touching Jonstin.

"*Darkness draws... draws... draws....*"

The bulge rippled, popped and a wave of white light poured out, enveloping all three of them.

"*Darkness. Dark....*"

Tashon stood in pure light. His splint was gone, his ankle healed. Jonstin floated to one side, and Ishlea the other. An immense weight pushed down on Tashon, and he hunched over in his attempt to bear it. Jonstin and Ishlea's forms bent forward as well, and each had a mass of fuligin bulging from their backs.

"Does my back look like Ishlea's?" Tashon asked.

"*Yes,*" Jonstin said.

"*Darkness has me. Has me, has me,*" Ishlea muttered over and over.

Tashon took a hesitant step forward, then stopped, the one movement forcing his heart to beat faster, his breaths come faster.

"*Do that again,*" Jonstin said.

"What?"

"*I saw something. Do it again,*" Jonstin said.

Tashon stepped with his other foot, then stopped.

"*When you move, some of the fuligin blows away. Watch me.*"

Jonstin struggled forward, and with each tiny movement, a flake of fuligin fell off and blew away in a wind Tashon did not feel.

Tashon nodded. "I think we're still in the pyramids."

Chapter 19

The buzzing on her wrist yanked Sheriff Pole from a dreamless sleep. She jabbed the screen with one finger without opening her eyes.

"What is it?" she asked.

"Sheriff, sorry to wake you. It's those three suspects in suits."

"They dead?"

"No, Sheriff—"

"They alive?"

"No. They're, uh, gone."

Sheriff Pole opened her eyes. "Gone?" More alert, she remembered another question. "Who is this?"

"Dr. Hinnish, Sheriff. And, yes, gone, no doubt. They were in the emergency ward, now gone. No patients or nurses or doctors saw them leave."

Pole sighed. "Did you ever get your security cams fixed?"

"Yes, yes, actually. The funding came through," Hinnish said.

Surprising, thought Pole. "What does the video say?"

"Disappeared."

Pole sat up and rubbed her eyes. "What's that?"

"They're there, in their beds. Then—poof—gone."

Pole bit her lip, then stood up. She trusted Hinnish more than she trusted most in Cody. But she couldn't just take his word for it. That'd be bad police work. "I'm coming down."

"Bring coffee?"

Pole ended the call. "House, bedroom lights on." She flicked a switch on the wall, and the room lit up, revealing her small studio apartment. On her meager salary, she'd never been able to afford smart home features, but she found a small joy with the pretending. "House, turn on Ginger's light." She walked to a glass terrarium in the corner and clicked a button on a dangling cord. A lamp hanging above the cage lit up, revealing a three-legged gecko. "Good morning, Ginger. I'll get some bugs or worms today."

Ginger licked her lips and Pole smiled. *If I can find any,* she thought. She walked to a small closet and opened it, revealing three uniforms, two sweat suits, and one pantsuit. She'd never worn the pantsuit, but it'd been a gift from her ex-girlfriend. It was worth a small fortune, more than a month of Pole's rent. She'd sell it, if she could find a buyer. If she ever decided to look for a buyer.

She grabbed a uniform, got dressed and jogged out the door without breakfast.

***

Bennet sat with his family at the bar of Cub's Den, cutting into a medium rare steak. With supplies running out and winter coming in the next few months, the town decided to butcher their livestock and have a feast, then freeze the rest. But this feast lacked the joy and revelry of past feasts. People talked in hushed voices or didn't talk at all. Some picked at their food, unable to eat while others ate more than their fill in attempt to cover up their anxiety.

Bennet half listened to a news broadcast on one the screens. "Reports from small towns across the country are still coming in," a woman said. "And no two have been the same. Strange, unknown characters inexplicably appearing. Some have caused serious harm, others have done nothing but provide curious entertainment or a problem to be solved. But they are popping up in more and more towns, while leaving major cities untouched by their presence. But the question on everyone's mind—"

"Is what's the connection to the *planes*?" Avet said mockingly.

No one laughed.

Leona took a sip from her bottle. "You're not sick of him yet, Claw?"

Claw smiled and shook his head. "Juth thick of not thewing. That thteak lookth fantathtic."

"I'll toss it in a blender for you," Bennet said as he dramatically took a bite. "Or Avet can feed you like a mama bird."

Avet shoved a piece of meat in his mouth, chewed it up, and then leaned in to kiss Claw.

Claw pushed him away, laughing. "Dithguthting."

They all laughed.

Cylindra stared blankly at her plate. "You know, lots of times while a mother bird is keeping the eggs warm, the father is the only one that leaves the nest to get food. He'll regurgitate into her mouth. It wouldn't be unnatural for Avet to do it for Claw." She looked up and grinned.

"I'm not a bird," Claw said, then made a gagging sound.

Gella looked up from wiping the other side of the bar. "Claw! Are you okay?"

Claw and the entire Gaines family laughed loudly.

Gella raised her eyebrows at Bennet, who winked and smiled back. She rolled her eyes and went back to work. The laughter died down as the news turned to the economy and supply shortages. Bennet turned his full attention to his steak, doing his best to enjoy it. To notice and feel its tender juiciness, to relish in the flavor he'd only ever tasted inside Cub's Den.

"Breaking news," the woman on the screen said.

Bennet looked up.

"Something new?" Avet asked.

"Not good." Claw scratched his cheek.

"We don't know that," Cylindra said, pushing her uneaten steak away.

"Shut up," Leona whispered.

The woman on the screen stared at her tablet, then looked up, eyes wide with surprise. "Multiple small towns across the country have been attacked... massacred... burned to the ground. All towns that reported having strange visitors. From what we know, the attacks were reactionary. Mass paranoia that these strange visitors were responsible for the biological attack, and that they would be responsible for more destruction. But it is unclear why entire towns were burned down, instead of the visitors alone being harmed." She paused and pressed a finger against her earpiece. "We have footage from a live InstaBook video from Bryson City, North Carolina. I'm being warned this footage is graphic."

"Turn that off," Leona called.

"Yes, Mayor." A waitress ran to the screen, turning it off before any footage was shown.

Bennet shook his head. "Entire towns... gone."

Leona stood up. "Let's go see our soldiers."

"Yeah," Bennet said. "Gella, I'll come by tonight."

"I'm going home," Cylindra said. "I don't want to see them."

Bennet didn't blame her. He didn't want to, either. When he saw them the night before, after returning from Lovell, he'd left with a sinking feeling that the world would never make sense again. But he knew his mom wanted him there, so he was going. He gave his sister a quick hug, and followed his mom out the door.

***

Avet sat in Sheriff Ling's chair, staring at the prisoners with Bennet and Leona standing around the station. Claw sat slouched in another chair, softly snoring. Avet smiled. Just having Claw there was a comfort, a safety net he knew he could always count on.

He turned back to the soldier prisoners. It was immediately obvious that they weren't soldiers — American or any other nationality. At least, it was obvious that their uniforms were fake. But he was also convinced they were insane, and he knew too well the insanity war could create in soldiers. The two women giggled softly to themselves while the man did aggressive, one-armed jumping jacks.

Avet looked at his mom. "They're not real uniforms. Doesn't mean they're not real soldiers, though."

"Homegrown militia?" Leona asked.

Avet shrugged. "Maybe. Or from somewhere else. Canada? Sovereign Alaska? Or they're just insane."

"Think there is a connection to the girl in Lovell? Or the juggler?" Bennet asked.

"How should I know?" Avet stood up. "Just because a lot of weird shit happens simultaneously, doesn't mean they're all connected."

"Language," Leona said. "But a good point."

Avet walked to the jumping soldier. "Attention!"

He stopped, slammed his legs together and one arm to his side. The other arm continued to flap up and down.

"What's your name, soldier?" he asked.

The man tilted his head back and forth, his neck cracking. "Name?" His head blinked in and out of sight as he continued his side to side bobbing. "No-no-no name." He went still.

Sheriff Ling walked through the front door. "Have we learned anything from them?"

"Nothing," Leona said.

The woman in the right-hand cell stopped giggling. "Nothing? I'm the queen president, bi-otches!"

"Yes, we are aware, Madame President," Ling said. "We are very honored to have you here."

A name tag appeared on the woman's uniform: "Madame President."

Avet stepped closer. The name tag seemed real. He could see it, and her, but did that mean they were real?

"Bouncing butts in an oven," Ling said. "Messes with my noggin every time nonsense like that happens."

Avet scratched his head. Strange, just like the juggler and the ballerina. But the juggler felt whimsical, the ballerina pure and innocent. These soldiers felt more complex than that. Not as bad as the suits, perhaps, but they still felt... wrong, somehow. Or was that just his PTSD talking? His deep-rooted mistrust of the military and soldiers who blindly follow orders? *Very possible,* Avet thought. *I can never know for sure.*

He walked to the woman on the far left, who was still giggling. "Are we sure they're dangerous?" he asked.

Ling nodded, then shrugged. "They're in here for butchering one of Patty's cows."

"My mom told me that," Avet said. "And if they're soldiers, or think they're soldiers, that's not completely unusual. We had to pull sh... shenanigans like that more than once in L.A. just to survive."

Claw stopped snoring and raised his head. "Ith true. I think thethe three are jutht odd."

Avet nodded. He trusted Claw with his life, and even if it didn't make sense, he trusted Claw's judgment with the faux soldiers. "I think so too."

"Are you suggesting, Mr. Gaines, that we let them out?" Ling asked.

"Not all of them," Avet said. "Just one. See if some freedom loosens their lips at all." He sat down. "Look, I want to understand who they are, too. But I was thinking about Bryson City. We need defenses, first of all. That's where most of our energy should be focused."

His mom nodded. "How, though? We don't have trees."

"We have buildings," Ling said. "Steel barns and carports. Wood ones, too."

"Exactly, Sheriff," Avet said. "Take them apart, put a wall around the main section of town. I don't think we'll have enough to protect—"

Leona's phone rang, cutting him off.

"Sheriff Pole," she said, answering. "Everything okay?" She listened for a moment, nodded, then put the phone on speaker and set it on a desk. "Go ahead, Sheriff Pole."

"Right, okay. Gaines boys. Is there anything more you can tell me about those suits? Or Claw, too."

The three looked at each other, shaking their heads.

"Nothing."

"No, ma'am."

"Can't think of anything, Theriff."

Pole sighed loudly. "They disappeared. One second there, the next gone. Poof. Out of sight."

"Wait," Bennet said. "I think... yeah, I remember something, Sheriff. I thought it was just adrenaline... but, when the woman was about to shoot me, something happened with her gun. It shook and I think it disappeared for a second, then came back."

"Our visitors have had some of the same idiosyncrasies," Ling said. "Though all three are still here."

Leona laughed. "Idiosyncrasies."

Avet rolled his eyes.

"Interesting." Pole clicked her tongue. "But I got no idea what to make of it."

Everyone nodded their heads knowingly. What could anyone make of it? Paranoia and conspiracy theories, and Avet knew nothing good could come from either.

"You'll tell me if anything changes?" Pole asked.

"Of course, Sheriff Pole," Ling said. "The mayor or I will keep in touch."

"Wait, Sheriff," Bennet said. "How do you want us to get your car back to you?"

"Don't," she said. "I've got my patrol car, and I don't think any of us should be driving that far. Not now. Maybe not ever, anymore."

A moment of silence followed the finality of that statement. *Is it really going to be that bad?* Avet wondered. *Can't be worse than L.A.*

"Right," Pole said. "Talk to you soon."

The call ended.

"All right, Mayor Gaines," Ling said. "What do you want me to do with our madame president and her friends?"

Leona rubbed her eyes and sighed. "Do what you think is best, Sheriff. We'll have a town meeting this evening about defenses."

"Build the wall, build the wall," Avet said.

"Shut up, brother," Bennet said, half smiling.

Avet shrugged and grabbed Claw's hand, helping him stand. "I'm taking him home to sleep."

Claw sighed. "All right. I'd jutht dithtract everyone with my thexth appeal anyway."

***

From Avet's War Journal, Audio Recording
click

Still in camp, doing nothing. Leaving tomorrow, though. Some government pricks came today. Almost would've preferred the enemy, but at least they brought some supplies. And some new tech. We're the first regimen to have the privilege to use it in real combat, they said.

Bullshit. We're their damn guinea pigs. And their tech is going to get more of us killed than the enemy, no question. And I don't understand it, really. Some sort of invisible shield that surrounds your body. It works. One of the government guys strapped it to his belt and turned it on. Let us shoot at him. It stopped every bullet. They say it's radiation protection, too.

Why the hell they think we need that? And the other question: if it's so good, why do they have to test it out on us? Why not just send it to all the troops? Something just doesn't feel right. Claw says I'm being paranoid. Maybe I am. Better paranoid than dead, though.

Going to L.A. tomorrow, finally. And yeah, I'll wear the new shield. But if it does any sketchy shit, I'm taking it off.

One night, then into the heart of the war.

...

That sounded too melodramatic. Ignore it.
click

Chapter 20

Tashon walked slowly through the brightness, each step feeling like an eternity. Jonstin and Ishlea moved along on either side of him, though he was barely aware of their presence. He took a deep breath, took another step forward. And just like all the steps before it, he felt a flake of weight leave his back as his mind was drawn to another place, another time.

He walked through the empty black of space, holding the hand of his father's bloated and frozen corpse. They walked for light years, passing over planets and under stars, through asteroid fields and around comets. At some point he realized he no longer needed to drag his father with him, and he let go, took a final step, and was back in the light.

Another deep breath, and he lifted his other foot. He was in the Ship of Nations, outside his old living quarters, surrounded by Crawlers, Singers and humans. All wanted him dead. He lifted his hands, a knife gleaming in each. He made the first move, leaping onto the back of a Crawler and slit its throat, laughing as the blood poured out. Pushing off the limp body, he turned against the onrushing horde. Slitting throats, disemboweling, and severing. Laughing all the while, finding joy in the swift death he inflicted upon the living. Within minutes, he was the only one standing, slick with blood.

A man emerged from the corpses, and Tashon was looking at himself. The two stared at each other. His smile faded and he dropped his knives. He looked down at his hands and wept at what he'd become.

Then he was standing amid the light, his burdened lightened, if even by the smallest amount. He had no idea how much longer he needed to continue, but he knew he would. And despite how long he'd been going, his physical form felt strong and energized. It was his mind and soul that dragged, sweating under the constant battering.

Another step and he saw himself dead in the Fourth before reaching his destination. His journey a pointless failure.

Step after step, tormenting vision after tormenting vision until he thought his entire life had been a sequence of horrifying events.

Then the weight was gone, light surrounded him, and he lay on the ground of the Fourth staring up at the wind. He sat up and looked around. The pyramids stood to his right, towering and majestic. Jonstin hovered, his form now intricate lines of whites, blacks, grays and fuligin. But of true darkness, there was no sign.

Ishlea hung just past Jonstin, appendages hanging limp from her main form. Like a tumor growing out of her back, a large clump of darkness clung to her.

Tashon looked from Ishlea to Jonstin, Jonstin to Ishlea. What about their experience was so different that the result had created such disparity?

"Tashon, are you okay?" Jonstin asked.

Tashon nodded. "Yes. Do I... look different?"

"No. Do I?"

"You do. There's no darkness in you. Or around you."

Jonstin examined himself as best he could. *"I see black and... fuligin, right?"*

"Fuligin, right," Tashon said. "Darkness and blackness and fuligin are different."

"Darkness is evil?"

Tashon pursed his lips. "Maybe. No, I don't think so. Not always, at least. Look at Ishlea. That darkness growing from her. Do you think it's evil?"

"I... No, I don't. What's the difference, then? Between evil and darkness?"

Tashon looked at Ishlea and the mass attached to her. She still hovered there, seemingly oblivious to anything happening around her. "I think darkness can turn into evil, maybe. The darkness on Ishlea, though. It's not evil. It's not actively trying to hurt or kill, like Aleron's monster. Did you live through... memories in there?"

"Yes. Not all real, though."

Tashon nodded. "I think your darkness is gone because of how you reacted to the memories. Mine, too. I look the same, but the weight of darkness is gone."

"And Ishlea reacted wrong?"

Tashon shook his head. "Just different. I think...." He paused, staring at Ishlea's lump of darkness. "I think Ishlea did the best she could with what she has. I think she has more weight than most." Tashon rubbed his leg, wishing the healthy ankle he'd had in his visions had stayed with him. *Do the best with what I have,* he thought.

Jonstin floated to Ishlea. *"Can you hear me? Ishlea?"*

Her appendages lifted slightly, her form tightening. "*It's a cruel universe, fellow traveler. Cruel and harsh and cold.*"

Tashon sighed. Something in her had changed again. "It can be, Ishlea," he said. "But not always."

"*All I've seen is cold darkness. Cruel violence. Even after death, that's all there is. Suffering, traveler. Suffering, plain and simple. No silver linings or lessons learned or strength found. None of that cliché, sentimental bullshit.*"

Tashon shook his head. He'd been in her place, felt the same feeling. But he sensed hers were rooted far deeper than his own ever were. It would take more than reliving cold, dark memories to release her from her burdens. It wasn't something he thought he could do, but he'd do the best with what he had. "Will you keep traveling with us?"

Her form whipped round to face him. "*What the hell else am I gonna do? Got nothin' else goin' for me, so might as well traipse around the universe following a silent call for help that only seems to lead to shit shows. But, yeah, sure, what the hell. I'll come. See what hole you fall into next.*"

Tashon laughed. "That's an accurate summary of the journey so far. Jonstin?"

Jonstin lifted him up. "*Which way, sage?*"

***

Tashon stared down in disbelief. A planet, with rolling hills of blue grass and purple flowers. Tall creatures with narrow bodies walked on six delicate legs, lazily chewing on the grass. A stream ran through the grass, cutting through the hills. Blue-gray clouds hung in a pale green sky.

Tashon looked in his bag. He still had water, but not much. He faired a bit better with his supply of food bars, but not by much. He would need more water and food before he reached his destination, and this might be his only chance to restock.

"Think I can breathe that air?" he asked.

"*How the hell would we know?*" Ishlea said. "*Go or don't go. Doesn't matter to me.*"

"It looks good, sage. But there's no way to know. You could catch a virus that will kill you in a decade, or one of those animals could attack you. They don't look violent, but there's no way to know."

Tashon nodded and shrugged. "All true. But I'll die of thirst if I don't. If I can't breathe, I'll be able to hold my breath long enough to pull back up."

"So much more shit could go wrong," Ishlea said. *"You're not the best at staying out of danger."*

"Yes, Ishlea. But I have to risk it. I only have so much food and water."

"Ha. We'll tell those animals down there to write that on your gravestone."

Tashon shrugged. "If I do die down there, my soul will just come back here and I'll still be with you."

Ishlea scoffed. *"Lovely."*

"Yes, you will. I wish I had the knowledge you do when I was in the Third."

"Even without that knowledge, you sacrificed yourself for Abe."

Jonstin's essence beamed. *"Thank you, Tashon."*

Tashon nodded.

"What about your ankle?" Jonstin asked.

"I'll drop right by the stream. I have a small filter to use to fill my bottles."

"Be careful," Jonstin said.

"Yeah, don't die, traveler," Ishlea said.

"I'll see you soon. I can talk to you from down there, too."

"Really?"

Tashon looked at the planet, closed his eyes and pulled himself down. The frigid air hit him hard, forcing the air from his lungs and for a moment he feared the air held no oxygen. But soon he sucked air back into his lungs and he did his best to breathe slowly, squeezing his hands between his armpits for warmth.

"Say something, Jonstin," he said with the part of him that remained in the Fourth.

"You look cold."

Tashon laughed, startling one of the nearby animals. *"I am. Don't make me laugh again."*

He sat up, his ankle twitching with pain, and looked to his right. The edge of the stream was less than a foot away. *Good start*, he thought as he shrugged his pack off and set it next to him. The lanky animals drank from the stream, seemingly oblivious to his sudden appearance. That, or they sensed his injury and knew he was no danger to them. Which also meant they might see him as an easy target, if they were carnivores. Or perhaps a different, carnivorous animal crept along, hidden in the tall grass.

Looking down as little as possible, he pulled out a filter and five empty bottles of water. The filter was a long, clear hose with a weighted nozzle, which was the filter itself, on one end and a button operated pump on the other. He tossed the weighted end into the water, slid the other end into a bottle and pressed the button. As the water slowly ran through the filter, Tashon looked down on himself from above. He saw the whole planet, and he was the only human on it. Most likely the only human who had ever been there, unless the Ship of Nations had sent a colony there. But it was obvious it hadn't. There were no signs of human activity, and the first five colonies had all been successful, as far as he knew.

Something leaped out of the stream and landed back in the water, sending soft ripples toward to the banks.

Fish, Tashon thought. *Food. Fresh meat.* His mouth watered at the thought of something other than stale food bars. But how to catch them? He'd never fished before, and wasn't even sure he understood how. *That's what a life inside a ship does,* he thought. He switched bottles and pinched a piece of blue grass between his fingers. It was warm to the touch, as if blood ran through it. He slid his fingers down to the the cold earth and pulled. The long strand popped easily from the ground, revealing a tangle of thin roots. Tashon placed it on the ground and pulled the food tester from his pack. It was similar to the one Ballas always had on him, though a bit larger and with more detailed analyses.

Tashon broke a piece off the grass. A soft powdery substance spilled out, staining his fingers blue. He split the blade of grass in half, shook all the powder off, and then placed it in the testing tube. After switching the bottles again, he looked down at his splint. He hadn't taken it off since putting it on, and by that point the pain hadn't lessened as much as he expected it to. *But how long has it really been?* he asked himself. He decided it hadn't been as long as it felt, given how much his ankle still hurt. He wanted to take the splint and give his skin a chance to breathe, but wasn't sure it was a good idea. *I'll just look.*

As gingerly as possible, he unwrapped the cloth, unwrapped one half and removed one side of the splint, keeping the other side pressed firmly to his legs. The bottom half of his calf, wrapping around to his shin and reaching down to his heel, was a swollen, purple-red bruise.

"Damn it," he whispered as he replaced the splint.

"Don't have any meds with you?" Jonstin asked from the Fourth.

Tashon shook his head. "Didn't even cross my mind. We didn't have that much on Aethera, anyway. It wouldn't have felt right to take it from them."

The testing tube beeped and Tashon picked it up. Edible, though it provided less calories than he had hoped. He broke off a piece and and placed it on his tongue. It was cold, almost like ice. He chewed slowly, focusing on the taste. *I'll probably never be on this planet again,* he thought. It had a faint earthy taste, but was, for the most part, bland. He swallowed, took another bite then scooped up a fingertip of powder, wiping it inside the tube.

As it ran its analysis, he switched the full bottle with an empty one, then stared at the water.

"Jonstin, you ever fish?"

"Never. Even on Earth. By the time I was born, hunting was outlawed. Nearly every species was endangered. Even if I did, probably wouldn't have caught anything."

Tashon shrugged. "Probably would've hurt myself—"

The tube beeped, and he picked it up. Also edible, with trace elements of a chemical that Tashon couldn't pronounce. He clicked the name, and learned it held minor pain-relieving and anti-inflammatory properties. He stared. Discovering a chemical that was exactly what he needed in the vastness of the universe was impossible. Yet there it was.

"Do you think the universe guides us, Jonstin?"

"You're the sage, not me," Jonstin said.

"No way in hell it does," Ishlea mumbled.

Tashon told Jonstin what the powder contained.

"Might be a coincidence," Jonstin said. *"But seems too specific to be just a coincidence."*

Tashon nodded, then noticed a second page of the definition. He clicked the arrow and read it aloud. "Warning: For some, this chemical has hallucinogenic effects. For others, it induces a strong drowsiness that can be overpowering. For a very few, these two have occurred in the same individual, resulting in vibrant hallucinations from which the subject could not wake. Use extreme caution, and consult a physician before use." Tashon laughed once. "Maybe the universe is looking out for me."

As he sat there, ankle throbbing, considering whether taking the powder was worth the risk, something brushed through the grass behind him. He turned to see a large shape leap out of the grass, straight toward him.

Chapter 21

Sheriff Ling slouched in his chair, legs stretched straight out, a cooling cup of coffee held between both hands. The sun had set long before, yet he couldn't sleep. The coffee was just to keep him focused. But on what, he didn't know. What was there to focus on? That three impossible soldiers had wandered into his town? He shook his head and took a sip, Madame President soldier copying the movement.

She'd been copying him since the sun set. Sitting the same way he did, sighing, coughing or sneezing right after he did. And it wasn't simple mocking. She matched each of his sounds perfectly in pitch, volume and length. He sighed again and tapped his foot.

She repeated both actions.

"You can stop, please," he said.

"You can stop, please," she said. "Madame President."

Ling rolled his eyes. He never should have indulged her by calling her by that name. The other two lay on their cots as if they were sleeping, but Ling got a feeling that whatever they were, they didn't sleep. And, to him, whatever they were wasn't human. In his mind, none of the visitors to the little towns were human. How could they be? But even if they weren't, he knew they were alive, and that meant they deserved whatever kindness he could offer them.

He stood up, bounced on his heels and vigorously shook his hands. Madame President, of course, followed him. He stopped, lifted his right hand in the air and slapped himself in the cheek as hard as he could. He swore, stepped to the left and looked up. Madame President stared at him blankly, then broke out in hysterical laughter.

"Piss in a Dutch oven," he said. "I'm obviously an idiot."

"And I'm the queen president, bi-otch!"

Ling groaned and dropped back into his chair. "You realize she never won, don't you? Never elected."

"I am the queen president," she said.

An idea came, unbidden as his best ideas always were. "You just don't talk like us," he said. "You're trying to tell me that you're in charge."

She stood up and grabbed the bars, pushing her lips and nose through the gap. A thin line of saliva dripped from the corner of her mouth. "The sun sets. The sun rises," she said, then slurped the spit back into her mouth.

"I'll take that as a yes," Ling said, wiping his chin as if he had saliva on his face. "You mean the leader of all the visitors that've been showing up, or just you three?"

She pulled her face from the bars and snorted. "Climb up the ladder."

"The latter," Ling said. "So just of you three?"

She sat down. "The sun sets. The sun rises."

Ling smiled. "We're getting to the moon, now. Okay, Madame President, where are you from?"

She stood up, sat down, and then stood up again. "From?"

"Where were you before here?" Ling tried.

"Before... mind... before...? Synapse, synapse, synapse."

"Houston, we have a problem." Ling scratched the scruff on his cheek. "Something with her brain, maybe? Maybe she can't remember."

He started to ask if she was suffering memory loss, but was cut short by voices shouting in the parking lot.

"Urine in my pancakes." He stood up. "What now?"

The door flung open and a large man in a ripped flannel shirt walked in, holding a beaten and bloodied Deputy Meerf by the collar.

"Sheriff, I—"

"Shut up," the man said.

"Flaming crap on my porch." Ling pulled out his gun and leveled it at the man's head. "What the hell is wrong in your brain, Mr. Rickerson?"

Two men walked in behind him, each brandishing a shotgun. Clint Veshre, tall and lanky with long hair. The other, Tim Durgeon, tall and pudgy, his head a mass of curly hair.

Mr. Rickerson sneered and held up a set of keys. "Protecting the town, *Sheriff*." He walked toward the cells, dragging the deputy behind him.

"Bi-otch!" The Madame President yelled. Then she whistled, like she was calling a dog. "Here, bi-otch! Over here!"

"Yeah, I'll come there, you—"

"Mr. Rickerson, do not do this." Ling clicked the safety off.

Mr. Rickerson motioned with a finger. Tim jogged over and pointed the shotgun at Meerf's head.

"Your deputy's life is in your hands, Sheriff," Rickerson said. "The safety of your town, too. If we harbor these... *things* here, we'll get torn down like the other little towns. But show them we've taken care of them." He shrugged.

Ling looked at the three men, quickly thinking through scenarios. He knew he could take care of at least two of them, but all options still ended with Meerf's skull blown apart. With a sigh, he clicked the safety on, ejected the clip and the bullet in the barrel and then tossed his weapon aside. He'd wait for his moment, and get Meerf and the soldiers to safety.

"It's clear!" Rickerson yelled.

The door burst open again and Cowley's local news crew stumbled in, the newsman dressed in a crisp brown suit and cowboy hat. The camera woman, dressed in dark blue coveralls, pulled out a remote control. With a few flicks of her thumbs, the small recording drone was in the air. She gave the spokesman a thumbs up.

"Welcome, viewer friends," he said, a too-big smile on his face. "We are here in the sheriff's station of Cowley, Wyoming." He dropped his smile and looked behind him. "Just one short day ago, these three strangers showed up on the outskirts of our peaceful town. We imprisoned them, and now one of our citizens will share our town's plan for these intruders."

The drone rotated to Rickerson, standing in front of Madame President's cell. Rickerson's lips turned up in a smile that churned Ling's stomach. *Not yet*, he told himself. *Not yet.*

***

Bennet sat at the small island of his mom's kitchen, sharing a glass of wine and food bar with a label the read, 'Birthday Cake—tastes like the real thing!' In the living room, Avet watched the news, the voice of the anchorman too quiet for Bennet to make out any words.

"It's not my birthday," Gella said.

Bennet shrugged and took a sip of wine. "Me neither."

She raised her eyebrows and grinned. "Why are we eating it?"

"I saw it in the pantry, wondered if it tasted any good... and when I picked it up I saw that it's expiration date was last week."

She swallowed the bite in her mouth. "Nice try."

He turned the wrapper over and handed it to her. "Last week."

She coughed and took a big gulp of wine. "What the hell?" She sounded somewhere between amused and angry.

"Hey, calm down." Bennet took a big bit of the bar, chewed and swallowed. "It hasn't changed in the last week. Probably not in the last year."

Gella looked at bar and bit her lip. "You're sure?"

Bennet laughed once. "Yeah, I—"

"Send my shit to hell," Avet shouted from the living room.

"Language," Leona called from her bedroom.

Something crashed, feet stomped and a door slammed. Then the garage door opened and Leona's Chevy sped away. Leona walked out of her room and into the living room, shaking her head in exasperation. "Damn that boy," she muttered under her breath.

Bennet grinned at Gella and broke the remainder of the bar into two pieces. He put one in his mouth and handed the other to her.

"Bennet," his mom yelled. "Out here now."

Bennet jogged into the living room, where his mom, sister and Clawman stood. His eyes immediately followed theirs to the screen. Mr. Rickerson stood in the sheriff's station holding the beaten face of deputy Meerf up by the hair, the young officer's breath wheezing in and out of a broken nose.

"...trying to protect these intruders," Rickerson was saying. "But Cowley does not stand for that, not most of us. We don't trust these intruders." He pointed to the cell behind him. "Doesn't matter what this *deputy* says. We're gonna protect our town and our nation, take care of these intruders."

Rickerson tossed Meerf off camera and lifted up a set of keys. "This one claims she's the Madame President." Rickerson laughed. "Dressed in a convincing military uniform, but fake to the trained eye." He yanked the prisoner out of her cell and slammed her against the outside of the bars.

"Shouldn't we go there?" Gella asked.

"Avet's already on his way." Leona shook her head. "We'd get in his way."

"And he took the car," Cylindra said. "Damn it, Avet. Claw, your boyfriend's an idiot."

Claw nodded and sighed. "Tho ith that guy on the tv. Who ith he?"

"Rickerson," Bennet said. "A prick, but he's usually harmless."

"He was a boxer," Cylindra said. "When he was younger."

Claw huffed. "Avet can handle that."

"Yeah, he can," Bennet said.

"You're not worried about him?" Gella asked.

"I'm worried about what he might do," Bennet said.

***

Ling sat on the floor, anger slowly rising. *Not yet, not yet.* Meerf lay in a corner, quietly weeping, blood and drool dripping from his quivering mouth. Ling locked eyes with his deputy, smiled and nodded. Meerf tried to smile, but it turned into a gurgling cough.

Rickerson swung the cell door open and dragged Madame President out. "Tim, come hold her."

Tim set his shotgun on Ling's desk and grabbed the woman by her elbows and held her tight against him. Her face showed no fear, not even a sign of understanding, her eyes lazily looking whichever way her face pointed.

"These intruders are not of our town, our state or our nation," Rickerson said. "Those watching, know that we do not harbor or accept them. They're...." He scratched his head and looked at Madame President. "They're a part of what's happened to our planet, and what might still happen."

He swiftly pulled his arm back and slammed a fist into the left side of her face. Her head snapped to the right, a few dots of blood spraying the drone. She turned back to Rickerson, her face still expressionless.

"Where did you come from?"

"Mind, mind. Kind, mind." She laughed.

Rickerson slammed a fist at her from the other side, sending a tooth into her empty cell.

She turned back to him, eyes narrowed, lips turned in a thin grin. "Bi-otch, bi-otch."

Rickerson's fist sped toward her face. Her head flickered as if a fading hologram, and Rickerson's fist passed through it, crunching into Tim's nose. He yelled in pain and surprise, then fell to the floor.

The front door banged open and Avet Gaines walked in, his pace steady, his eyes calm. He jerked an elbow into the side of Clint's face, then ripped the shotgun out of his hand and slammed it into his gut. Clint collapsed.

Now. Ling pulled a knife from his boot, jumped to his feet and leaped at Rickerson, getting his knife on the man's throat before he had a chance to react.

Avet nodded at Ling and walked toward Rickerson, shotgun hanging loosely at his side. Tim lay on the floor clasping his nose, blood seeping through his fingers. Avet gave him one good kick as Madame President moved away from Rickerson.

"The hell's wrong with you, Dickerson?" Avet asked.

Ling couldn't help but smile, despite the bodies and blood on the ground. Rickerson's old nickname, back to haunt him.

The drone pulled back, its engine softly whirring.

Rickerson's eyes narrowed. "We're taking care of our town," Rickerson said through gritted teeth.

"So now you're Judge Dickerson? And Sheriff Dickerson? Your own jury, too, huh?" Avet took a step forward. "Where's your damn evidence?"

Rickerson blinked. "Evidence?"

"Proof, Dickerson. That these three are what you say they are. That they're our enemy, or will be. *Evidence.*"

Rickerson looked around the room, eyes wide. "It's not, not just that we think they're our enemy... everyone does. Towns are being destroyed for having them. I'm, I'm trying to protect our town. Show them that we're not harboring them."

Ling nodded, but kept the knife where it was. "You have good intentions, my friend. But you're also showing the world you no longer believe in innocent until proven guilty."

Rickerson looked at the ground, chest moving slowly up and down. When he looked up, his eyes were narrowed in a firm glare. "This is *war*, Avet. Ideals like that can't always be followed."

Avet took a step forward and backhanded Rickerson across the face. "Don't talk to me about war, *Dick*. You were never a soldier. You've spent your entire life in this town, dicking around."

"Avet's right," Ling said. "Using war as an excuse for harsher violence is what makes war the hell it is."

Rickerson spat blood into the floor. "If we let them live, this town's going to burn."

"You'd rather have innocent blood on your hands?" Avet asked.

Rickerson shrugged, then spat again.

"Trust me, Dickerson. You don't."

Ling released the knife, shoved Rickerson into the empty cell and locked it. He turned to the drone. "Looks like this broadcast is going to make it national. So, everyone who sees this, pay attention. Don't let fear and paranoia lead to more death and violence than we've already had. Calm souls and sharp minds are what will get us through."

Avet snorted. "Poetic."

Ling shrugged. "I thought so."

Avet lifted the shotgun above his head and slammed the drone to the ground.

"The hell?" The camerawoman dropped the ground and collected the pieces.

"Get out," Avet said. "*Now.*"

She gathered her gear in her arms and ran out, tears treading down her face.

"Was that strictly necessary, Mr Gaines?"

"Probably not." Avet sighed. "But they turned this scene into entertainment for the world. Disgusting."

Ling nodded. "Madame President," he said. "We need to put you in the cell with one of your friends, for your safety."

She nodded, flickered and then disappeared. Seconds later, she was in the far left cell with her fellow woman soldier.

"Flatulent herd of cows," Ling said. "Looks like they could all get out whenever they want."

Tim and Clint moaned as they clambered to their feet.

Avet brought the shotgun back up. "Don't try anything stupid."

"They won't," Ling said. "Now that Mr. Rickerson's locked up. Leave, both of you. If there's any more of this from you, you're joining Mr. Rickerson."

"Yes, sir."

"You have my word, Sheriff."

The two stumbled out, clutching their faces.

"Sometimes I wish I could be as forgiving as you," Avet said.

"Then you wouldn't be you," Ling said.

Avet laughed. "Violence makes you deep, Sheriff."

"Then get ready for prophet-level deepness, Mr. Gaines. I fear this is just the beginning. Help me with my deputy."

The two lifted a trembling Meerf into a chair. He coughed and gurgled, then dropped his forehead onto the desk.

"You all right, Deputy?" Avet asked.

"Of course he's not, Mr. Gaines." He placed a hand on Meerf's shoulder. "We need to get you to the hospital."

The male soldier coughed in his cell. His entire body vibrated and then he walked through the cell bars and sat on the desk by Meerf.

"My soldier friend, what are you doing?" Ling asked.

The soldier leaned forward, pursed his lips and blew a thin stream of green smoke into Meerf's face. The smoke swirled around the deputy's head, then slid into his nose and disappeared. His body went limp. The soldier blinked out of sight, then reappeared in his cell.

"Fecal matter soup, what did you do to him?" Ling stomped to the cell.

"Looks like I was right," Rickerson said.

"Shut up, Dickerson," Avet said.

The soldier held up his hands as if in surrender. "Zero, zero."

"Sheriff," Avet said. "He's waking up."

Ling glared at the soldier, then turned around to see Meerf standing up and stretching. Dried blood covered his face, but his broken nose was healed, the bruising and swelling in his face gone.

"Deputy, how you feeling?" Ling asked.

"Starving," Meerf said.

"Me, too," Avet said. "Sheriff, I'll take him to the Den."

Ling nodded. "Thank you, Mr. Gaines. For all your help. I think I should deputize you."

Avet laughed. "You'd have to get Pole to end my parole early. Let's go, Meerf."

Meerf stared at Rickerson as they walked out, almost tripping over his own feet. He mumbled something under his breath, and they were gone.

Ling laughed once and dropped into his chair, shaking his head. "Bigfoot clog my toilet. Bigfoot. Clog. My toilet."

***

"That wasn't as bad as I expected," Gella said to Bennet as they sat on the couch.

Clawman and Cylindra stood on the patio, waiting for Avet to return.

Bennet shook his head. "You're right, Gella. He showed some self control."

Gella rested her head on his shoulder. "He's not a bad guy."

"No, he's not. I've never thought he was."

"A lot of the town thinks he is."

Bennet shrugged. "After that, I hope some will see he isn't. But others will take Rickerson's side, I bet."

"I wish I could disagree with you," she said. "Buts it's not black and white."

Bennet let out a sharp breath. "Not black and white? It's three innocent lives. Dickerson was plainly wrong."

Gella sat up straight. "Hey, calm down. I agree with you, but it's not as simple as that."

Bennet took a deep breath, trying to calm himself. "Why not?"

"Look, like Ling said. Rickerson had good intentions. He was trying to protect the town. You can't say protecting the town is bad."

Bennet nodded cautiously. "Truth there. But at the expense of potentially innocent lives?"

"I think Rickerson got stuck on the potentially innocent part of that. And you can't say you know for certain those three are innocent and harmless."

Bennet sighed. "You're right there. But assaulting Deputy Meerf, then attempting to torture the female soldier? There's no gray area there."

"Maybe not. But Rickerson was doing it for the greater good of the town."

"The ends justify the means?" Bennet asked.

"I don't agree with his means, in any way," Gella said. "But, Bennet, you're kind. I know you'd never hurt anyone. But... the way the world's going, anyone who wants to survive is going to have to swim in the gray areas."

Bennet looked down. He liked to think he'd die before hurting someone else, but the encounter with the suits already showed he had a more sinister survival instinct than he expected. And that terrified him more than anything.

The toilet flushed in the bathroom, the faucet ran for a short time and then Bennet's mom walked out and sat on the couch.

"Mission successful, Mother?" Bennet asked.

"That joke's never been funny," Leona said.

Bennet smiled. "That joke's *always* funny."

Leona rolled her eyes and looked out the window. "You think they're human?"

"What?"

"The visitors." Leona kept her gaze on the window. "The ballerina, the suits, the soldiers, the juggler. Are they human?"

Bennet hadn't once considered otherwise, but if they weren't human, it would make sense. How had he not considered it before? The ballerina girl obviously did things no human could, as did all the others. "It all seemed so normal when it happened," Bennet whispered.

"That's what Claw said, too." Leona looked at him, asleep on the recliner. "But the suits disappearing... and the girl in Lovell. Did you see someone got it on video?"

Bennet shook his head.

Leona told the screen to find and play the 'Lovell Ballerina' video. It all played out exactly as Bennet remembered it. Her graceful innocence as she leapt from the building, flying over the crowd, then falling to the ground. Even as he watched it, no questions of how or why came into his mind. It didn't matter, because whatever it was he was sure it was *real*. Perhaps more real than anything he'd ever witnessed. The video ended, and Leona shut the screen off.

Gella shook her head and wiped a tear from her face. "Beautiful."

"It is," Leona said. "But human?"

"How can we know that?" Bennet asked. "Without drastically violent measures?"

"Sheriff Pole is getting what little information the hospital got from the suits in Cody," she said. "But you're right. We can't know for sure without invasive surgery, at the best. Autopsy at the worst."

"And if they're not human?" Bennet asked. "What then?"

Leona sighed. "No idea. And this is all just speculation. My gut tells me they're human, despite everything we've seen. Maybe they're just altered in some way."

"We still don't know why, though," Gella said. "Why are they here? What's their purpose?"

Maybe they don't have one, Bennet thought. But the idea seemed too ludicrous to even mention. Of course they were there for a reason. *Or maybe not.*

***

A young deputy, his belly poking over his belt buckle, ran into Sheriff Pole's office. "Sheriff, we've had sightings."

"The suits?"

The deputy nodded. "The two men. Maverick's parking lot."

Pole stood up. "Deputy Lethrop, there's over a dozen Mavericks in a two-mile radius."

"Uh, Sheridan and Ninth. And Sixteenth and Wyoming."

"Deputy those are nowhere near each other."

"Multiple reports for both, Sheriff," Lethrop said.

"We'll head to Sheridan. Send Alione and Saunters to Sixteenth."

Without lights or sirens to alert the suits of their coming, Pole sped toward their destination, refusing to stop for anything. She screeched into the parking lot, stopped in an empty charging station and ran inside.

Bags of chips, candy and jerky littered the floor, but no suits. The clerk stood behind the counter, blue-lined eyes staring wide at the mess. Lethrop slowly walked through the isles, examining the disaster.

Pole looked at the girl's name tag. "Madri, are you okay?"

She slowly turned to Pole. "I'm not hurt. But look. They took hundreds of dollar of product. Sal's going to be pissed."

"Don't worry about that. It was the suits?"

Madri nodded.

"Don't worry about Sal. You couldn't have stopped them."

"They just zapped in here, shoved their bags full and zapped out."

"How many?" Pole asked.

Madri held up two fingers.

"Both men?"

Another nod.

Pole shook her head. "See anything, Deputy?"

"Nothing, Sheriff. I got the munchies now, though."

Pole laughed once. "I do love chips. Grab me some salt and vinegar and some barbecue."

Lethrop brought an armful of chips to the counter. "Do you have security cameras?" he asked.

Madri nodded as she mindlessly scanned the bags. "Yeah. Don't think you'll see anything though. They weren't here long."

"We'd still like to see them," Pole said.

But Madri was right. Even going through the footage frame by frame, there was nothing useful.

They left the store. Pole shoved the charger into the car and the two got in. As they waited for it to charge, they ate chips in frustrated silence. Who or what were the suits? And what could they do about them?

Chapter 22

Tashon lay on his back, a thin line of blood trickling down his forehead from where the creature's claw grazed him as it jumped into the stream. Now it stood in the water, its three front legs and two back submerged to its first set of knees. Its hair matched the blue of the grass, the edges drooping into the water. Its wide, flat face stared down, moving back and forth, up and down. Tracking its next meal, from what Tashon could tell. Which meant it hadn't meant to hurt him, and thus didn't see him as prey. At least, that's what he hoped.

But he remained prone on the ground, hope accompanied by a fear that any sudden movement would result in an attack. He could pull himself to the Fourth, but that meant leaving his equipment behind. More than that, though, he simply didn't want that moment to end. The only human on an undiscovered planet. The only human to ever breathe that air, to lie in that grass, to watch that creature hunt.

The creature opened its mouth, baring dozens of sharp, tiny teeth and shoved its face into the stream. It shook back and forth, cold water spraying Tashon. A large, reptilian head burst from the water and bit its assailant's neck. The five-legged creature reared up on its back legs, squeezing a five-foot long, one-foot wide snake in its jaws. Blood dripped from its neck as the snake bit harder. A high-pitched squeal rang out from one of them, and the snake went limp. The victor trotted out of the water, down the bank and out of sight.

"Good thing you didn't try to fish," Jonstin said.

Tashon smiled. *"No other human's seen that."*

"I'm human and I just saw it," Ishlea said.

Tashon rolled his eyes.

Jonstin laughed. *"You coming back up?"*

Tashon shook his head. *"I need to rest. Can't think of a better place to do it. Wake me up if something's going to attack me."*

"I'd just as soon let you die," Ishlea said.

"I'll watch out for you," Jonstin said.

Tashon nodded as he took in the fresh air and the beauty of the world that surrounded him. All the pressures of his journey and the fear of failing melted away. He fell into meditative nothingness, aware of only two things: the cool air surrounding him and the pain in his ankle.

The pain meant the injury was getting worse, and he knew in his gut trying to use the blue powder would make his life worse. And even without the risks, it wouldn't heal his ankle, wouldn't mend the bones any quicker. Just mask the pain.

But maybe I can, Tashon thought. *I've expanded my mind outside myself, so why can't I do the opposite?* He took a few deep breaths, calming himself until his body was nothing but dead weight. He knew he couldn't completely bring his Fourth essence back to the Third, but he was confident he could still make more use of it than he had in either dimension. He focused on the ball of essence in the higher plane, invisibly tethered to his three-dimensional form. It swirled and turned as he grabbed the smallest speck from it and slowly pulled it toward the lower dimension. It slowed at the ground of the Fourth, making a dent, then refused to break through.

Tashon took a deep breath, flexed his mind and pulled, his head pounding with the effort. Then it popped through and his body relaxed as the fourth-dimensional speck floated into his physical mind. He turned it around. It emanated countless lines of calming energy, each far thinner than a strand of hair. But they moved without reason or purpose, swirling through and around his neural pathways. For the speck to have any effect, he'd have to maneuver it to the right spot.

He took a breath and pinched one of the strands streaming from the speck. Then another, pulling it toward the first. Strand after strand, until they were all one strand, still smaller than a hair. Another pause and another deep breath, sweat dripping off his head. Exhaustion swept over him, but he wasn't done. He couldn't stop now. If he did, he was sure all his work would fly back to the Fourth.

Another breath and he stretched the strand back and down to his brain stem, the speck trailing behind. From his brain stem into his spinal column, slowly from vertebrae to vertebrae. He paused at the bottom of his spine, unsure of the best route to follow. And nervous that pulling the speck out of his spinal column was going to hurt. But none of it had hurt so far, so he took a deep breath, fighting to stay within himself and his meditative state, and continued.

Down the nerve endings, through his hip, past his knee and to his broken ankle. With a gentle pull, the strand and speck popped out of the nerve and into the crack of his bone. A vibrating pain erupted from the fracture, firing up the nerves, into his spinal column and up to his brain stem. Salty sweat dripped into his mouth, dripped from his chin, soaking his clothes, but he didn't have the strength to wipe it away. He grimaced, trying and failing to calm the convulsions. Light flashed and darkness loomed, light and dark, light and dark. For days or weeks, or perhaps only seconds, his entire existence was nothing but anguish.

Then it stopped, replaced by a sudden stillness. The speck hovered in the crevice of his bone. After a few deep breaths, he reached for it again, turning one strand into two and connecting one to each edge of the break. Cautiously, waiting for the pain to return any second, he pulled the gap closed. The bone reattached a nanometer at a time, and with each nanometer, the speck shrunk, its light and warmth fading. He did his best to will it on, repairing as much of the break as possible, but by the time it faded completely, less than a quarter of the break was repaired. Still, he'd done something no other human ever had, and it was better than waiting for it to heal on its own.

Pure exhaustion swept over him and he fell into a sleep deep enough to rival the rest of the dead.

***

He awoke to cool night air, his clothes and hair still drenched from sweat.

"You're awake." Jonstin's voice screamed into his mind.

Tashon pressed a hand to his temple. *"Quieter, please."*

"Sorry. I was worried about you."

Ishlea laughed. *"I wasn't."*

Tashon sat up, shivering against the cold. *"Was I out for that long?"*

"The sun set, rose and set again," Jonstin said.

"Makes sense," Tashon said.

"It does?"

Tashon looked up to the sky. *"Yeah. I... exhausted myself, trying to heal my ankle."*

"You...what?"

Tashon paused, momentarily shocked that Jonstin and Ishlea had seen nothing of what he had done. But of course they hadn't, he realized. It had been an entirely internal struggle, and one they would know nothing about unless he told them. *"I tried healing my ankle. I did heal it – part of it."*

"*Bullshit,*" Ishlea said.

"*How?*" Jonstin asked.

As best he could, Tashon told them what he'd done with the speck of his essence from the Fourth. When he finished, he partially undid his splint. The swelling was down and the bruising lighter. Much farther along than it naturally would have been in that time. He gently wiggled his foot back and forth, up and down, and sucked his breath in. Still painful, but less so.

Ishlea twisted above him. "*Tashon, that is amazing! Do that a few more times, and it'll be completely healed.*" The sincerity in her words was unmistakable, and Tashon couldn't help but smile.

"*Impressive,*" Jonstin said.

Tashon nodded and put his water and equipment back in his pack. He pulled another blade of grass from the ground and broke it in half. The blue powder poured out, and he put the two pieces of grass in his bag. He continued packing the fresh food, watching the water flow lazily in the stream. He'd miss it there, he realized. Being back in the third dimension was more refreshing than he could've imagined. The third dimension was his home, and being out of it for so long was taking its toll. But the cry for help still rang on. So Tashon pulled his pack on, closed his eyes and rose back to the Fourth.

He opened his eyes. A gentle red wind blew past, carrying small spheres of blue and white.

Ishlea's form twisted and brightened. She sped toward Tashon and lifted him into the air. "*Tashon, welcome back! I'm so glad you're here. I'm ready to get moving. Are you ready to get moving? Let's go answer that call. Which way? I'll carry you. We'll give Jonstin a break. Come on. Which way, which way?*"

Tashon looked at her and at the lump of darkness grafted onto her back. What if she changed to someone more dangerous while she was carrying him? Or into someone who didn't want to help him, and took him farther from his destination? But she held him already, and he didn't feel right questioning her when she was only trying to help. He looked at Jonstin and nodded at him. If anything went wrong, the former pilot was there to help.

Tashon pointed. "*That way.*"

Ishlea squealed and flew off, turning tight barrel rolls as she held Tashon tight.

Chapter 23

Bennet stood in a front corner of Town Hall, listening to the mixture of whispers and shouts of the gathering crowd. Anger and paranoia, yes, but Bennet was also glad to hear words of hope and kindness. Voices offering support and encouragement, refusing to give in to the hateful fear that could tear the town apart. He nodded at Claw and Cylindra, sitting in the front row. Avet stood in the other front corner of the room. A side door opened and his mom walked to the podium. The hall fell silent. *At least they still respect her*, Bennet thought.

"We were supposed to be making plans for our town's defenses," she said. "But after the disaster at the station, looks like we have some other things to cover."

A woman in the back stood up and lifted a sign that read, 'Free Rickerson!'

"He's where he belongs," someone shouted at her. "He almost committed murder in Cowley's name."

"He was trying to protect us," another yelled back.

Avet stood up. "Shut up and let the mayor speak."

Leona cleared her throat. "Thank you. And that is exactly what we need to discuss. But I'll be blunt. I'm shocked we have to. That anyone in this town would be willing to murder just to protect ourselves." She raised her hand to stop the shouts. "I'm telling you the soldiers will not be murdered."

The majority of the crowd nodded their support, but others shouted how the soldiers were not to be trusted.

The woman with the sign jumped back to her feet. "This is supposed to be a democracy, not a dictatorship."

Leona gripped the side of the podium and shook her head. "Democracy was never meant to give the people the right to vote on *murder*. The soldiers are in jail for the crime we know they committed. Anything else is speculation. They are protected. Anyone who harms or assaults them will be punished for their crimes."

The woman dropped her sign and sat down.

"Okay," Leona said. "We need to get a barrier up around town. The first step is deciding which structures we can take apart and repurpose for our defenses. Then we need to figure out how much of our town that'll cover, and so on. There are going to have to be sacrifices here, folks. Neighbors are going to need to move in with neighbors if we all want to be safely inside. And if you have a barn or anything that you can part with, let us know."

"Are we really protecting these soldiers?" a man asked.

"Yes, but that's not the only thing. We can all see it's getting worse. Even if the soldiers weren't here and we weren't under threat of being attacked because of them, I think we'd still be strengthening our defenses. We don't know what else might be coming."

"Do we have any news about food deliveries? Are trucks on schedule at all?" someone asked.

Vinley, the town's grocery store owner, stood up. "No word. All they tell me is there's supply shortages. We need to make do with what we have."

"Good thing we got a lot of dead cows frozen up," someone said.

"That just might be what saves us," Leona said. "All our dead cows. Any other questions?"

"Are you keeping the soldiers locked up?"

"For now," Leona said. "For their crime and for their own protection. Anything else?"

The lights in the room flickered and went out. Gasps and screams filled the air. Slowly, phone and watch flashlights lit up the faces of the crowd.

"Don't rely on those," Leona said. "Don't know when you'll get to charge them again, but we'll be okay. Cowley will get through this. Let's stick together, and do our best to keep fear and paranoia at bay. We have, maybe, another hour of sunlight. Get home safely. Watch out for each other. Meet outside this building at first light."

The crowd slowly dispersed, the occasional citizen thanking Mayor Gaines for her words. She nodded graciously and offered her own kind words, smiling as if politicking was her favorite pastime. Before long, only the Gaineses, plus Claw and Gella, remained in town hall.

"Good thpeech," Claw said.

Leona nodded and rubbed her temple. "Never wanted to deal with this kind of crap."

"Mother, language," Avet said.

Cylindra smacked his arm. "Avet, knock it off. Gella, you want to stay at our place tonight?"

She nodded. "Please, if I can. I also wanted to say you can use my house. You can take it apart for the defenses."

"Gella," Bennet said. "Are you sure? That was your—"

"I'm sure," she said. "It's what my parents would've done. It's just a house, anyway."

"No," Claw said. "You jutht want to move in with Bennet."

Bennet blushed and coughed. "I mean, uh, you can't blame her, can you?"

"Hell no," Claw said. "You're the thexier brother. A thame you're hetero."

"I like my men hetero, Claw," Gella said.

Claw laughed and shrugged.

"All right, let's get home," Leona said.

"I need to get my horses first, if that's okay," Gella said.

"Of course, Gel," Bennet said. "We'll see you guys at home."

"Wait," Cylindra said. "Can... uh, can I come with you?"

"Of course, sis," Bennet said.

***

The three walked back from Gella's house, leading Olive and Coop by the reigns. The plodding of feet and hooves rung out in an otherwise silent night. Bennet glanced at Cylindra, entirely aware of the desperate exhaustion under her red eyes. They were all feeling it, but none more than her. She'd always treated Earth like more of a home than anyone Bennet ever knew.

He wrapped his free arm around her and pulled her close. "I love you, sis."

She nodded and sniffed. "I love you, Ben."

"You hanging in okay?"

"No," she said. "We're making all these plans as if we're going to save the Earth. There's no saving it, or is... I'm sorry, that's pessimistic, but it's true. Oxygen levels are going down. Species will be extinct soon. We can't live on lab-enhanced everything. Why bother?"

Bennet shrugged and nodded. "Something might happen to change the path things have taken. It hasn't been that long. Maybe the soil will recover quicker than we think. Maybe some kid scientist in his mom's basement will find a solution and save us all. We're still here, sis."

"She knows that, Ben," Gella said. "But it doesn't make it easier. The possibility of cure doesn't make the fear disappear."

"Yeah," Bennet said. "I know. Look, Cyl, what can I do for you?"

"Just be with me more, Ben. I've hardly seen you since we all got back. I know you were helping Avet, but... I need help, too."

A lump formed in Bennet's throat, and he had to force it down. "Im sorry. I'm here for you."

"I am too," Gella said. "For both of you."

Bennet smiled at her as they turned a corner.

"Do you really this is it?" Gella asked.

Cylindra nodded. "How can it not be? I don't see any way to fix it. We can't plant any new trees. The ones we do have won't produce enough oxygen. Not for long. And all the shortages are already making people anxious. It's going to get more violent, too. It already has. If we don't die in a violent attack, we'll die from suffocation, thirst or starvation."

Bennet hadn't considered the true scope of the world's plight. Not fully, at least. But hearing it from his sister put it all in stark perspective. And when he looked at it that way, what the hell could any of them do? Plod on, fighting for survival, knowing one day soon they'd all face miserable and painful deaths?

"There has to be more than that," Bennet said.

"*Has* to be?" Cylindra asked.

"There is," Gella said. "I like to think there is."

"But what is it?" Bennet asked.

"Our time here. Our relationships. Our memories."

It sounded nice, but Bennet wished she'd given a more concrete answer.

"It sounds too sentimental to be true," Cylindra said.

"Things don't have to be deep or pessimistic to be true," Gella responded.

Bennet raised his eyebrows and glanced at Gella. She flashed a bright smile at him, and he couldn't help but smile back. Maybe there was some truth in her sentimental words. Maybe.

***

With everyone else asleep, Bennet sat in the cold midnight air just outside the front door, Olive and Coop by his side. His finger moved lazily through the dirt.

***

The world around, falling apart.
Worlds inside, falling apart, breaking in darkness.
Seeking light, connection, hope.
Connection to stave off the breaking darkness.
Connection alone won't keep it at bay.
Can't.
Cannot stop what's coming.
But can(?) make it better, they say.
I think they're right, perhaps
Connection can(?) help the world inside.
But what can help the world outside?
It still dies, falls apart, darkens.
And when all dies in darkness, and no light remains to shine on our meager memories –
What then?

***

Bennet stood and put a hand on Olive's back. She neighed softly as if in approval and Bennet slowly moved his hand back and forth through the coarse hair.

"What can we do, Olive? To keep the world alive?"

Olive snorted and shook her head. Bennet looked at the absence of trees, thought of what had caused that absence. *Who* had caused it. And of who had been causing the death of the natural world for centuries. He knelt down again and resumed writing.

***

What then?
All the things made by human hands would slowly crumble, rot away.
Once all those memories are gone,
The first blade of grass will return, followed by another, another, another.
Green will blanket the Earth again, once our hate and fear and violence have all gone.

***

He looked at Olive. "Sounds damn cynical," he said.

Someone walked up beside him. "Or hopeful." Cylindra's voice was a whisper.

Bennet turned to her. "Hopeful?"

She nodded. "It's hopeful to think that Earth could recuperate from all the hell we've caused her."

"It can't recover from us," Avet said as he groggily stepped outside. "You guys are loud, by the way."

"You don't think she'll ever recover?" Cylindra asked.

"Maybe from this," Avet said. "But there's so much more we could do to our home than this. Things that'll make this shit look small. Hell, L.A. looked worse than this. It *was* worse than this. But this shit hit everywhere."

It was the most Bennet had ever heard Avet say about L.A. at a single time, and he didn't want to cut him short. Not if he was ready to talk about it.

"Yeah, there'll be worse shit coming," Avet said. "And I'm afraid all of Earth is gonna start looking like L.A."

"What'd it look like?" Cylindra asked.

Avet spit into the dirt. "You don't want to know. Just came out to tell you two to hush your holes." He turned and walked back inside.

"Guess I should get some sleep." Bennet wiped his words from the dirt and walked his sister back into the house.

***

From Avet's War Journal, Audio Recording
click

    Made it to L.A. and shit's way worse than they said. Those pricks told us all the civilians had been evacuated. We were walking through the dust and rubble and we came around a corner, Claw in front. Something moved and Claw went into his training. Fired before any of the rest of us had our guns out.

    Problem was it wasn't the enemy. Humphreys killed a civilian. A kid, just because the higher ups gave us bad intel. Just because they wanted the world to think we weren't risking civilian lives coming here. Pricks. And damn, you shoulda seen Claw's face when we saw it was a kid. All our faces. Damn, seeing my Claw's face like that, too. And you try to tell him it's not his fault, that he was told we'd only see enemies here. He'd done exactly what he was trained to do. Did it better than any of us. Tell him all that. Not your fault, Claw. Not your fault.

He doesn't believe it. I wouldn't, either. Man, I felt guilty just burying the kid. Claw... he went for a walk.

...

The sun's almost down, and he's not back yet.
Hey! Anyone seen Clawman?
No, soldier.
Nope.
Think he headed west.
I don't want him to be stuck out there.
Hey! Who's coming with me?

...

...

Yeah, I'll come.
Me too. Hate to lose a good fighter.
click

Chapter 24

They sped through a maze of floating ellipses and twirling spheres, Ishlea giggling as she twisted and spun, narrowly missing every shape she could, Jonstin doing his best to keep up. With each turn, Tashon found himself somewhere between thrilled and terrified. It wasn't the gut-wrenching, life-ending pit in his stomach he got when the Ship of Nations went down. It wasn't a calm walk through the yellow forest, either. They came up over a twirling egg and nearly slammed head-on into a sheer wall. Ishlea adjusted last second, shooting upward near enough the cliff Tashon could've licked it, had he been so inclined. Up they went, higher and higher, until at last they reached the top.

"Stop," Tashon called, breathing heavily.

Ishlea obliged, placing Tashon down on the cliff's narrow top. A sea of spinning shapes and swirling lines stretched out on all sides, some glowing brightly and others densely fuligin. Tashon pulled out a food bar, staring at the view as he ate. In the distance, a cylindrical ridge glowed a dim purplish-yellow.

"*How's your ankle?*" Jonstin asked.

Tashon rubbed the splint. "Better than it was."

"*You going to try and heal some more?*" Ishlea asked. "*I'd love to see that.*"

Tashon breathed slowly as he considered. "I might. But I don't think you'd actually see anything, Ishlea."

"*Maybe not. Doesn't matter. What you can do is amazing. Capable of healing yourself by thought alone? The stuff of fringe theory when I was alive. Reserved for comic books and hero movies.*"

Tashon smiled at the mention of comic books, thinking of Johann and the society he'd left behind. He would probably never see how Aethera turned out, how the foundation of mercy impacted future generations. Then the question came to his mind: *am I doing the right thing?* He closed his eyes. The plea was closer, more dire. It wasn't calling for Tashon specifically. But as far as he knew, he was the only one who could hear it. And the pull he felt toward whatever begged for help was overpowering.

For whatever reason, he would follow the sound. But damn if he didn't miss those on Aethera.

His ankle twitched. "Are we safe here? For me to try and heal it more?"

"Yes," Jonstin said.

"We'll keep an eye out," Ishlea said. *"Think your ankle better."*

But before Tashon could do anything, shapes appeared over the ridge.

"What are those?" he asked.

"No idea," Jonstin said. *"I've never been here before. Could be anything. Ishlea?"*

"Don't know either. I'll get a closer look." Ishlea took off, ducking behind shapes as she went.

"I like her right now," Jonstin said.

Tashon laughed. *"Me too. I always like her. Just don't always like being around her."*

"Very sage of you, Tashon."

Tashon shrugged. They watched as Ishlea got farther away, the gap between her and the coming shapes lessening. As they got closer and closer, a sense of familiarity creeped up Tashon's neck. What were those shapes? No, not shapes. Beings. A horde of them, tumbling over, under and around the floating shapes.

"Do you know any of them?" Tashon asked.

"I... shit. They're still after us."

"Who?"

"From before. The pyramids."

Tashon's mouth fell open as he watched Ishlea, unable to help her. She stopped behind a thin tower, no bigger than Tashon's index finger from that distance. But it seemed she'd figured out who the horde was, too. She stayed behind the tower as the horde poured under, over and around the floating shapes. A surge of fear burst into Tashon's chest. What if they got Ishlea before she was able to rid herself of the darkness that clung to her? If Tashon had a choice, he'd rather Jonstin or himself get taken and Ishlea got free.

"We need to help her, Jonstin."

Jonstin flashed with fear for a moment, then burned with resolve. He burst off the edge of the cliff, stopping behind each shape briefly, then soared around to the next. Closer and closer until he was only a few small shapes away from Ishlea. But he wasn't fast enough. The first of the horde was coming over the tower that hid Ishlea.

With a mind-piercing screech, Ishlea exploded upward as strings unfurled from all around her form. Each shot out, latching onto beings and tossing them into the air, leaving them dazed and motionless. Jonstin flew out of his cover, extending the few strings at his disposal. They marched to their targets, pushing them out of the way.

The horde kept coming, pouring as one mass over and around the tower. Ishlea quickly fell into a brutal and ruthless pattern, latching onto news beings before the ones she tossed aside even came to a stop. Jonstin tried to keep up, clumsily latching and throwing, latching and throwing. He caught hold of a large, conical form and pulled on the string, but the being didn't move. It shot out a thick rope of its own that wrapped around Jonstin and cinched tightly around him.

"Jonstin!" Ishlea yelled.

She whipped around and quickly freed two of her strings. The bulge of darkness on her back expanded as she stuck two string into Jonstin's attacker and one string into Jonstin himself. Fuligin traveled down the first two and seeped slowly into the conical being. It went limp and released Jonstin. Ishlea flung it away. Then, harder than she had with any other, she threw Jonstin away. He sailed into the distance, over the far ridge and out of sight.

Tashon jumped to his feet, ignoring the pain in his ankle. "Jonstin!" Gripping the necklace around his neck, hoping for it to bring help as it once had, he stared helplessly, unable to walk or run. Even if he could, all he'd be able to do would be to walk to the edge of the cliff just a few feet in front of him.

Ishlea screeched again and the tumorous fuligin grew and grew. Twice her size, four times, six times. It exploded, sending out a multidirectional ripple of darkness that pushed everything away. Beings were shoved into beings, shapes crashed into shapes. Towers, diamonds and spheres cracked and shattered. The movements slowed, and Tashon saw each being that had been attacking was now nothing more than a statue rendered in the deepest fuligin. The ripple stopped and vanished, far too close to Tashon for comfort. He stepped back, hoping the precipice held firm.

Again, Ishlea screeched. Another ripple, and each being it touched exploded in a cloud of dark dust. Each shape shattered more still as the ripple spread out, faster and faster. The dark force of it slammed into the cliff Tashon stood on, then ripped through. It shook, tilted, and then collapsed.

Tashon fell.

***

Jonstin fumed with anger as he soared through the air away from Ishlea. Away from the fight. Away from Tashon. He knew, or thought he knew, that Ishlea had done it to protect him. What if she had meant to hurt him, though?

He soared over the ridge and came to a sudden stop when he slammed into another cliff. He hovered, dazed for a moment, and then rose up. Maybe Ishlea had meant him harm, or maybe she hadn't. Either way, he wouldn't leave Tashon behind. He'd stopped not far beyond the ridge, and was confident he could make it back before much else happened. Back he flew, up to the top of the ridge to find... nothing.

Not precisely nothing. A vast field of shrapnel floating in all directions, but not one being. The enemies he was sure would capture them were gone, as were Ishlea and Tashon. It had been but moments since Ishlea tossed him away, hadn't it? He sighed and slowly floated into the battle's aftermath. An ending to a hopeless battle that simply made no sense. How could it? He looked up and down, left and right, ana and kata. No sign of anyone. He went on, zigzagging through the floating shrapnel. As he came around a jagged chunk of cylinder, he found Ishlea, sitting silently on a small, broken sphere. The fuligin lump on her back had grown and cracked, darkness leaking into the air, blowing away in the wind, drop by drop.

"Ishlea," he said as he inched closer.

"*Jonstin...? Why would momma make this simulation? It's not right. Now she's gone. I can't find her. Jonstin? What's happening?*" The fuligin lump pulsed as if it were an independent creature, breathing of its own accord.

"Ishlea, I don't know what happened. We were fighting those zealots. I got thrown out of the fight."

Ishlea turned to him. "*I threw you out, didn't I? I'm sorry.*"

"It's okay. Do you remember what happened after you threw me?"

"*I was scared and angry. I screamed, then everything went dark. And now I'm here. The same place. But it's changed.*"

Jonstin looked at the broken cliff where he'd left Tashon. "Do you know where Tashon is?"

"*Tashon?*" Ishlea shot up. "*Tashon! Where is he?*"

"Damn it," Jonstin said.

The two flew quickly to the broken cliff, swerving in and out of the obstacles.

"Where's the ground?" Ishlea asked.

Jonstin looked down. Below them and the sea of crumbled shapes, nothing. No ground as far as he could see, down and down.

"Tashon... Either they took him away, or he fell," Ishlea said.

"If they took him, they would've taken you, too. He fell."

"Can you seen him?" Ishlea asked.

"No." Jonstin descended, knowing now that he'd go as far as he needed to find Tashon and help him with his journey.

Ishlea followed. "The simulation is wrong. Mother?"

Jonstin looked at her. "Ishlea... this is real."

"What?"

"It's not a simulation," Jonstin said.

Ishlea looked around, grabbed a small hunk of rubble and threw it at what remained of the cliff. It hit, bounced, rolled through the air then came to a stop. "This is all real?" She continued to follow Jonstin down, reaching out and touching everything she could. "If it's real... what did I just do to those who wanted to hurt us?"

"You made them... disappear?" Jonstin glanced at her as they descended below the lowest shapes and entered open air. In every direction but up, there was nothing in sight other than the two lone beings.

"I think I did something to them." She looked around, her form shifting. "Why... How am I here, Jonstin?"

"You've been following Tashon. You helped us escape back at the point of creation. I don't know why, though."

They continued down, Ishlea's form flickering constant changes. "Momma did this, damn her. All Momma's fault...I hurt them, Jonstin. I caused the pain. Now I have no idea where I sent them. Why did I do that? What's the point of harming others?" Her form sagged, then stiffened. "The point is survival. This is war, and I did what I needed to survive. I'd do again, don't doubt that. Where am I? Who the hell are you? What's wrong with my body? Am I...?" The darkness on her back grew. "You mean death isn't the end? I was supposed to be dead. I wanted... no, no, no...." She fell silent, sinking faster.

Jonstin stopped and watched her fall. Had her life on Earth been so bad that she had hoped the afterlife was a lie? And what traumas had she suffered since she'd been in the Fourth? There had to be a significant amount, Jonstin felt, for her souls to be so disjointed. Then he thought of some of the hell he'd suffered in his three-dimensional lifespan, and of what others had suffered. The shit some of them went through in their physical life alone was enough to destroy the soul.

But how to repair a soul so broken and confused? he asked himself as sped down and rejoined Ishlea.

"Ishlea, I'm here," he said.

"*No shit, I can see,*" she said. "*Sorry, I...shit, no shit, I see. No. I'm sorry, Jonstin. No sh...sorry...shit on you....*"

Jonstin reached out and touched her. For a moment her form and her lump brightened, but as soon as it came it was gone, even darker than before. She screamed unintelligible sounds, flailing her appendages in every direction. Jonstin moved away to avoid getting hit, but stayed nearby. He'd told he was there for her, and he wasn't lying. But he hoped Tashon was okay.

Chapter 25

The lights flickered within the packed Cub's Den. People talked nervously, passing glasses and bottles around their tables. The air was thick with worry and fear. Something had happened, but no one knew what. Clawman worked furiously at the keyboard of a vintage laptop, its screen brightening and darkening of its own accord.

Avet sat down next to Claw and handed him a glass of water. "Anything?"

Claw took a long drink, then shook his head. The lights crackled.

"Sigs, you sure the generator's good?" Avet asked.

A short, thin man huffed. "Sure as we can be, friend. It's the worst of the generators we got. But we're gonna need the better ones for winter."

Avet nodded. "Good thinking, Sigs."

The man shrugged. "Was your momma's idea."

"Of course it was," Avet said with a smile.

"Wait," Claw said. "Quiet."

The restaurant fell eerily silent.

"You get something?" Avet whispered.

Claw pointed at the screen. "Power plantth were hit. Loth of them, lookth like."

Avet quickly read the short article. Dozens of power plants across the country had been taken out, all within a single hour. The attacks had been timed perfectly, but as of yet no one had taken responsibility.

"Wait, found a link." Claw moved his finger on the track pad, then huffed. "Damn it. Lotht connecthon." He slammed the screen down and rubbed his eyes.

Avet wrapped an arm around him and kissed his temple. "It's okay, Claw. At least we know more now than we did."

"Are they going to get it fixed anytime soon?" someone asked.

"Not that I thaw," said Claw.

Mumbles and groans. Then the front door swang open, revealing the dark, windy dawn. Bennet, Leona and Cylindra walked in, each wearing a smile.

"The hell is all this?" Leona said. "You're all supposed to be tearing down homes and barns to build the perimeter."

"But, ah, Mayor," a man said. "We have limited power. Our tools and machines won't last long. We, ah, don't want to waste the power supply."

Leona scoffed. "Our defenses are paramount, my friends. And yes, we should save what power we have. But you all have hands. Shovels, hammers. Manual tools, friends. When did this town get so lazy?"

Everyone glanced at each other, then back at Leona.

"You heard her, lazy shits," Avet said. "Let's get to work."

"You've been sitting here doing nothing, too," Gella said as she stepped from behind the bar.

"Yeah, yeah. I'm a lazy shit too."

"Let's go," Bennet said.

Avet grabbed Claw's hand and helped him to his feet. "You good to work, my Clawman?"

"Yeth," he said. "Leth get to it."

Cub's Den slowly emptied, Leona giving each person orders as they left. The Gaines children, along with Claw and Gella, went to tear down Gella's house. They walked silently, Claw's hand resting soft but firm in Avet's as the sun rose.

Gella sniffed and wiped her cheek.

Bennet wrapped his arm around her, pulling her close. "You don't have to take apart your parents' house."

"I do," she said. "They would've done it. And it's just me living there. I don't need that house." She paused and smiled. "And, like Cylindra said, now I have an excuse to move in with you." She playfully shoved her shoulder into his.

"I knew it," Cylindra said.

Claw through a fist in the air. "Yeah, get thome!"

Bennet blushed and shook his head.

"Bennet's saving himself for marriage," Avet said.

"He ith?" Claw said.

"Really?" Gella looked at him, eyebrows raised, a thin smile on her face.

Bennet shrugged. "I... yeah, I am. I was a... late bloomer, anyway. Never cared much about sex in high school."

Gella smiled. "I like that," she said.

"You thaving yourthlelf?" Claw asked.

Gella blushed and giggled. "Starting now, sure."

They all laughed, and for a moment Avet felt as if they were teenagers again, walking home after a night of illegal drinking. *Simpler times*, he thought. But he hadn't known Claw back then, hadn't even known himself. Was simpler always better? Looking around at the laughing faces and gleaming eyes. Maybe simpler wasn't always better, he decided. Or maybe the chaos that surrounded them made the simple moment more pure, more *alive* in some way.

They soon arrived at Gella's house and her face hardened. She nodded, wiped a tear from her cheek, walked to the shed and pulled the door open. She handed out tools. Crowbars, hammers, a saw and a pickax.

"I know none of you are stupid," she said. "But we all have pent up fear, and all that shit. We're *not* destroying my parents' house." She lifted a mallet and knocked the shed door off its hinges. "We're dismantling it, putting it to a different use. If any of you decide this is demolition time, expect this mallet in your scrotum."

Avet raised his hand. "Ah, Cylindra doesn't have a scrotum."

"You think I'm worried about your sister?" Gella said. "That speech was mostly for you." She smiled happily and went to work dismantling the shed.

Claw laughed. "I like her."

Bennet smiled. "Me too. Me too."

"Both of you shut up." Avet grabbed his crowbar and walked to the house, trying to ignore the laughter behind him. Despite his feigned anger, he smiled to himself.

***

"Sheriff, I gotta piss," Rickerson moaned, gently bouncing up and down in the dim light.

Ling stretched and leaned back in his chair. "Thanks for the update, Mr. Rickerson."

The three soldiers coughed quietly to each other.

"This is inhumane," Rickerson said.

"You have a toilet right there, Mr. Rickerson." Ling opened a box of day-old donuts and handed one to each of the soldiers. "Have you had donuts before?"

Madame President sniffed hers, licked it, and then shoved it in her mouth. The other two followed. Ling watched, waiting for any resemblance of a natural human reaction. Madame President coughed, gagged and spit the donut into her small toilet.

The male soldier, who Ling now referred to as "Healer," swallowed his, then sneezed.

"Bless you, Healer," Ling said.

Healer wiped a string of snot from his upper lip and laughed.

The third soldier swallowed, frowned and rubbed her gurgling stomach.

"Meat, meat," the unnamed woman soldier said. "Meat."

Ling set the box of donuts down, opened a drawer in his desk and pulled out a bag of beef jerky. As soon as he opened it, the woman soldier flickered out of her cell and appeared in front of him. She grabbed a handful of the dried meat, shoved it in her mouth, and then popped back into her cell, chewing loudly.

"All right, then," Ling said. "I'll call you Carnivore for now."

Carnivore beamed an open-mouth smile, bits of chewed up meat falling to the floor. She bent down and hurriedly shoved them back into her mouth.

"Hey, uh, Sheriff," Rickerson said. "Any food for me?"

Ling looked at the vintage clock that hung on the wall. "Not meal time." He dropped into his chair and grabbed a donut from the box.

"Sheriff, come on, I'm hungry here. And you fed those—"

Ling slammed his open hand on the desk. "Methane gas on my lover's breath, Rickerson. You assaulted my deputy half to death, and almost tortured an innocent woman on live TV. I don't give a rotten horse liver how hungry you are. Sit down and close your gaping hole."

Eyes wide in shock, Rickerson slowly sat on his cot and turned away. The three soldiers smiled, and Healer covered his mouth in a failed attempt to hide his soft laughter. Ling nodded to himself, and nearly tossed more harsh words at the man, but stopped himself. It wouldn't do any good. *Though it might feel good,* he thought.

The front door swung open and Meerf walked in, his face free of injury. "Hi, hi, Healer. Sheriff. Madame President." He set a small grocery sack on his desk and whistled softly.

"The other one I'm calling Carnivore now," Ling said.

"She, uh, likes meat?"

Ling shrugged. "More than she likes donuts."

"Meat is *always* better than donuts," Meerf said.

Rickerson swore under his breath, stood and turned to his stainless steel toilet. He dramatically sighed and unzipped his pants. Ling did his best to hide his amusement at the small indignities Rickerson had to suffer.

Meerf sat down. "You plan on unlocking their cells soon?"

Ling clicked his tongue and sighed. "I don't know. They're in there for their safety, not ours. They wanted to hurt us, they would have already."

"Unless it's a long con," Rickerson muttered under his breath.

"Think I'll keep their cells locked," Ling said. "For their safety."

"Do they need our protection?" Meerf asked.

Ling laughed and shook his head. "Probably not, Meerf. Probably not."

"What about me?" Rickerson asked.

"You've been proven guilty," Meerf said.

"In what court?"

"Mine," Ling said. "The world's changing, and no lawyer is going to defend you right now. Not when you broadcast your pitiful show of force."

"I have a cousin lawyer, in Cheyenne," Rickerson said. "Where the hell is my one call, Sheriff?"

Ling wiped his fingers on a napkin. "Phones are down. Internet, too. Cars aren't gonna be going far, either."

"You're just leaving me here, no trial?"

"No trial," Ling said. "If the world gets back to normal, you'll get one. But, Rickerson, do you think that's going to happen?"

Rickerson grabbed the cell bars and squeezed. "I was trying to help our town," he whispered.

Ling sighed. "I know you were, and that's why I haven't knocked you out. But we all know you crossed a line, Rickerson. And most of Cowley refuses to take it that far." Ling stood and walked to the front door. "Deputy, Madame President. Healer, Carnivore. Keep my station in tact and connected to Earth's gravitational pull, huh?"

"Yes, Sheriff," Meerf said.

The three soldiers made various sounds that Ling thought indicated understanding. But Ling knew Meerf could handle it himself if he needed to. Despite what most of the town thought. The door swung shut behind him as stepped onto the sidewalk, narrowly avoiding a collision with a tall, dark-haired woman carrying a large wood pallet.

"I'm blinder than a cow in the womb, Kachee," he said. "I apologize."

"No apologies, Sheriff," she said without stopping.

Ling fell in step next to her. "How's the barrier going?"

"Good, I think," she said. "But I'm still not sure how much we're trying to enclose. Or how quick they think this is supposed to go."

"Just following orders?" Ling asked.

"Just following orders," she said.

Ling nodded and looked ahead to see a neatly organized stack of pallets, doors, planks and other lumber higher than his head. The town had been working quickly while he sat lazily in his office, watching Rickerson. He'd have to remedy that.

"Can I carry that for you, Kachee?"

She laughed. "You know me well enough not to even ask that," she said.

Ling shrugged. "I know. My body's just itching like a mouse covered in cat hair. I need to get moving."

"Find the mayor. She'll have something for you to do."

Ling found her at a folding table outside town hall, a few candles illuminating a large map of Cowley, its borders covered in lines and numbers. She watched Pethie Sans, Cowley High's wild-haired math teacher, nodding intently as she spoke.

"Lots of variables, situations, numbers to consider," Pethie said. "Need enough buildings to live in, need enough material to encircle all of us. Populations, living arrangements, wall...." She scribbled on the paper, then looked at the sky, closing her eyes in thought.

"Miss Sans," Mayor Gaines said. "How large of an area can we protect?"

The teacher muttered numbers under her breath, then looked down. "Need shelter. Farm land, in case Earth revitalizes."

Ling sighed. He had little hope of that happening.

"Less than half, certainly. Encircle, protect, perhaps two hundred acres of land."

The mayor nodded. "Thank you, Miss Sans." She turned to Ling. "Hi, Sheriff. Which two hundred acres should we cover, in your opinion?"

Ling smiled and nodded. "I hope some of our land becomes viable again, but I doubt it. And... you know, we don't know how all of this is going to change our winter. My opinion is whatever two hundred acres gives us the most shelter."

"I agree," Leona said. "Miss Sans, can you figure out which two hundred acres that would be?"

She nodded and muttered under her breath, then started scribbling on the paper.

Leona walked to Ling. "Sheriff. I saw Deputy Meerf. He looks like nothing happened to him."

"Like nothing happened." Ling shook his head. "The soldier just zapped out of his cell and healed him."

"Do you think they're here to help us for some reason?"

Ling inhaled deeply and considered the question. "Can it be that simple? For us or against us?"

Leona shrugged. "It'd sure as hell make all this easier."

Ling laughed. "It would. But then it wouldn't be real."

"I hate reality." Leona sighed and rubbed her eyes.

Ling smiled. "'Reality is merely an illusion,'" he quoted.

Leona raised her eyebrows. "What?"

"Albert Einstein," Ling said. "'Reality is merely an illusion, albeit a very persistent one.'"

"Didn't he create the atomic bomb?" Leona asked.

Ling shook his head. "That's a myth. The government thought he would be a security risk."

"You know that, but not that Shakespeare wrote comedies," Leona said with a smile.

"Which one had more of an impact on the human race?" Ling asked.

Leona tilted her head and clicked her tongue. "No idea. Let's get to work."

"Right," Ling said. "Where do you need me?"

"Sheriff, right now I need you wherever those soldiers are."

"You want me at the station?" Ling asked. "Stuck there like a goat stuck to an electric fence?"

"Sure. Only less painful." Leona smiled. "We need to know what's going on with the soldiers at all times. Even if they're not connected to what's happening, they could provide a lot of answers. And we don't know why they're here. Keep them safe, and try to get some answers."

"Yes, Mayor," Ling said. "Stay safe."

Without warning, Leona stretched her arms out and pulled Ling into a tight hug. "You too, Sheriff." She pulled away, then turned her attention back to the map.

Ling made his way back to the station, a smile on his lips and tear in his eye as he tried to remember the last time someone had hugged him.

***

Pole and three of her deputies approached the warehouse slowly, under cover of a cloudy night sky. All the intel they'd gathered indicated the suits had made the warehouse their home, and most often spent their nights within its wall. As they closed in, Pole drew her gun, her deputies following her lead. They stopped outside the front door, one of two. Pole motioned for two of the deputies to circle around to the rear door.

The unspoken truth within their minds was that every movement they made was nothing more than ritual. Block the entrances, storm in and demand the criminals to put their hands up and drop their weapons. But that wouldn't work with the suits, or any like them. Why, then, did they still go through these motions? For Pole, it provided a sense of comfort. And her deputies did it because they would never question her lead.

"Cops!" someone screamed from inside.

Shots and shouts followed. Pole kicked the door in. The two deputies lay dead just inside the other entrance, surrounded by at least a dozen people. She shoved her deputy to the left behind a pallet stacked with packs of cocaine. She dove to the right, firing twice, hitting her mark once, and landed behind an upturned table.

Her mind spun as she registered the faces she'd seen. Most were nameless lackeys, but two she knew from multiple wanted memos. Alexi and Celeste Hanith. Twin sisters, one with hair died white and the other black. They'd been smuggling weapons and cocaine for decades, and here they were in Pole's city. There Pole was, with about twenty less deputies than she would've brought along had she known the twins were there.

She looked at her deputy and counted down with her fingers. Three, two, one. They jumped to their feet and fired, shot after shot. Four bodies went down, then the black-haired one, bouncing on her heels with excitement, shouted for everyone to stop.

"What're you doing, Alexi?" the blonde one asked.

"Having some fun, Celeste," she said.

"Fine, psycho bitch," Celeste said. "But give me the deputy."

"Fine. I want the sheriff."

Pole aimed and fired. The bullet sped to its target, yet just before it hit, the smallest flicker disturbed the air, and the bullet disappeared. Frantic, she emptied her clip at her but not one bullet hit.

Celeste ran at the deputy, who fired, but with the same result as Pole's shot. Celeste leaped over the stack of drugs and flicked a knife from her pocket. The deputy threw his gun at her head, but it didn't slow her momentum. Laughing, she landed on him. Pole turned and fired at Celeste, but, again, the air snatched her bullets away.

"Shit," she said.

Her deputy was dead, Celeste laughing and soaked in his blood.

The air around Alexi shifted. Two figures appeared on either side of her—the men in suits. Pole had fallen for their trap. Cursing her stupidity, she dropped her gun, raised her hands and stepped out from behind the table.

"What do you want with me, Alexi?"

The suits snickered, eyeing each other like two giddy school boys.

Alexi tilted her head, but said nothing. She wouldn't give Pole the satisfaction of an explanation, or the opportunity to find an escape. Instead, she slid a knife out of her sleeve and threw it. Pole ducked, but Alexia had aimed low. The knife sunk into Pole's hip. Not fatal, but painful. She bit back any sound, determined to show as little weakness as possible. With a smile, she straightened and pulled the blade from her leg.

Alexi laughed, drew another knife and charged. Fast. She slammed into Pole, grabbed her by the collar and forced her against the nearest wall. But she was stupid. Or, more likely, arrogant. Pole got her knife through Alexi's ribs and into her heart before her back was even against the wall. Warm blood dripped down the handle and onto Pole's hands. She let go and shoved Alexi away. She dropped, motionless.

Pole looked up, her victory short-lived. Each nameless lackey had a gun pointed at her.

Celeste screeched, loud and high enough to shatter glass, it seemed.

Pole took a deep breath, released it and waited for death to come. The guns fired. The bullets never reached her, swallowed up in the air. Then the woman suit was there, moving in a blur from lackey to lackey, until they lay on the floor, each missing at least one limb.

Celeste screeched again and turned to run, but the woman suit appeared in front of her. Her arm flickered into a half-visible limp. She slammed her open palm through Celeste's skull, and stopped with her hand, invisible, inside Celeste's brain. Then her arm flashed solid, then disappeared completely. Blood dripped from Celeste's eyes, nose and ears, and she collapsed.

The woman suit turned to her male counterparts. "Wrong. Inaccurate. Broken." She walked to them, arms outstretched. "Wrong. Inaccurate. Broken." She grabbed each by the hair and ripped their heads off. No blood spilled, just a *whoosh* of mist as the dismembered heads laughed hysterically. Their bodies slumped to the floor and disappeared, followed by their heads and then the woman suit.

Pole stood there, alone, breathing heavily. She'd made it out, thanks to one of the suits. She'd thought all three of them were trouble, but now she wasn't sure. There was something different—*better*—about the woman, and Pole couldn't help hoping that she would see her again.

Chapter 26

Tashon had been falling for so long that the idea he would ever stop falling seemed insane. When the cliff crumpled, he fell headfirst into a slow, never-ending somersault. He spun and spun. For a time he passed shapes, vainly groping for them in an attempt to stop the spinning. Then he fell below the shapes, into an empty void, with nothing around him but sparks of untouchable light.

On he spun, down and down, the lights getting dimmer every moment until at last they disappeared. He was surrounded by darkness, ever falling, ever twirling. Yet it was not like the darkness growing from Ishlea. No, it was merely an absence of light. And something about knowing the Fourth wasn't always filled with light comforted Tashon. It calmed the logical part of his mind, the piece that told him if light exists, then so must darkness.

But the comfort was fleeting, and he soon longed for stillness. The constant twisting, though not fast, pulled his blood from his feet to his head. Both tingled and buzzed, as if he'd been sitting on his feet, then he stood up too fast, sending his head spinning.

He passed out of conscious awareness.

And found himself, his higher essence, completely alone. Not even his third-dimensional form was in sight. He hung, frozen still, the only source of light in a sea of darkness. *True* darkness. It poked and prodded, jabbed and stabbed in an attempt to pierce his essence, to drain his light. He struggled, trying to move his arms or legs or even his head, but no movement was possible. He tried to open his mouth to scream, but his lips remained shut.

The darkness deepened, sinking into him from all angles, pressing his essence smaller and smaller. Panic gripped him and he tried to gasp for air, though his essence didn't breathe, had no need for oxygen. Completely and terrifyingly helpless, then. The darkness compressed him, smaller and flatter until he was nothing but a one-dimensional plane. The darkness continued to crush him, pinching Tashon's plane of essence into a thin line. He ached to scream, to stretch, to do *anything*, but still the darkness squeezed, pinching until his line of essence was nothing more than the tiniest speck of inconsequential light amidst the darkness.

Then that, too, was snuffed out.

***

Gasping, Tashon's eyes shot open. He rolled to his side and vomited, then rolled away from it. He lay on the ground of the Fourth above a swirling green nebula in the Third. He rolled onto his back and sat up. The air was dimly lit by an unseen source in the distance, creating the sense of being in a dense fog. He was completely alone. No beings around him, not even a colorful wisp of wind.

Turning his gaze, he realized his pack was gone. His splint, too. Then, as if waking from a drunken stupor, he realized everything tangible that had been with him was gone. He sat in the leering fog, entirely nude. No embarrassment flushed through him, nor anger. Just a calm confusion. A simple curiosity about what had happened after the darkness broke him down into nothing.

He touched his face, his chest, his legs. His form was still physical, still three-dimensional. He tried bending his ankle and winced. Still able to feel pain, too. The swelling had gone down, and it seemed the repair he'd made was holding. But in the hazy fog, he dare not turn his attention inward in an attempt to complete the healing. Though the air around him was still, it seemed to move at times. He felt a presence lurking just out of sight. A heaviness that always seemed just beyond sight.

The call was still audible, if only barely. It gave him direction, purpose. He rose to his feet, swearing as he put weight on the fractured bone, then staggered forward into the darkness. Given his lack of clothing and the creeping mist, he felt he should be cold. But it seemed there was no temperature at all, just as it was in the rest of the Fourth. His skin felt no different, no goosebumps or shivers spread across his body. Yet something about the space he walked through exuded an icy chill that penetrated his thoughts and sank into his heart. His thoughts slowed, his legs moved automatically, his body following the call out of habit. Were it not for the pain in every other step, he would've lost awareness of himself.

"The painfulness of use," he mumbled. "No, that's not right. Or... not wrong? Right, wrong, right, wrong."

His eyes fell shut. He continued to shuffle forward as he mumbled and whispered whatever came to mind. "Rightfulness...wrongfulness. Difference? No. No, Rosa, not same, but...what? Oh... We...did something wrong?

Too much mercy? No, Theresa, no. Just the...right amount, I say...yeah. Mercy, I mean, can't get any better than...than... Damn, cold. That isn't cold. Like... I don't know. You ever felt something like this, Smith? Abe?"

The words collapsed into unintelligible sounds. All he knew was that he had to keep moving, convinced that stillness would invite an attack.

An electric crack shot through the air. Tashon lazily opened his eyes.

Something moved in his peripheral. He jerked his head to the right, but whatever it was had left. If it had even been there. But the almost-glimpse of it lingered with him, his heart pounding as he continued on, wincing with each step. Hoping that the mental chill wouldn't render his brain useless. Soon, his eyes fell shut again as he blindly limped forward.

***

Jonstin and Ishlea hovered over a ground littered with the rubble from Ishlea's explosion. Darkness continued to drip from her lump, yet it did not shrink. Jonstin wondered what darkness within her kept it alive, but he wasn't sure he wanted to know. Even if he did, it wasn't his place to ask her. One must make their own choice to divulge the darkness within. It couldn't be forced.

Instead, he asked a question with an obvious answer. *"You see any sign of Tashon?"*

"No, unf— The hell I give a sh— Fortunately not. We saw it, you ass...him fall here...that, damn piece of—ah! Sorry, I'm sorry." Her entire form quivered as she turned away from him, fully exposing her tumorous mass of darkness. It was leaking faster now. The lump itself beating as if the darkness were blood pumping through a massive heart.

"It's okay, Ishlea." And Jonstin meant it. He felt no anger toward Ishlea, nor any fear of her. He knew that maybe it would've been smart to fear her, that she could do to him the same she did to their attackers. But he also knew she risked herself to save him. That wasn't something easily forgotten. *"Which way did he say that sound was?"*

Ishlea trembled, then stiffened. *"That way,"* she said, pointing. *"If the shit brain isn't crazy. I mean, damn it, I mean, yeah, let's see if we can find him."*

They moved on, Jonstin doing his best to keep Ishlea beside him. He knew he didn't want her behind him, but he didn't want to hide behind her and let her think he was scared of her. No, he needed to show friendship and support. And, hopefully, he'd help her find a way to rid herself of the crippling darkness.

"*See something,*" Ishlea said.

Jonstin looked, but saw nothing. Ahead, the ground disappeared, leaving only a vast cloud of translucent emptiness. The wind swirled high above it, but it stretched out of sight in all other directions.

"*Let us ascend over the top,*" Ishlea said. Then, after a pause, "*Shit's tall. Damn tall.*"

Jonstin rose up, unable to keep from staring through the glass-like wall. No wind swirled inside. Nothing moved or lived at all. And it stretched seemingly forever. Below where he floated, he could still see down to the third dimension. But when he looked into the emptiness, the Third did not appear at the bottom. There wasn't a bottom at all, as far as he could tell.

Jonstin wondered if the surface was solid, or if he could move through it. What if Tashon had come upon it? He would've had no way to climb over the emptiness. Would he have been committed enough to walk into the emptiness? *He wouldn't hesitate,* Jonstin thought.

He looked up, then over at Ishlea. "*It just keeps going up,*" he said.

"*No shit, this damn –* " Ishlea paused and twitched. "*Momma always went hiking up these high mountains. Took me with her when I did somethin' bad. Force me to flip over animal dung 'til I found this fungus, then she'd shove it down my throat.*" She shook and twitched. "*Damn, Jonstin. Don't know why I'm sticking with you.*"

"*I don't know, either. But I'm glad you are,*" Jonstin said.

"*That's sentimental bullshit. I know you're scared of me.*"

Jonstin paused for a moment. Was this the *real* Ishlea, fully aware of herself and her ever-changing personality? "*I – yeah, okay. I'm a little scared, sometimes. But you've saved me. Twice. And you took care of Tashon. I don't think you'll hurt me.*"

"*I hope not,*" she said. "*I mean you better hope not, you prick. I'm only staying with you 'cause I got nowhere else to be. And I'm hopin' to see those freak fanatics again and can send more away to – Where did I send them, Jonstin?*"

Jonstin looked at Ishlea, then his gaze followed a drop of darkness as it spilled from the mass and slowly fell to the ground far below. "*I don't know, Ishlea. But you did it to survive.*"

"*But they weren't going to kill me, we're they? You can't be killed here, right?*" A pause, then a flicker. For a moment, she seemed like she had more to stay. Instead, her form slumped and the tumorous mass pulsed.

They reached the top suddenly, unaware it was the top until they were staring at an emptiness in the middle of the fourth dimension. A sea of nothing. Not black or fuligin, white or any other color. An inexplicable emptiness, stretching as far as he could see, at once drawing him in yet repelling him. And somewhere on the other side of it, the cry for help that guided Tashon.

"I think he's in there," Jonstin said.

"The dumbass probably is," Ishlea said. *"Shall we go and get him, Jonstin?"*

J.S. SHERWOOD

PART TWO

Chapter 27

One Earth Month Later

Bennet and Gella stood at the top of the recently completed barrier, watching the sun rise over the dead earth. It had been the best kind of night for watch duty: quiet and uneventful. Bennet smiled and looked at her profile, lit by the rising rays. After tearing her house apart, she'd moved in with him and his family, bringing only her parents' food storage and one small bag of clothes.

The first week had proven less awkward than he'd expected, and they quickly fell into a comfortable routine that ended each night with Gella retiring to Bennet's room, and Bennet sleeping in the living room. It wasn't that he didn't want to sleep with her—of course he did. But he'd spent so long committed to waiting for marriage that the thought of giving up on that, while exciting, also made him nauseous.

Then, that morning, Avet had asked him, "What's the point of waiting when we don't even know if Earth will be here tomorrow?"

"Because it feels right to me," Bennet said. "That's the only way I can explain."

Avet shrugged and walked away, leaving Bennet questioning whether the state of the world made marriage more, or less, important.

"What are you thinking about?" Gella asked.

Bennet blinked and pulled himself back into the moment. "Us, I guess. Our future."

"We haven't been together *that* long." She smiled. "Already thinking of ending it?"

"Not at all. I don't want to find a new place to live."

She smiled. "They *would* choose me, huh?"

He nodded and looked away. "Do you, at some point, ever want to get married?"

"I think so, yeah," she said. "You do too, right?"

"I... yeah, I mean...." He paused and looked into her eyes. "Is marriage still important, you think?"

"You mean with all this"—she spread her arms out, encompassing everything in sight—"Going on?"

"Exactly. I mean, is it worth it? All the pomp and circumstance? All the planning?"

She nodded. "You mean, what if the world ends before the planning is even done? Before even getting married? Let's just skip all that. Go to town hall and seal the deal today."

Ben stared at her. "Wait, what?"

"That wasn't a proposal?" she asked, then broke into laughter.

Bennet looked away. "Nope, never getting married," he said with a smile.

She grabbed his hand, pulled him close and kissed him on the cheek. "I wouldn't say that."

Footsteps clamped up the ladder. Clawman pulled himself onto the wall, followed by Healer.

"Your time's up," Clawman said. "See anything interesting?"

"What?" Bennet asked. "I can't understand you without your lisp."

"Hey." Healer raised a fist. "Be nice. Claw is friend."

Bennet raised his hands in surrender. "You're right, Healer. I'm sorry."

Healer lowered his hand.

Bennet didn't know much about the three soldiers, but it seemed treating them like children was always the best tactic. At first, he'd been against letting the three free. More for their safety than anyone else's. But once the barrier was complete, the town voted to set them free. And, so far, no fanatics had come to pillage Cowley for harboring them.

Before the decision was made, there had been—and still were—countless discussions about who or what the soldiers were. And, by extension, all of the strangers who appeared in towns across America, perhaps across the world. The theories were as endless as the discussions, though Bennet clung to none of them wholeheartedly. Why fervently support a theory as true when a theory, by definition, had not been proven true? The one that made the most sense to him was that that the soldiers were some type of biomechanic robots brought to existence through a fusing of virtual reality and human cloning. Bennet hadn't any idea how something like that would actually work, but he knew human cloning had been done across the world, to varying degrees of success, for the last few decades. And if they were simultaneously part of the real world and a virtual one, it would explain the sometimes hologram-like state of their bodies. What mattered most to Bennet, though, was that the soldiers had proven to be valuable members of their town. Three more bodies on whom he could rely.

Bennet and Gella climbed down the ladder and walked, hand in hand, to town hall to collect their morning rations. Cylindra stood at the entrance, passing out small bags of food with Madame President. The line was over fifty people long, and Bennet wasn't sure he wanted to wait.

It wasn't the actual waiting that bothered him. It was the number of people. With them all crowded together, waiting for their meager rations, he sensed their anxiety and desperation. Cowley had remained a mostly peaceful town, save a few small drunken bouts. But Bennet felt an eager darkness building.

"Cyl seems happy." Gella's voice broke into Bennet's thoughts.

He smiled. "She is. Madame President is the first friend she's had in—I don't know—years."

Gella nodded. "I'm starving."

Bennet shrugged. "I could wait."

"You want to head back? I'll bring our rations back."

Bennet examined the crowd, taking in every nervous twitch or agitated glare. Would it be the day the darkness would show itself? He shook his head. "No, I'll wait with you."

She leaned in and kissed him. "Great. Thanks, Ben."

Bennet wrapped his arms around her, wondering if she hated being apart as much as he did.

Was hating being away from a person enough of a reason to make a lifelong commitment? If the world ended and he died in a few months, or even years, the answer for Bennet was yes. So the real question was this: if he and Gella both lived to be one hundred, did he still want to spend the rest of his life with her?

Someone screamed.

Bennet instinctively squeezed Gella tighter as his heart beat faster.

"It's unbearable!" A teen boy, half of his head shaved, yelled as his mother shook her head. "I'm bored all the time. And, worse, we don't know shit about shit. No visual, audio or textual communication. No info. No entertainment."

Bennet rolled his eyes. They'd all been frustrated with the absence of outside information, but comparing that with the lack of entertainment seemed ridiculous. At first.

"We all want to know what's happening, Lem," the mother said. "But you can live without your virtual world."

"And do what?" Lem tossed his hands in the air. "All my friends are in other towns. I don't even know if they're alive, Mom."

The woman smiled sadly and wrapped her arms around her son, whispering words only the two could hear.

"Being a teenager while the world ends," Gella said, "would be hell on Earth."

Bennet nodded but said nothing, as a poem that would never be put to paper, or even dirt, came to mind.

***

> *It must be toughest on the kids, the dying of a world.*
> *At least those old enough to remember what it once was.*
> *Yeah, the world wasn't great before.*
> *(The worst it'd ever been, according to some.)*
> ~~~
> *But even then it had been*
> *A living world*
> *A breathing world*
> *A world full of possibility*
> *A world that would soon be theirs.*
> ~~~
> *But now look*
> *At the burning hellscape*
> *They get to inherit.*
> *An optimistic question:*
> *Will their bright-eyed excitement for the future*
> *Be enough to guide them to a better tomorrow?*
> *Less optimistic:*
> *Will the world be around long enough for them*
> *To even try?*
> ~~~
> *I'll choose to believe the former*
> *And fear the latter*
> *To hope that they will find a way*
> *For humanity to coexist with each other*
> *And with the Earth.*

***

Lem looked around the crowd, then walked to another teen boy, this one with long, thick hair.

Lem nodded. "I'm Lem. Looks like we need new friends. Gotta have people, right?"

The other boy laughed nervously. "Yeah, sure. I'm Stan!"

Lem examined Stan's abstract T-shirt. "You like art?"

"Yeah, sometimes," Stan said.

Lem grinned. "Wanna go paint random crap on the barrier?"

"Hell yeah," Stan said, pulling a can of spray paint from his bag.

"Now, wait," Lem's mother protested.

Surprising himself, Bennet stepped out of line. "Ma'am, I think it's a great idea. Liven up the place a bit."

The woman raised an eyebrow. "And you'll make sure your mother or the sheriff don't call it vandalism?"

"Our sheriff's department, and my mom, have bigger problems than that." Bennet turned to the boys. "Nothing obscene. Got it?"

The boys agreed and walked away, discussing their artistic plans.

***

Avet sat at his desk in the sheriff's station wearing his dirty deputy uniform. He hadn't washed it since he'd been deputized three weeks earlier. Didn't want to waste the water. And he figured he looked more intimidating in a blood-stained shirt than a clean one.

"Hungry," a man grumbled from the middle cell, his thick beard obscuring the movement of his mouth.

"You'll get your rations," Avet said, "after the rest of the town, Mr. Mance."

Rickerson huffed. "It's inhumane."

Avet almost jumped to his feet, almost yelled about the real inhumanities he suffered in the war, but he knew it wouldn't do any good. "Life's inhumane," he said.

The woman in the first cell sat up in her cot, sweat-soaked hair caked to one side of her face. "Humans are inhumane. I am inhumane." She wept, shoulders shaking. "I'm sorry," she whispered. "I'm sorry."

Avet took a deep breath, trying to calm himself. "I know, Santi. I know." What else could he say? In a drunken rage, she'd killed her husband for having an affair. But he wasn't cheating, and had been seeking understanding of himself and the changed world they all found themselves in. To be fair, he had cheated before. Her suspicion wasn't out of line, even though her resulting violent outburst was.

The front door swung open and Meerf walked in with two handfuls of meal bars. He dropped them on Avet's desk.

"We got all the flavors," Meerf said. "One salty espresso left."

Avet picked it up, tore it open and took a bite. "Damn good bar of coffee. Damn good."

"Uh, gross, Deputy Gaines," Meerf said. "Gross."

"What's your flavor, Meerf?" Avet asked.

Meerf dug through the pile of foodstuffs, lips pinched in thought. "It's all terrible."

Avet laughed, but the sound was cut short as Carnivore stumbled through the front door, the left side of her head twitching in and out of view.

"Sheriff," she said. "Sheriff. Gone, gone. Sheriff gone. Poof, poof. Gone, gone."

"What?" Avet stood up. "Where? How?"

Carnivore shook her head. "Not know, don't know. With sheriff, pat... pat... petroleum around the barrier—"

"Patrolling," Rickerson said. "Patrolling, dumbass."

Without hesitation, Avet grabbed an open pen from his desk and threw it across the room. It sailed between the bars and clacked into Rickerson's forehead, leaving a solitary blue dot.

Rickerson swore. "Some officer of the people, you prick."

Avet ignored him. "Carnivore, take me to where you saw him last."

Leaving Meerf behind, the two hurried toward the nearest of Cowley's two exits.

"Tell me what you can, Carnivore."

"Walk around wall with Sheriff Ling. Was next to sheriff, then shook and twitched, bounced far in front of sheriff. Went back to find sheriff. No sheriff. Walk around whole wall, no sheriff."

"Damn it." Avet thought of the dread he shared with Bennet. That shit was going to get a lot worse before it got better. If it ever got better. And what did "better" even mean? Cylindra had chimed in, saying that Earth would probably be better without any human life. Avet knew humanity could be evil. He knew they could be good, too. But would humanity as a whole choose to be better? No way to know.

By the time they stood outside the wall, they'd been joined by Avet's two favorite people: his mom and his boyfriend.

"So, you didn't see anything, Carnivore?" Leona asked.

"No. Already said, nothing."

"Where'd you last see him?" Claw asked.

She pointed and they headed east, sticking close to the wall. Avet tried to ignore the complete absence of life around them, but it was impossible. The world was dying and there was no blocking that out.

"Did you see his footprints?" Claw asked.

"Footprints?" Carnivore asked. "Footprints are...?"

Claw and Avet exchanged glances.

"Look at the ground behind us," Leona said. "See the marks our feet leave?"

Carnivore smiled. "Oh! Did not look." She quickened her pace.

Avet rolled his eyes. The soldiers were different, there was no question. But how could she not think of footprints? She was a grown human, after all. Or, at the very least she seemed to be an adult. Avet was reminded of something else Bennet had said about the soldiers.

"Sometimes they seem just like children," he whispered.

"What was that?" Claw asked.

Avet shook his head and smiled. "Nothing."

Claw grabbed his hand and they walked until they came across a mess of footprints.

Leona crouched and examined the evidence. "Ling's footprints. And a bear, I think."

"Funny, Mom," Avet said.

"Not joking. Look."

Avet joined her. A random scattering of boot prints lay right in front of him. To the right, nearer his mom, were massive paw prints that couldn't be anything other than a bear. Farther to the right Ling's prints disappeared, replaced by a wide, shallow indentation that trailed into the distance.

"Shit in a river," Avet said.

Claw pointed. "Blood."

Sure enough, a line of blood ran along the path left by what must have been Ling's unconscious body. *Unconscious, not dead,* Avet thought.

"Your sister said it was coming," Claw said.

Avet stood up. "What?"

"What else the bears got to eat?" Claw said. "No vegetation. Fish and whatever other small animals that bears eat are getting harder to find."

Carnivore bounced on the balls of her feet. "Search party, search party." A flickering smile spread across her face.

"No point," Leona said. "I'm sure the beast was starving. No way that man's still alive."

Her words were true, Avet knew, and she spoke them as if that truth didn't hurt. But he saw the glint of sadness in her eyes, the hint of a tear. She'd hold it together until she thought no one could hear her sobs, the way she'd done half a dozen times during his childhood.

"Gone? Forever?" Carnivore said.

"Dead," Avet said. "It's called dead."

Carnivore vibrated violently, flickered out of sight then reappeared a dozen feet away. She flickered in and out, there then not there, the entire walk back to town. Once inside, they split up, Avet and Claw making their way to the sheriff's station. To give Meerf the news.

Claw cleared his throat. "Ready to be sheriff?"

Avet stopped walking. "What?"

"It's you or Meerf. And Meerf won't want it."

"But... I'm still on parole, technically." It was a poor excuse, he knew. No one in town cared about that when Ling deputized him. And he'd done nothing to upset anyone but the criminals since then. He looked at Claw. "Damn it, I'm going to be sheriff."

***

From Avet's War Journal, Audio Recording
click

We found Claw. Fifth floor of some building that used to be important. It was blown apart above the sixth floor. He was just standing there, silent. Could tell he'd been crying. All his guns were on the floor, disassembled and useless. He had his claws on. The first time I've seen him with them on. Usually, he just sharpens and polishes them. I always thought they were a good luck charm. He made them with his dad as a kid. Hand-forged blades welded to brass knuckles.

...
...

We didn't have much time to talk it out. Enemy soldiers shouted at us from outside. Telling us to surrender or die or some shit like that. Ten of them, four of us. Only three willing to use guns. We made it out. Mostly thanks to Claw, really. He stayed quiet, hidden in the shadows while we drew fire. Clawed five of them to death. I took two out, a single shot each.

...
...

sniff

Shit, man. This killing shit sucks.

sniff
click

Chapter 28

Nothing. Ishlea was all that existed. Herself, her present and her past. She hovered in complete absence, absorbed in her past, her fears and her hopes.

Young again. A child, she played with the neighbor's dog on the front lawn. The brown, dead grass poked her bare feet as she ran through it. She smiled as her dad ran outside, picked her up and twirled her around. Faster and faster until they collapsed, breathless laughter bursting from their lungs. The dog jumped on her chest, licking her face, turning her laughs into squeals.

A shadow of a man blocked out the sun and ripped the dog away from her. "I told you to leave it alone," the dark voice said.

Ishlea jumped up. "Viola is a she!"

The shadow turned to her dad. "Tell the little bitch it's an animal that's going to be my dinner in a few months."

Ishlea lunged for the dog. The shadow's fist slammed into her face and her nose crunched. Screaming, she fell to the ground. Her dad screamed words she wasn't allowed to say. The shadow dropped the dog to the ground, then pulled out a gun. Two loud cracks echoed through the air. Her dad dropped to the ground. The shadow ran away.

Blood, tears and snot soaking her face and neck, Ishlea crawled to her dad. His head was gone, a pile of red-gray mush in its place. He wouldn't move. She screamed at him to wake up for hours, until a man in a car with flashing lights picked her up and took her to a home full of more shadows.

In the Fourth, Ishlea screamed. Her tumor of darkness pulsed, and her form sagged. These visions of the past, always haunting her. She stretched an appendage back and touched the black ooze that dripped from the mass. It stuck to her, and no matter how hard she tried, there was no getting it off.

She sunk lower. Only her in that emptiness. Her own memories from a distant place. Why was she there, in complete absence, and not back where her dad had died, or where the man in a uniform had taken her? Where was she?

Confusion filled her. The tumor pulsed and grew. Hadn't someone else been with her? Why was she alone?

"Because I've always been alone," she said.

She disappeared back into her past. Bigger, now, but far from grown. She walked down a sidewalk that was nothing more than shattered concrete stamped into the dirt over decades of neglect. In her young mind, it was nothing more than the trail that would lead away from the city, a place with no shadows to torment and abuse her. Where it would be her and the animals. Animals were the only ones she could trust.

A car drove past, a large shadow at the wheel, and Ishlea jumped behind a bush until the buzz of the electric engine vanished. But as she stepped from her hiding place, a hand grabbed her shoulder. She screamed and tried to run, but to no avail. Ready to kick, spit and bite she turned around. It wasn't a shadow at all, but a boy, not much older than her.

He looked her up and down. Not in the leering, sickening way the shadows did, but with a look of concern. Ishlea decided the boy was kind. She relaxed, if only a little.

He let go. "You're running away."

She looked away and shrugged.

The boy took off his backpack. "Braver than I am, girl." He opened the bag and gave her a wad of cash, followed by a sack full of junk food. "This should help. Good luck."

She looked at him, but chose to say nothing. The shadows always got angry when she spoke. And what if the boy was nothing more than a shadow in disguise? After a moment of silence, he turned and jogged away.

Ishlea's essence trembled in the higher plane.

"Not always alone." She looked at all the emptiness. *"But alone now. Almost always alone."*

She slumped and hung forward, the weight of the mass suddenly too much to bear. It crushed her into ground and refused to go.

Where am I? Where has that other place gone?

The mass shoved harder, then grew until it enveloped her in its darkness. Images flooded her mind.

A man, or maybe a woman, hazy and ghost-like, towered over her. Fingers wrapped around her throat, then she flew and slammed into a wall. Air burst from her lungs, her eyes closed and everything went black.

Alone, high in the branches of a pine tree, the smell of forest filled her lungs. A hawk hung above her in the cloudless sky, a squirrel sat two branches below, unfazed by her presence. Footsteps crunched below her. The boy, pretending not to see her, emptied his backpack of food into the dirt at the base of the tree. Once the sun set, she climbed down and ravenously tore into her meal.

Yelling at the top of her lungs as a large gleaming machine barreled into the forest, tearing trees from the ground. Birds took to the air, squirrels leaped from tree to tree in an effort to escape. She clambered down from her perch as the machine neared, oblivious to her screams. Frantic and unaware, she missed a branch and fell, hitting the ground just in front of the machine. It rolled on, and crushed her.

When she opened her eyes, her body was gone. She was a thing of light and air, without physical form, surrounded by animals with forms just as hers. She wandered and wandered, encountering beings of light, dark and the always confusing "middle grounders." Anything that wasn't full of light reminded her of the tortuous shadows, and she stayed to herself as much as possible.

Until she found a boy that still had a body like the one she once had. And despite his physical form, light and kindness streamed off him. So pure was the light that she had no choice but to follow.

In her present, Ishlea screamed into the dark shell that trapped her.

"*Tashon,*" she said. "*Jonstin.*"

She forced herself up and the darkness cracked against the new force she found within herself. She rose and, with the tumor still clinging to her, she went to the find the only real friends she'd ever had.

***

Tashon still struggled through the mist, dragging his broken ankle behind him despite the pain and exhaustion. He hadn't stopped walking since he took that first step deeper into the hazy darkness. How long had it been? In Third time, he had no way of knowing. But the swirling nebula that had been below him was long gone, and he'd passed at least a dozen galaxies since leaving it behind.

If he could've stopped to rest, he would have. But something wouldn't let him. He thought it was the presence that lurked just out of sight, somehow forcing him on like a puppet as a new form of torture. But how was his physical body still alive? Certainly it had been long enough for him to have died of hunger or thirst. His stomach and throat thought so, at least. Then there was his ankle. The repairs he'd made on it were undone, and the pain was worse than it had been when he'd first injured it.

He tried, yet again, to fall onto his stomach hoping, at least, to be allowed to crawl. Again, the force held him up as it forced him onward. He tried to access that part of his mind that healed his ankle, but with the state of his physical body, it was impossible. All he could do was let his body be forced on, and try to keep his mind busy.

But what the hell could he think about? What possible thought could be strong enough to pull him away from the torture he was enduring?

Rosa. Her face filled his mind, her smile and piercing eyes, reminding him that she never lost faith in him. Then his mind was full of faces, his soul filled with the hope they'd all put in his words. His head beamed with the memory of their warmth and kindness. They'd cared for him, and he for them.

So why had he left them? To traipse across the fourth dimension, chasing after a sound that probably wasn't even real? Doubt and guilt, both more crushing than his pain and exhaustion, enveloped him. He walked on, the emotional pain overpowering the physical tenfold, and Tashon wished he would've stayed focused on his exhaustion. The pains of hunger and a broken ankle were nothing compared to the weight that now sank into him.

He sludged forward, a numb puppet with no understanding of why he'd begun this ludicrous journey in the first place. *Damned, delusional idiot,* he thought. And he knew thinking that way would only make matters worse, but he was too tired to fight it. Even though he couldn't give up with his physical body, he was more than able to call it quits heart and soul.

He screamed until his breath ran out, paused, and then screamed again. Screamed and screamed until his throat burned and no sound escaped his gaping mouth.

He passed over young stars and galaxies alive with the excitement of sentient life. Saw dead planets, the civilizations that had once been there nothing more than faded etchings on a tombstone. Walked over asteroid fields so large they encircled Aethera a hundred times over. All this he saw, but couldn't appreciate. The beauties and complexities of the universe meant nothing, *were* nothing to him. Then, as he crossed over a dying star, the force released its hold and he collapsed. He was certain he would die in seconds, but his heart kept beating, his lungs kept breathing.

Something twitched in the shadows to his left. Then something slithered in the misty air to his right. Then the twitching, slithering began to move, circling him. It moved slowly, without any sense of urgency. Tashon knew he had no chance of getting away. He could barely walk.

The two separate movements stretched out and connected, corralling Tashon in a dense circle of fuligin. A dense breathing echoed from behind the circle. A gasping, clicking breath without any rhythm. It sunk into Tashon's chest. His breathing slowed, quickened, and then slowed again. A chill ran through him, then a wave of sweltering heat. Despite his exhaustion, he forced himself to sit up. He needed to be as alert as possible for whatever was coming.

Nothing happened. For what felt like hours, the circling remained constant and the breathing consistently unpredictable. The only thing that changed was the level of Tashon's fear. With each passing moment, his heart beat faster and his pores released more sweat. There was nothing he could do. He sat there with no food and no clothes. He sat, utterly exposed, waiting for the inevitable moment when the source of the breathing revealed itself.

***

While the emptiness had eagerly swallowed Ishlea, it had denied entry to Jonstin, shoving him away when he tried to enter. He watched as her body slowly changed from visible to invisible as it entered the vastness until she disappeared completely. Then he waited for countless, agonizingly long moments for her to return.

When she didn't, he realized they'd said they would travel through the empty space to the other side. When she came out, it would be on the other side. If he was lucky, she'd already be out by the time he got there. He looked forward, but couldn't tell how close the edge of the emptiness was. He flew over it as fast as he could, keeping an eye below to catch a glimpse of more than emptiness. He never did.

The questions arose, as they always did. What was the emptiness? What purpose did it serve? Or, more likely, did it just exist? Jonstin knew his understanding, even the questions he could think to ask, weren't enough to make sense of everything. Though now that it seemed existence, in one form or another, would continue forever, he hoped to one day achieve a full understanding of everything the universe had to offer.

What would that be like, he wondered. Would he be able to truly understand right from wrong, and the ambiguity in between? Would he have access to all dimensions, including those lower and higher than the

Fourth? Those abilities seemed godlike, and for a moment Jonstin felt blasphemous for even having those thought. He hadn't been religious, but his grandmother had always told him there was only one God, and all must humble themselves before. Imagining he could attain the powers of God, or a god, definitely wasn't humble. And, he realized, such imaginings were most likely too human, too narrow-minded, to be the reality. Because almost everything humanity's religions had said about the afterlife was wrong.

He reached the edge of the expanse and looked down. Then up. Left and right, ana and kata. No sign of Ishlea. No sign of anyone. Beyond the expanse lay a long stretch of flat ground. Glowing eggs were scattered about, each covered in various two- and three-dimensional shapes. Millions of beings wandered amid the eggs. Jonstin got the feeling they were the essences of animals and not sentients, but one thing he did understand was that sentience took far more forms than he'd previously thought. Or perhaps animals in the Third gained sentience in the Fourth. Another question without an answer.

Some of the beings looked exactly how he imagined a horse or a dog or a bird to look like in the Fourth. Most of them had no resemblance to anything he had a name for. But they were all alive, all beautiful and all seemingly content. Not one bothered another. Each gracefully and slowly meandered about, as if their only purpose was to exist and find peace in that existence.

Shouldn't that be everyone's goal, he wondered as he settled in to wait for Ishlea. He hoped she showed up before he felt the need to force his way into the emptiness. If that was even possible.

Chapter 29

Gunshots. Screams. Shadows creeping in under doorways, through windows. Encompassing. Enveloping. Consuming. A suffocating pressure.

Sheriff Pole jerked awake, cold sweat soaking her face. No malevolent shadows. But two more gunshots sounded. Those were real. She rolled out of her bed, still in uniform, and grabbed her gun off the nightstand. After a quick glance at the glass box her gecko used to live in, she ran out of her apartment, shrugging on her backpack. Another gunshot as she ran down the stairs and into the parking lot. No suspects or witnesses in sight. She slowly examined her surroundings. The same cars that'd been unmoved for the last two weeks. No power meant no charging cars. Pole had half a charge left, but wouldn't use it unless she had to.

Clouds hung heavy in the sky, litter blew across the deserted street. A can fell over behind her. She whipped around smoothly, gun held to fire. A feral cat leaped onto a fence and ran out of sight.

"Bang," Pole whispered, lowering her gun.

She was sure the shots had been close, not more than a couple of blocks. But which direction? She got the feeling eyes were watching her, carefully analyzing each step she took. She'd heard rumors and seen hints of evidence in the last couple weeks. Zealots had wandered into town, looking for the "fakes," as they called them. The ones that flickered in and out of your vision, the ones they blamed for the death that covered Earth.

The problem was that in their search they were taking innocent human lives. People she'd grown up with. Real humans. And so far no they hadn't caught anyone. Other than the bodies, at least. Pole wondered if some of the zealots were just psychopaths using the fakes as an excuse to carry out their demonic deeds. The way some of the bodies had been mutilated.... She shook her head and clambered to the top of her patrol car.

No more gunshots. No screams. The silence deafening, she climbed back down, opened the trunk and pulled out a bicycle. The clouds above parted, sending down a sliver of sunshine. She looked up, assessing the time.

She hopped on the bike and rode off, pedaling slowly enough to peer between buildings and inside windows. Nothing suspicious, until a drunk man staggered out of an alley. With the state of the world, she was surprised there weren't more drunks staggering around. Surprised, but pleasantly. Of course, she never knew what other vices people might succumb to in the privacy of their own homes. She pulled up to the man as he vomited into the gutter.

"You all right, sir?" she asked, unfazed by the putrid smell. She'd seen and smelled worse.

"Arrest me?" he mumbled as he wiped bile from his lips.

She shook her head. "The world's past arresting people for trying to numb themselves to the shitstorm. I say better to help them." She pulled a bottle of water out of her backpack and held it out to him.

Standing up, the man reached for the bottle and nodded his gratitude.

"Did you hear the gunshots?" Pole asked.

He swished water in his mouth and spit it out, drool dribbling down his chin. "Wha? Huh? Shotsa here?" He shook his head. "Din't hear no-ah shotsa." He gagged and bent over again, adding to the puddle of vomit at his feet.

She looked away, scanning nearby windows. Were those blinds across the street closed a minute ago? "Did you see anyone strange? Maybe not from here?"

He shook his head.

Pole got the feeling he wouldn't have the desire, or capacity, to talk for a while.

"Sit down and catch your breath." She held out a hand and helped him settle onto the curb.

The curtain in the nearby window flashed.

Pole whipped out her gun and shoved the drunk to the ground. The window flung open and an arrow shot out, skimming the edge of Pole's shoulder, drawing a thin line of blood. She ran across the street, snatching a large rock on her way. Another arrow flashed into sight. She dove behind a parked car just in time, the arrow sailing over her head. Up again, she threw the rock into the window, shattering it. Before all the glass had settled, she was at the window, pulling out a body by the shoulders. She dropped it, hard, on the sidewalk and looked down. Just a kid. Fourteen, maybe fifteen years old. His black hair covered one eye, and the visible eye darted back and forth, refusing to meet Pole's gaze. Scared or defiant?

"You shot an arrow at an officer, kid."

"No, at a fake." He paused, scratching his chin nervously. "You're a fake, a fake."

The accusation hurt Pole more than she would've expected. She took a deep breath. "I'm a real human," she said. "Who else is with you? I heard gunshots."

"The fakes shot at me."

Pole took a deep breath. "How many?"

"Two."

"And how do you know they were fakes?"

The boy looked at the ground. "Same way I know you're one."

Pole laughed. "And how's that?"

"They were in hiking clothes, but they weren't hiking."

"That's normal in Wyoming," she said. "You should know that, kid."

"But they were having a rap battle."

Pole's eyebrows shot up. Unusual, no question. "Rapping hikers. Doesn't mean they were fakes."

The boy huffed and mumbled something under his breath.

"You think I'm a fake too?"

The boy nodded.

Pole crouched down. "Why?"

"You didn't arrest the drunk. Cops arrest drunks."

Pole sighed and shook her head. "So someone's a fake if they don't fit your stereotypes."

"No, that's not...." He trailed off, lost in his thoughts.

"I'm guessing you shot at the rapping hikers first?" she asked.

The boy nodded.

"Thought so."

"But the fakes are real, right?"

"Real fakes?" Pole laughed at the phrasing. "Yeah, they exist. But I don't think they can be killed. And I don't think all of them are bad."

The boy spat. "What makes you say that?"

Pole hesitated. She hadn't told anyone what had happened. But if the story could help the boy, how could she keep it to herself? "Did you hear about the first fakes in Cody?"

"The suits."

Pole nodded. "We were trying to track them down after they disappeared. Following rumors and possible sightings. I think it's impossible to catch a fake if they don't want to be caught, by the way."

"Says a fake," the boy mumbled.

"We were chasing ghosts, like they say. All around the city. Me and a few deputies ended up at a drug handoff, unprepared. They killed my deputies, each taking a bullet to the head. I took a few of theirs out before one of their leaders got me pinned in a corner, knife to my throat. That smile on her face. The look in her eyes. She wanted to show me, the sheriff of Cody, wasn't in charge anymore." She paused, calming her breaths.

"What happened?"

"She tried to kill me. I fought her off. Killed her. But then I was surrounded by her sister and her people, a dozen guns pointed at me."

"You're lying," the boy said with a scowl. "You would've been dead."

"That's what I thought. But then someone flickered out of nowhere and knocked each one out. A suit. The woman. She took all their weapons and tied them up. Didn't kill one of them. She didn't even say anything to me. Just nodded, smiled and flickered out of sight. We got all of them locked up. Got drugs and weapons off the streets. They tried to give me an award, but I didn't do shit." She was bending the truth, sure. Not telling the whole story. But she wanted the boy to understand that not all fakes were dangerous.

"What's your point?"

Pole looked into his eyes. "Not all fakes are out to destroy humanity."

The boy shook his head. Across the street, the drunk sprayed vomit. Pole glanced to check on him and saw movement in a window.

"There's someone else with you," she said to the boy, keeping her eyes on the window.

"My dad," the boy said, his confidence rising. "He's the fake killer."

The window shattered and a gun fired. Pole dropped to the ground and raised her weapon, but only silence followed. She was alive and unharmed. Either the gunmen had terrible aim, or she wasn't the target. She rolled over. The boy's head was gone, blood and brain matter spattered everywhere. She stood and turned to the window, but the presence was gone. Ready to continue the chase, she was shocked when someone walked out of the front door of the building holding a gun. An older man with a fading hairline and a braided white beard.

"Sheriff," he said, holstering his weapon.

Pole raised hers. "On your knees. You're under arrest."

He tilted his head. "For what?"

"Murder."

The man laughed. "Murder? That boy was a fake. An imitation of my son."

Pole tried to calm herself before she shot the man, but complete calm was impossible. "That boy was your son. Shit, I've seen fakes get killed. They don't bleed."

The man looked at the boy. "All the ones I've killed did. That's not my son. He never would've treated the sheriff like that. I voted for you, by the way."

So this was her man. The one killing all of them, believing they were fakes. "Thanks for that. On your knees."

He slowly lowered himself. "That's why I voted for you. No matter what, I knew you'd fight for the right. But it appears you've been confused. There are fakes among us. They will destroy the world." The man undid his belt and pulled it out, letting the holster and gun drop to the ground. "I'm not going to hurt you. But I can't say the same for my friends." He spread his arms out wide and over a dozen windows slid open, each revealing a person with a gun aimed at Pole.

Pole shrugged. "Better to die in a rain of bullets than by cancer."

Shots fired. Time slowed. Ripples flashed in the air, swallowing each bullet, saving Pole's life. Shouts and swears, then the female suit stood between Pole and her attackers.

"Stop," she said.

The gunners laughed. The suit flashed into a window, threw the man out headfirst then flashed into the next with same result. Window to window until, seconds later, every gunmen lay crumpled on the sidewalk. Some moaned, others obviously dead from the impact, their necks bent at unnatural angles. The man stayed on his knees, eyes and mouth wide in surprise.

The suit turned to Pole. "Go. Now."

Everything in Pole's training told her to stay, to see this through to the end. But to what end? She couldn't call for backup, couldn't call an ambulance to see if any of them could be saved. They'd tried to kill her, but she still didn't feel they deserved death. They were acting out of fear and paranoia, brought on by the dangers of the unknown. She'd felt the same fear. What was happening to her city, her planet? And what would happen in the coming days and months?

"Go," the suit said again. "Many more."

Pole's eyes narrowed. "More?"

"More." She pointed at the incapacitated and dead gunners. "Like them. All over."

All over. Pole had suspected that. Feared that her city would be overrun by the violent and paranoid. How long could she hold out? Was she willing to die in an effort to save Cody, Wyoming?

Maybe. She pulled out her handcuffs, clasped them onto the man and yanked him to his feet. She pushed him forward and they made their way to the station. She'd send her deputies for the rest. In their state, they wouldn't get far.

"This city isn't yours anymore," the man said.

Pole said nothing, fearing the man might be right.

***

Ling opened his eyes. He hovered over a translucent ground. Beneath it lay the dead Wyoming earth. A mama bear stood with her cubs, all chomping on Ling's body in the shade of pine tree. A cub ripped off a finger and danced away with it, its sibling chasing after. His soul, as he thought of it, shook at the sight and he wanted to vomit. When he realized he couldn't, he looked at his hands. What once were mere three-dimensional appendages were now multifaceted works of ethereal art. *No longer a physical being*, he thought.

Elation filled him as he looked back at the bears, finding survival by eating what he now realized had only ever been his shell. What he had only sometimes hoped for was confirmed: death was not the end of life, only a transition into something new. Or was it something old? Had his soul existed before it merged with his body at birth, or in his mother's womb? And what happened now?

He looked around. Where was the welcoming committee? Nowhere to be found. No judge and gavel. Nothing but colorful, beautiful air around and above him. The Earth that had been his home for so long. His soul wept at the loss, trembling for a time before his thoughts turned to Cowley. He turned his head to the left, and there, not far away, lay the town he loved.

On Earth, the journey would've taken a day of steady walking, but the simple thought of floating above Cowley pulled him quickly to his destination. He looked down, and it appeared nearly the whole town was gathered outside his station, the parking lot packed with gas grills and people telling stories about him. There were tears, yes. But Ling was happy to see more smiles on lips and twinkling eyes as the people recounted their memories about Sheriff Ling. He'd always thought the town liked him, hoped he'd done right by everyone. But hearing those hopes confirmed, for Ling, felt better than being welcomed to the afterlife by a saint or god he didn't know.

Eventually, the crowd dispersed as the sun set. Ling looked around this new place. Another dimension? A spirit realm? He didn't know what to call it, but he knew he wasn't ready to call it home. He was, more or less, okay that he had died. Leaving Cowley behind to explore the new realm just didn't feel right, though. No, he would remain over Cowley to see how they would overcome the challenges they faced. Because, despite his death, the thought that they wouldn't overcome never entered his mind.

***

Avet sat on their front steps, staring at the night sky, the emptiness left by Ling's absence a palpable presence. And the fact that Avet had officially been chosen as the new sheriff. Given the state of things, they didn't take the time to vote. Meerf brought it up after the funeral, and their mom, as the mayor, supported the motion. To Avet's surprise, no one argued the appointment. He'd always seen himself as the one the town tolerated but didn't really like. Now, though, they seemed to support him as their protector. He looked down at his new gun lying next to him on the concrete, then picked it up with a sigh. Images of Los Angeles flooded his mind. Sure, he'd held a gun since then. But he'd yet to fire one. He told himself that was because of his parole, but he knew it was a lie. With he sigh, he put it back down.

The door behind him opened, and Claw and Bennet came out. Claw sat beside Avet. Bennet leaned against the house.

"It feels like snow," Bennet said absently.

"What?" Avet asked.

"The air. It feels like it's going to snow," Bennet said.

"It's still summer," Avet said.

Bennet shrugged. "There's something rolling in."

Claw looked at Bennet. "Can you give us some space?"

"Yeah, yeah. Just wanted to say congratulations, Avet. You'll be a great sheriff."

Avet nodded and lazily waved a hand as Bennet went back inside.

Claw grabbed Avet's hand. "Still don't want to shoot?"

Avet looked down and sighed. "No. I mean, I know I've hurt plenty of people since L.A., letting the anger get the best of me. But I haven't killed anyone. I don't *want* to kill anyone. I don't want to shoot anyone." He picked up the gun with his free hand and stared at it. A part of him knew it seemed contradictory. He had hurt plenty of people. He'd even used a gun to hurt the suits, even though he didn't shoot. Something about shooting another person put a lot in his stomach.

"You don't have to shoot anyone," Claw said.

Avet shook his head. "But what if I do? To keep you and my family safe. I don't want to kill anyone. I'll beat them unconscious if I have to. But I promised myself I wouldn't kill anyone again."

"You're not the only one who can keep us safe," Claw said, gently putting a hand on Avet's cheek and turning his face until their eyes met. "Don't put it all on yourself."

Avet nodded. "I know. I'm scared, you know? L.A. was hell. But something worse is coming."

"We don't know that," Claw said.

A chill breeze blew through them, carrying the smallest specks of white. Avet held out his hand. One landed on his palm and melted almost instantly.

"Snow in summer. It's getting worse, Claw."

Chapter 30

Eventually, Tashon realized the airy sound around him couldn't be breathing. Beings in the Fourth didn't breathe. But what if it was a creature from the Third traveling in the Fourth? Something like him? No. Something from the Third wouldn't be able to do to him what this thing had. He had been a puppet at its mercy, and now he was left defenseless in the midst of its circling. But his fear faded as his need to continue his journey grew.

With his mouth dry and his stomach rumbling for want of food, he rose to his feet. He heard the call that was his beacon and his compass, if only faintly. In that moment, it was all he had. The hint of a path, perhaps only the illusion of a goal. But he would follow it. Perhaps following it was the only thing that could keep him alive.

He took a step forward and the circle of darkness shrunk. The breathing sound intensified. Another step, then another and another until the darkness was within reaching distance and the gasping breaths vibrated into his bones. Another step, and he would come into contact with the darkness. Was it a solid form, or not? Would he pass into it, or run into it like wall? He stretched out his hand, his fingers disappearing into cold fuligin.

He let his feet follow. Then his nude body was encircled by piercing, frigid darkness. Shivers shook his body immediately. He looked in all directions, but all he saw was darkness. No sign that anything but the dense darkness existed. Snot dripped from his nose and froze immediately. He inhaled deeply, pulled his arms around his chest and continued toward the faint beacon.

For a moment, he thought the breathing had stopped and hoped it had only been the noise of a rushing wind inside the darkness. His heart slowed and his mind calmed. For whatever reason, he was still alive. Despite starvation, thirst and temperatures that would have killed any other human, he was still alive.

Or he thought he was. A thought occurred. *What if this is hell?* No, it couldn't be. He still existed in his physical form, so he couldn't be dead.

Unless, of course, only those not in hell shed their physical forms, leaving behind pain and hunger. And hell was suffering through cold, feeling the pains of starvation but unable to die or fill your body with sustenance. If hell existed, Tashon decided that's what it must be like. Yet he was confident hell, as understood by humans, did not exist. If it did, though, he also believed it wasn't the place he would end up. No, his life had not been one that would lead to hell.

So, why then was he in that shivering darkness? Was it because of his actions, or had something put him there? Or maybe it was just part of the path he was on. He almost laughed. What path? All he was doing was following a sound he thought was a cry for help, but might only be in his head. He'd bounced all over the Fourth with nothing to show for it besides his naked, starving, frozen body. What was the point? As his feet moved him forward, he closed his eyes and his mind went back to Aethera.

The sun hung high in the sky as he sat on top of the downed ship, a soft breeze blowing through his hair. A hand squeezed his shoulder and Smith sat next him. Then Rosa and Abe joined, and the four sat in warm, contented silence.

His bare feet shuffled on through frozen air.

"You've done good things for us, Tashon," Smith said, spreading an arm out.

Crowds bustled around the trees below them, going in and out of newly constructed buildings seamlessly integrated with the natural landscape. Humans, Crawlers and Singers going about their simple and harmonized lives.

"The knowledge you've given them of an afterlife, and of the peace they can create in themselves, has created a beautiful culture," Rosa said.

Tashon smiled and nodded. Below, a human child slipped and scraped her knee. Tears filled her eyes as she called for her mom. A crawler gently picked her up, told her she was strong, then passed her to her mother.

On moved his frozen feet.

"But we still have questions," Abe said. "Where did you go? Why did you leave us? Was it worth it?"

Tashon's head dropped as guilt filled him. "You were all okay. You were going to be okay without me. You don't need me."

"We'll get by without you," Rosa said. "But we miss you. And no one else can see into the Fourth. Are you sure it's worth it?"

Tears formed in Tashon's eyes.

Shaking, joints creaking, he continued to walk.

He wiped his cheeks. "No," he whispered. "I'm not sure. I thought the cry I hear needed *help. I thought I could help it. But I'm no closer to finding it. It's not any louder. I haven't done anything worth leaving Aethera for."*

Smith, Rosa and Abe disappeared. Jonstin floated in the air in front of Tashon.

"*What about me? What about Ishlea?*"

Tashon opened his eyes, then stopped short. Something was visible through the darkness, just barely. Countless specks of light in a color Tashon had never seen, blinking in and out of sight. They were somehow dark yet full of an internal light that Tashon felt more than saw. They sang out a sense of warmth and comfort, an airy breathing. To Tashon, the flickering lights seemed to be his only chance at escape. He stumbled and shuffled toward them, reaching a trembling hand out, hoping to feel a glimmer of the warmth their color promised.

A few more shaky steps, and the flickering lights swirled around him, emanating a warmth that filled his mind and his heart, yet left his body shivering. One speck landed on his palm. He closed his hand quickly, holding the warmth tight in his fist. His stomach churned, his throat burned and he was certain his skin would crack and freeze off any minute.

"*Was it worth it?*"

"*I don't know.*"

The plea that had been his guide seemed farther than it ever had, now little more than a vibration in his eardrums. But it was there. It had to mean something. If not, what was the point? If nothing else, Tashon could make meaning of it, couldn't he? Or would that just be one big lie? He didn't know, feeling at that moment that he had no answers.

The speck bounced around in his fist, trying to move, to get *somewhere*. Did it care where? Did it have a plan, a goal? Or was its only purpose to exist, spreading its warmth and light to any soul lost enough to find themselves in that frozen hell?

That thought brought the smallest of smiles to Tashon's face. He took a deep breath and closed his eyes. Then, only because it *felt* right, he opened his mouth, tossed the speck in and swallowed. It slid down his throat, smooth and warm, then stopped at Tashon's center. Warmth spread through his essence, filling an inner hunger and quenching a central thirst he didn't know he had.

With his physical body still weakened and shivering, he lifted his head up and limped on, his ankle shooting pain up his leg, yet confident he would find his way out of the darkness.

***

Ishlea sped toward the wall at the end of the emptiness, the black mass stretching and flapping behind her, but still clinging on. Dark images flashed into her mind. Shadows yelling at her, hitting her, leaving her for dead. She forced them out with her most recent memories: following Tashon through the Fourth, helping him escape the beings that sought to destroy him and Jonstin. How both had always been nothing but kind to her, though she knew she rarely did the same.

The end of nothing neared, a semi-translucent walk through which the shapes and wind of the Fourth were visible. The sight of something other than nothing boosted her morale and a small chunk of the tumorous mass broke off, flying back as she sped toward the exit. She burst through the barrier, but her dark burden caught and she slammed to a stop. She pulled and tugged, jerked forward and eased away from the wall. Nothing worked. She wouldn't be able to escape unless she freed herself from the mass.

But how? She stretched an arm back and grab at the black. As soon as she touched it, the dark sucked her mind in, pulling her into the fears and uncertainties that had ruled most of her life in the Third.

Towering shadows chased her through a vast cityscape, weaving around buildings thin as twigs, wrapped in staircases, topped in circular doors. She charged up the nearest one, then tripped and rolled down. A shadow descended on her, covering her in a memory she'd forgotten.

The shadow in a house they sent her to after her dad was killed. A place where she was meant to be safe. The shadow crept into her room in the dark of night and took the one thing that should never be taken from a child—from anyone.

She screamed and was back on the staircase, the shadow reaching out for her, almost wrapping its arms around her. She screamed and kicked, then a force exploded from her, dissipating the shadow and buildings.

Another dreamscape, another shadow, another memory no one should have to endure. She fought off memory after memory, each nearly enough to crush her soul completely and eternally. Yet she refused to give in, to give them power over her. Eventually, after what seemed like an eternity, she put them all behind her. Didn't forget them—couldn't forget them. And why should she? They didn't cause her any pain, not anymore, and remembering them only gave her more of a reason to fight for the good she did have.

Her arm came free and the mass crumpled away from her in chunks, leaving behind a smooth, black sheen that felt to her like strength rather than burden. A form sped toward her and her entire essence burst into a smile.

"Jonstin," she said.

His essence smiled back. *"Ishlea! You're okay."*

"I am," she said. *"Finally. Still haven't found Tashon?"*

Jonstin's form sagged. *"Not yet."*

"We will, Jonstin. We will."

Chapter 31

The chill wind whipped Pole's face as she sped down the street on her bike in civilian clothes, the woman suit running alongside, showing no sign of cold or exhaustion. If what the suit had told Pole was true, then it was too late. Cody was lost, and she'd be dead soon if she didn't leave. But before turning her back in her city, she had to be certain.

They turned a corner and a police station came into view. Just like the others they'd seen that day, this one was burnt to a crisp, officers' bodies piled up in the parking lot next to the words, "No Fakes in Cody" painted on the pavement.

"Damn it," she said as she rode past.

"Now leave?"

Pole turned toward her apartment and her car, considering her options. It was likely she would die if she stayed. The fanatics were somehow convinced all cops had been replaced by fakes. She guessed that whoever led the group didn't believe that, though. Most likely the leader was looking for a way to take control of the city, and figured to use people's fear and paranoia to take out any potential opposition. *Smart and idiotic,* Pole thought to herself. Something her grandpa used to say about any above average criminal.

A group was gathered two blocks from her apartment at a small park, all listening attentively to a woman standing on a picnic table. Her companion disappeared, and Pole came to a stop, pulling her hood up. She walked over casually and stood at the back of the audience.

"We've taken care of most of the fakes here. We know there are more out there, though. Some towns have even accepted them as their own. As if they were *real.*"

The crowd booed and jeered.

"But we'll take care of that, won't we?"

The crowd cheered.

"This is war, you hear? We're sending troops out all around. The next group leaves in the morning, heading for Byron, Lovell and Cowley."

Pole swore under her breath, turned and started walking, but was stopped when someone recognized her.

"Sheriff Pole," a man yelled.

"Not Sheriff Pole," the woman on the picnic table said. "She's gone, remember? Like all the other officers. She's a *fake*." She said the last word with disdain.

Pole turned around and dropped her hood. "I'm not—"

"Get her!"

The crowd charged. Pole ran to her bike and pedaled off as two shots fired. One missed, but the other grazed the knuckles of her right hand. She ducked her head as she pedaled behind a row of parked cars, then turned down a side street, heart pounding. Screams echoed from the park, but as far as she could tell, no one had followed her. She quickly made her way to her apartment, and her half-charged car, knowing there were valid reasons for her to leave Cody behind.

First, to warn Byron, Lovell and Cowley.

Second, to stay alive.

Thirty minutes later, she was in her car, Cody in her rearview mirror. The female suit ran outside the vehicle, keeping pace, showing no sign of exhaustion.

Pole rolled down her window. "Get in. You freak me out with that."

She flickered, disappeared, and then reappeared in Pole's passenger seat.

"Better," Pole said. "Thanks for saving me. More than once."

"Yes, you are welcome."

"Do you have a name?" Pole asked.

"Name? Call me... Juggernaut38."

Pole glanced over. "What?"

"Name I was given."

"Who gave it to you?"

Juggernaut38's face flickered out of focus, then return to normal. "They did."

"Who's they?"

Juggernaut38 flickered again but said nothing.

Pole sighed. Something like an answer, but not quite. "Okay. I'll call you Jugger. Does that work?"

"Change name?"

"If you're okay with that."

"Prefer Naut."

"Okay, Naut," Pole said. "Can I ask you some questions?"

Naut nodded.

"When you first came here, you were with the other two. You hurt people. You were violent. Why did you change?"

"They wanted to."

"But who are they?"

"They is they," Naut said.

Pole took a deep breath, calming her frustration. She got the sense Naut was answering her questions as best as possible. And then the question Pole asked herself: could she trust Naut?

They soon rolled into Byron, Pole readying herself to warn the town of what was coming. A juggler in full jester clothing stood beneath the "Welcome to Byron" sign, tossing at least a dozen live chickens in a smooth, never-ending circle. For a moment, his leg flickered out of sight. A fake, then. Though Pole felt he was harmless. She waved as she drove past, receiving a smile and a nod in return.

"Have you seen him before?" Pole asked.

"Yes," Naut answered. "Before left them, all us together."

"Where?"

"Home?" Naut looked out the window.

More vague answers. Pole had the beginnings of an idea about the source of the fakes, but those ideas were nothing more than images. Nothing concrete enough to turn into words.

She realized they were halfway through Byron, but hadn't seen anyone since the juggler.

"Where is everyone?" Pole asked, rolling to a stop in front of the town hall. She opened the door and got out. "Hello?"

No answer. She pulled out her gun, holding it steady by her hip. A cold wind blew from the west, followed by a gentle falling of snowflakes.

Naut phased out of the car, then was opening the hall of town hall. "Empty."

"Every room empty?" Pole asked.

"This room, empty," Naut said. "Hello? Hello?"

Pole walked into the darkened lobby. Perfectly empty, and perfectly clean. Not a speck of dust or dirt anywhere. They walked from room to room, each revealing the same, empty cleanliness. Pole holstered her weapon and the two walked out. A thin layer of snow had formed on the dead ground, bringing a sense of life to the world that Pole had missed deeply. The sight almost brought a smile to her lips, but the silence surrounding the town was too great for her to feel contentedness, let alone joy.

They climbed back in the car and drove on. Pole turned on her megaphone, calling for anyone who could hear her to come out, that she meant no harm. No one answered and, just before leaving town, she turned around to inspect some of the homes. All of those she checked were empty, and she would've assumed the residents had fled to Lovell or somewhere else, except for the fact that each home she entered still had food and water supplies. She grabbed as much as she good, loaded her trunk and left town.

"Not checking rest?" Naut asked.

Pole shook her head. "If there was anyone here, they would've come out. Besides, I don't think there's much time before those zealots from Cody catch up with us. Gotta warn Lovell, then Cowley."

Lovell was surrounded by a chain-link fence, topped with barbed wire. Men and women with semi-automatic and fully automatic weapons patrolled the border. The man at the gate recognized her, making her entrance easy.

"What's happened to Cody?" he asked. "You wouldn't leave for anything small."

She quickly told him what happened, warning them of the oncoming horde.

He nodded. "We can take care of them. How many you think?"

"Hard to say," she said. "A few hundred, at least."

"Okay. We'll get ready. You want to hole up here?"

She shook her head. "I need to get to Cowley and warn them."

"We'll stop them here," he said.

"I'm sure you'll stop the ones who come here," Pole said. "But this isn't the only road to Cowley."

"Copy that, Sheriff," he said. "You know the way through town. I'll spread the word here. Stay safe."

"You too," she said. "Thanks."

Halfway to Cowley, she thought she heard gunshots behind her. She floored the gas pedal, breaking many traffic laws to get there quicker.

***

Sheriff Avet Gaines sprinted down neighborhood streets, the sun setting behind him, a thin layer of snow coating the dead yards. He chased a man carrying a backpack full of stolen rations. The man was Grenad Houds, the only one of his family still in Cowley. He'd lost contact with everyone he loved when the power went out. Despite that, he'd always seemed okay, helping where he could and being an active part of the community. Avet couldn't understand why he stole the rations in the first place.

Grenad dove behind a parked and useless car, then poked his head out, gun aimed at Avet. "Stop!" Grenad yelled.

Avet obeyed, lifting his hands above his head. "You're not going to shoot me, Mr. Houds."

Grenad shrugged.

"Where you running?" Avet asked.

Grenad shrugged again, then spat onto the hood of the car.

"There's nowhere for you to go. You walked in."

"I want to leave," Grenad said.

Avet tried to hide his surprise, but knew his eyebrows had shot up. "Leave Cowley?"

"That's what I said, Sheriff."

Avet shook his head. "And go where?"

"I got family out there. A sister and her kids. She doesn't have anyone."

Avet sighed. It made sense. Grenad, like everyone, wanted to make sure his family was safe.

"How many days of rations did you take?"

After a moment, Grenad said, "Three."

"Grenad," Avet said.

"Damn it. Five."

Avet considered his options. He could arrest Grenad, and toss him in an already overcrowded jail. He could let him go and be out five rations, but then never have to feed him again.

"Where's your sister live?"

Grenad slightly lowered his weapon. "Cheyenne."

Avet whistled. "That's a long way. Planning to walk it?"

"I got no other way."

Footsteps pounded down the street behind Avet, and Meerf stumbled onto the scene, breathing heavily.

"You okay, Deputy?" Avet asked.

Gasping, hands on knees, Meerf nodded. "Don't remember running."

Avet laughed. "You're a good deputy, still."

Meerf shrugged, then looked at Grenad. "He's got a gun."

"He's not going to shoot anyone. Right, Grenad?"

"Haven't decided yet. You going to let me go?"

"Maybe," Avet said. "Meerf, how many in Cowley have loved ones other places?"

"Everyone, Sheriff," Meerf said.

"In Cheyenne?" Avet raised an eyebrow.

"Huh. A lot, I'd say," Meerf said.

"Grenad, I think we could get at least a few to go with you. Maybe a horse or two, if anyone's willing."

Grenad lowered his weapon. "You'd let me do that?"

"Can't promise it," Avet said. "But give me your weapon and let's go to the mayor. I'll plead your case."

Grenad slid his weapon across the hood of the car. It clattered onto the ground.

"Deputy," Avet said.

Meerf walked over, picked up the weapon and released the magazine.

"Let's go, Grenad."

At sunrise, ten men and women, with three horses and a week's worth of supplies, walked out of town, beginning their long journey. Avet stood on the wall with his mom, watching the cloud of dust the group kicked up behind them.

"You handled that well, Avet," Leona said.

Avet shrugged. "Thanks." The truth was, he was terrified what he would have done had he tried to take Grenad out rather than talking him down. He didn't want to become so embroiled in "fighting for the right" that he turned into the raging, violent soldier he'd been during the war.

The memories flooded into him. Instances of bodies and hands drenched in blood. Acts he'd committed, and never repeated out loud. Not even to Claw. As far as his boyfriend knew, everything of significance was told in Avet's audio recordings. But Avet had left out those times he'd lost control. Gunning down unarmed soldiers. Taking them out with knives and fists in violent outbursts when his bullets ran out. He looked down and, for a moment, blood dripped from beneath his fingernails, dripping down his fingers and palms.

They watched silently as the group faded into the horizon. Then, just as Avet was ready to head home, a car sped down the freeway, straight toward Cowley.

"Shit," he said.

"Language," Leona said. Then yelled, "We have visitors from the west. Gunmen at the ready."

Six bodies ran along the wall and stopped above the gate, rifles trained on the incoming car. When the car stopped thirty yards in front of the gate, Avet recognized it.

"It's Sheriff Pole," he said, smiling.

Pole stepped out of her car and waved.

"Mayor," she said. "Avet."

"He's sheriff now," Leona said.

Pole laughed.

"Why aren't you in Cody, Sheriff?" Avet asked.

"Long story," she answered. "Can we come in?"

"We?"

Pole motioned to the car and the passenger side opened. A woman in a suit stepped out. Avet swore and whipped out his gun, all thoughts of never using one again fading from his mind.

"Son!" Leona yelled. "Lower your weapon."

"Mom, she's one of those who almost killed Claw, and attacked Bennet and me."

Leona looked at Pole. "Sheriff, is that true?"

"It is, Mayor. But something's changed about her. She somehow killed the other two she was with. And saved my life — twice."

Avet shook his head. "I don't trust her."

Pole sighed. "I get that, Sheriff Gaines. But do you trust me?"

Avet slowly lowered his weapon and ordered the gate opened, hoping he wasn't making a deadly mistake.

***

Bennet, Gella, Cylindra and Claw sat around the coffee table of his mom's home playing Uno.

Bennet placed a card down. "Sorry, not sorry, Gella."

"Hey! Another draw four? You really don't want any tonight."

Bennet shrugged. "It's not like I'm getting any anyway."

"That's not my fault," she said.

"You're right. Which is why I can give you all the draw fours I want." He leaned toward her and kissed her head.

She rolled her eyes and picked up her cards.

Claw was next, but he stared blankly at the table.

Cylindra put a hand on his shoulder. "You okay, Claw?"

He blinked, then looked up. "Yeah. Just tired. Sorry. My turn?"

"Yeah," Bennet said. "You sure you're okay?"

"Absolutely. What color?"

"Red," Cylindra said.

Claw put down a card, and his gaze quickly faded again.

Cylindra placed another card. "Reverse. You're up again, Claw."

Claw silently put down a card.

Gella quickly slammed down a 'plus four' card. "Ha! Got you, sucker."

Cylindra laughed hysterically, as if nothing more funny had ever happened.

Gella smiled as Bennet playfully nudged her shoulder with his.

Claw threw his cards across the table. "How are you laughing? The world's going to hell and shit's about to hit the fan."

The room fell silent. Cylindra scooted closer to him and gently pulled his head onto her shoulder. Both women looked at Bennet, as if he would have all the answers. But what was there to say? With no better options, he decided the truth would have to do. But what was the truth?

"I don't know, Claw," Bennet said. "Shit's definitely going to get worse. I can feel it. We all can. But, I don't know, there's something simple about being together like this."

"Our planet dying isn't simple," Claw said.

"No, it's not," Cylindra said. "What he means is our way of life has become simpler."

Claw shrugged. "I don't know about that."

"You loved owning your own bar, right?" Bennet asked.

"You know I did."

"But it was stressful and complicated at times, wasn't it?" Bennet asked.

"Yeah, okay," Claw said.

"But now, what's truly important is *all* that's important," Bennet said.

"Huh," Gella said. "I hadn't thought of it like that. There aren't all the distractions, or stresses that ate at me but really didn't matter."

"Just one big stressor that we shouldn't be ignoring," Claw said.

"The death of our planet," Cylindra said. "We're not ignoring it by finding some joy."

"Maybe," Claw said. "I just can't seem to feel that same joy I see in you guys. I'm... I don't know." A tear fell down his cheek. He stood up and walked to the bathroom.

Bennet sighed. "Maybe he's right."

"You think so?" Cylindra asked.

"Hell no," Gella asked. "If we don't find joy despite the struggle, then what's the point of struggling in the first place? If we're not fighting for joy, then what are we fighting for?"

Claw walked back into the room. "Survival," he said, staring out the window. "Avet and your mom are back. And, shit, no." He threw open the front door. "What the hell is she doing here?"

Bennet and the girls ran out behind him to see Avet, Leona, Sheriff Pole and a woman in a suit standing in the dead yard.

Avet walked up to Claw and put a hand on his shoulder. "It's okay."

Claw pulled his eyes away from the woman. "She almost killed me."

"Sorry," the woman said. "Had bad protocol."

"What the hell does that mean?" Claw asked.

"We're not sure," Pole said. "But she's saved my life. I trust her."

Claw's body slackened. "Don't let her get close to me." He turned and walked back into the house.

"Okay, then," Leona said. "Let's head inside."

The group gathered in the living room, and Pole told them everything. By nightfall, the wall around Cowley was lined with all those willing and able to fight.

Bennet sat at the base of the wall, writing in the dirt, deciding if joining the fight was for him and contemplating the role joy would play in their struggle.

The words in the dirt read:

***

A battle comes
And after that a victory,
Or a loss.
Followed by a war,
And maybe death.
The struggle is real, they say jokingly.
But what do they mean?
And what of joy?
Is that not real too?
Or is joy just a construct, an impossible goal?
Something created to convince us
The struggle is worth the pain?
~~~
A battle comes, and I want to survive,
As long as those I love survive.
But fight? Kill?
I'm sure I will
When the time comes.
If I must to protect my family, my friends.

*They bring me joy. That's no construct, not an impossible goal.
I find joy with them now, despite the struggle.*

***

Footsteps crunched from behind, followed by Avet's voice. "I'm tired of fighting, of war, Ben."

Bennet stood and turned around. "You have seen it more than most of us."

"I didn't just see it, I participated in it. The shit I did...." Avet looked at the sky.

"That why are you not on the wall or at the gate?" Bennet asked.

"I need to help," Avet said. "I'll hurt as many as I have to, but I don't want to kill again." His eyes darkened, and it seemed he would break into tears any second. But then his eyes refocused. "Some of us are going to scout it out, see how far they are."

"They'll see you," Bennet said. "No trees to hide behind, and it's a full moon." He shook his head. "It doesn't sound smart."

"Maybe. But we're taking the old dirt road between here and Byron. Hide behind the rocks, get a view from the hill." He turned and walked away.

"Wait," Bennet said. "I'll come too."

***

Avet crouched in the snow behind a boulder atop the rocky hill. Claw, Madame President, Bennet and Gella were with him, along with three black horses. Gella had been a later addition than Bennet, and an awkward one at that. She caught them walking out the gate, obviously hurt that Bennet hadn't thought to tell her he was leaving the safety of the town. Bennet apologized and tried to convince her to stay, but it was useless. She joined the group, and Avet knew the young couple would have an interesting conversation about it later. The kind of conversation that would bring them closer or farther apart. Avet had his hopes on the former.

"Lights," Madame President said.

Everyone peaked over the boulder. Avet lifted a set of binoculars to his eyes. Twenty cars stood still at the intersection of the 14A and the 789. All were trucks and SUVs, each capable of holding at least seven passengers, and that was if they gave each person a seatbelt. Avet figured they didn't care about seatbelts. Then the ones in front rolled forward, turning south for Lovell. For a moment, hope filled Avet's chest, but after the first ten headed south, the next ten turned north, straight for Cowley.

"Looks like at least sixty," Avet said. "Most likely all armed. Damn, I wish Pole knew what kind of weapons they had. We gotta move out quick to beat them to Cowley."

A shadow crept along the top of the boulder and Avet jumped back, raising his gun. A mountain lion crouched low, growling. It jumped and Avet fired, but missed. The animal hit him head on, slamming him to ground. The gun flew from his hand, and teeth sunk deep into his shoulder.

"Shoot it," Gella screamed.

"Might hit him too." Claw pulled his metal claws from his pocket and slid them onto his knuckles. Fist pulled back, he charged forward and slammed into the beast's side, knocking it off Avet as his metal claws sunk deep into the animal's throat.

They rolled to a stop, laying side by side, animal and man huffing with the effort. The mountain lion gurgled as it breathed, in obvious pain and discomfort.

Avet sat up, putting pressure on his shoulder to stave off the bleeding. Tears filled his eyes as he watched Claw pull his gun out, place it against the animal's skull and fire.

Claw crawled to Avet. "Hey, hey, you okay?"

Avet nodded. "Thanks. You?"

"Bruised up, but I'll be fine," Claw said. "Let's wrap up the shoulder and get back."

Avet nodded again, overcome by a numbness as Claw tied a tourniquet on his shoulder. The world around Avet faded away. He was aware of the pain in his shoulder, knew that he'd been helped onto Claw's horse and that they were heading back to defend their town.

But none of it mattered to him. All he could think of was the animal that almost killed him. He could've felt fear of the mountain lion, or even anger at it.

All he felt was sympathy. The creature must've been starving. Its usual diet of smaller animals was surely dying out as they were unable to find vegetation to consume. The mountain lion was trying to survive. Just like all of them.

He thought of the poem Bennet had written in the dirt before they left. Was the mountain lion fighting for survival alone? Or did it have its own cubs somewhere out there? Had it been fighting to survive to keep its own source of joy alive, or out of pure animal instinct? He turned his head around, looking at the mountain lion carcass.

"We gotta go faster," Claw said. "Your shoulder going to handle it?"

Avet turned his head around and nodded. "I'll be fine. Let's go."

The group broke into a gallop, hoping to get back to Cowley before the cars.

***

While the town was readying for battle, Cylindra stood in her backyard, a shovel in her hands, staring at the absence of life. She loved the dirt. It was still part of what she considered to be her Earth. The Earth she'd fought so hard to protect. Sure, she found some solace in the company of those she loved, and those she loved all thought she was doing okay. "Better than we would've expected," she'd heard them say when they thought she wasn't listening. But that's because that's what she wanted them to think.

That was by design. She didn't want them to know that as her Earth was dying, so was she. That her soul felt like it was slowly fading, and that she would soon be an empty shell of flesh if something didn't change. She screamed and stabbed the shovel into the dirt, scooped up dead earth and flung it to the side. Screaming and crying, she dug deeper and deeper into the soil, hoping to find some sign of life. A root, a seed. Something to show that her Earth wasn't completely dead. Something to give her some reason to hope.

She found nothing. Two feet down. Then three, the top of the hole just above her waist. She closed her eyes and screamed as loud and as long as she could, imagining the air of that scream spreading out and down into the soil, down through each layer. When she opened her eyes it seemed to her that the hole had widened, as if the vibrations of her scream had shaken, the earth of the walls of the fresh hole. She screamed again, this time with her eyes open. But the hole remained the same. She tossed the shovel out of the way and collapsed, pulling her knees to her chest as she lay in the bottom of the hole.

She knew she should be locked in the house, just in case those coming made it through the walls. She didn't care, though. All she wanted was to feel that closeness to the Earth she hadn't felt since she was last in the rainforest. Closing her eyes, she pictured the Earth closing the circle around her until it was just tight enough to bring a calming comfort, but not suffocate.

Soon, she fell asleep.

Chapter 32

Tashon's stomach churned. His ankle throbbed, sending searing pain up to his hip. His head spun, his eyes were blurry with exhaustion and his frozen skin felt as if it would crack. Yet, somehow, the light he'd ingested kept him moving. Step by agonizing step, the darkness slowly thinned until Tashon stumbled into blinding white and collapsed on the translucent ground of the Fourth.

He looked at his hands and arms. Stick thin, nothing but skin and bones. He needed food and water, fast. But his pack and supplies were gone, along with his clothes and body fat. At least he still had his mind and his soul. At least he knew that if he died from thirst or hunger, he would still exist. Though something told him that without his physical form he wouldn't be able to help... whatever was making the plea through the cosmos. A laugh escaped his lungs. He had to be insane, he realized. He was nearly dead, following a sound from an unknown source that only he could hear. Why the hell had he left Aethera?

He had no answers that made him feel any less insane.

Then two things of note burst into his awareness. First, a planet lay below him with green grass and a lone blue tree sprouting some sort of pale yellow fruit. Second, the plea for help was louder and clearer. He was closer, though he felt he was still a fair distance away.

"Not insane," he whispered. "Maybe."

He closed his eyes, readying to pull himself down to the planet in the Third. Despite his shriveling physical form, the Fourth part of his mind was still solid. He dropped to the planet's surface, his back slamming into hard ground. The wind burst from his lungs and he rolled to his side, gasping for air. Once he caught his breath, he rolled to his hands and knees and crawled through the thick grass to the tree. Haltingly, he rose to his knees and grabbed the bark, then tried to use it to pull himself to his feet. But the bark was wet and slick, and his fingertips found no purchase. He dropped onto his side, staring up at the moist, unattainable fruit. He felt his body dying second by second, and the source of his salvation no more than a few feet out of grasp. If he'd been in better condition, perhaps he would've been able to get the fruit he was sure meant his survival.

Or maybe the fruit was poisonous and would kill him rather than save him. Given all the variables of the universe, that did seem more likely. Though maybe, at the very least, the poison would kill him faster than the thirst would.

He faded slowly, or maybe quickly. He wasn't sure. Time meant nothing. His vision blurred, then his eyes closed. Flickered open, then closed again. Footsteps crunched toward him. An animal, he hoped. Something to attack him and end his misery.

The footsteps slowed, then stopped in front of him. He opened his eyes. Through blurred vision, he saw two bare human feet. He rolled onto his back and smiled. Rosa stood there, glowing in a robe of shimmering gold, smiling back at him.

He said her name, told her how good it was to see her.

She nodded, then looked up at the fruit.

Yes, that's what he needed. Would she get him one, please? Could she reach?

She let out a gentle laugh a lifted her arm up. At first, the fruit was far from her grasp. Then her body stretched upward, and she plucked two fruits from the tree. She shrunk to normal size and set one fruit on the ground and gently lifted Tashon's head in her free hand. She told him to open his mouth, then lifted the other fruit and squeezed. A crystal clear liquid shot out, filling Tashon's mouth with the sweetest water he'd ever tasted. He gulped it down greedily, burping loudly when he was done.

Rosa tossed the squished fruit to the side, then picked up the other fruit. She broke this one in half, revealing a blue, crystal-like fruit. With her index finger and thumb, she pinched a chunk out and placed it in Tashon's mouth. He chewed the tender, salty fruit slowly, then swallowed. Rose fed him until the fruit was gone.

Rosa smiled. The moths appeared above her, descending on her from above. They flew a perfect circle around her head, forming a multi-winged halo. At their appearance, Tashon's necklace glowed warm and vibrant. It rose away from his body, taking with it his hunger and thirst. Then Rosa, moths and necklace burst apart into millions of multicolored shards that slowly floated away.

"Thank you, Rosa. Thank you, my moth friends. Bye." Tashon closed his eyes and fell asleep.

***

"Is he dead?" Ishlea asked.

"I don't think so," Jonstin said. "If he was, wouldn't his soul be up here?"

"Okay," Ishlea said. "We came all this way to find him. I don't want him dead."

Jonstin agreed. After they'd found each other outside the emptiness, they'd set out to find Tashon. Ishlea emerged from that space of nothing renewed, and Jonstin felt it was how Ishlea was meant to be. The soul she was before life in the Third beat her down, over and over.

The two headed quickly in the direction Tashon had always said the sound was. The only obstacle they encountered was a vast, swirling mass of black. They flew over it easily enough, but as they did, Jonstin couldn't shake the feeling that if he'd found his way in there he might never come out. Which begged the question: was it better to be lost in nothing, or in blinding darkness? He considered the question as they silently floated over the dark cloud. His first reaction was that lost in nothing would be better. He could at least see, but then again, there would be nothing to see. Nothing to feel other than what was already in your mind and soul. Perhaps lost in the darkness. At least he would know what he was fighting against. Wouldn't he? It was either fighting the darkness of your past in nothing, or fighting new darkness right in front of you.

Not an easy choice, and Jonstin simply decided he was glad it was one he didn't have to make. Though Ishlea hadn't had a choice. She'd been forced to fight the darkness that had been forced on her due to the cruelty of the third dimension. She told him her entire, short life story as they looked for Jonstin. A heartbreaking tale. He glanced at her. Despite all of that, she'd still come through. Left the Third a child, but now with a wisened soul. He smiled. What wonders the Fourth had shown him. What wonders would he still find?

They passed the dark hurricane and found Tashon, completely in the Third, and completely still.

"He's naked," Ishlea said.

"And starved. He doesn't look good."

"Looks like he's breathing."

"He is."

"Can we do anything?" Ishlea asked.

"Neither of us can go between dimensions," Jonstin said.

"Do you think he'll still be able to, even if he dies?"

A good question. "Maybe," Jonstin said. "I'd like to think so. I saw a fourth-dimensional being in the Third. That's what killed me, actually."

"Really?"

Jonstin nodded.

"*I'm not leaving Tashon,*" Ishlea said. "*Might as well tell me the story.*"

Jonstin gave every detail he could. The Ship of Nations breaking down, the dark being following it into the Third. Its dark and brutal collection of three-dimensional bodies. He considered being overly humble and leaving out his sacrifice for Abe, but that was a significant part of the story. A significant part of *his* story. By the time he finished, Tashon still hadn't moved.

After a stretch of silence, Ishlea said, "*The human body is weird.*"

"Huh?" Jonstin turned to Ishlea.

"*We've been sitting here, staring at Tashon's naked and dying body. And, I mean, look at it. It's weird.*"

Jonstin laughed.

"*I'm not joking,*" Ishlea said.

"I know, I know. The truth is usually funnier than fiction."

Below, Tashon coughed and rolled onto his stomach, then rose on one knee.

"He's alive," Ishlea squealed.

Tashon coughed more, then started heaving. Once, twice, then he vomited specks of light that floated into the air like ash. He rolled to a seated position, looked up and smiled.

"Jonstin, Ishlea, you found me."

"*You're alive,*" Ishlea shouted.

"I am," Tashon said.

"And naked," Jonstin said.

Tashon laughed. "That too."

"What happened?" Ishlea asked.

Tashon told them everything as best he could, though there was much he didn't understand.

That was one thing Jonstin appreciated about Tashon was that he was never afraid to admit he didn't know something.

"But how are you still alive?" Jonstin asked. "*How didn't you starve?*"

Tashon looked at the tree. "Rosa helped me get some fruit."

"Rosa?" Jonstin asked. "*How?*"

"No idea," Tashon said. "No idea. Maybe it was a hallucination. But I was dying of thirst and starvation. Now I'm not."

"That's great," Ishlea said. "*Now get up here and let's get you where you need to go.*"

Tashon looked up and smiled. "I will. I need a few days to rest. And eat. Maybe make a loin cloth out of some grass."

"*We'll be ready when you are,*" Jonstin said.

***

Tashon awoke to a night sky. Three moons hung in a sea of stars, two nearly full circles and the third a mere sliver of yellow light. With his stomach full and his thirst quenched, he sat up and smiled. Ishlea and Jonstin looked down on him, obviously anxious for him to return to the Fourth.

"Give me a minute," Tashon said. He took a deep breath and blew it out, then examined his ankle. "Damn it," he said.

Ankle and foot were swollen, and a deep purple bruise stretched nearly to his toes.

"*Can you heal it?*" Jonstin asked. "*Like last time?*"

Tashon shrugged and closed his eyes. Something had happened while he'd been asleep. Where his physical body was rejuvenated, that part of him in the Fourth had shrunk to a wonky, haphazard sphere the size of his fingertip. Perhaps he could pull enough from it to heal his ankle, but if he did he feared he wouldn't have enough energy left to return to the Fourth. At least not for a few days.

"I don't think so," he said. "My essence is drained. I think," he said, then paused, "maybe my body drew from my essence automatically to fill my hunger and thirst."

"*You sure?*" Ishlea asked. "*What about the woman who helped you?*"

It was a good point. What had been the source of his renewed body? He should've been dead from thirst and hunger a dozen times over.

"I'll try it," he said, closing his eyes.

He focused in on his essence in the Fourth, examining its new disheveled roundness, its dimming light. Was there enough left in it to pull into his physical form?

Maybe. He reached for a speck of his essence, just as he had before. He pulled. His essence trembled and pain shot into his brain, sending electric convulsions to all of his appendages. He released the speck, and the pain stopped.

He shook his head. "It won't work."

"*We'll carry you,*" Ishlea said. "*You have to find out who or what needs your help.*"

Tashon nodded and smiled, wondering what had happened to Ishlea. She seemed different. Calm, confident and eager to help. He reached again for the Fourth, lifting himself into the higher dimension. Again, pain shocked his brain, but this time he didn't relent. The pain grew, and his entire body tensed and shook. He plopped on the ground of the Fourth, trembling and soaked in sweat.

"*You okay?*" Jonstin asked.

Tashon nodded, but he wasn't okay. His connection to the Fourth was weakening, and he didn't know how long it would last.

"*You don't look okay,*" Ishlea said. "*Let me carry you.*"

She picked him up, a warmth spreading from her that surprised Tashon.

"You've changed, Ishlea," he said.

"*I'll tell you about it. Which way?*"

He pointed, and off they went, Ishlea telling of how she faced the demons thrust upon her in her short life on Earth.

When she finished, Tashon was left wondering at the purpose of the Fourth. Even more than before, he believed this afterlife was a place where souls continued to progress. What seemed off was the lack of any structure or system. But then why would there be? Systematic bureaucracy was a human invention, and Tashon now realized there was nothing natural about such things. No lines of souls waiting to be sentenced to heaven or hell. No tallying of good and bad decisions.

The afterlife is what you make of it, he thought. *The choices we make here make it a heaven or a hell. And we're not permanently consigned to one or the other.* He smiled. Ishlea had turned it into a heaven for herself. Though she lived a short life on Earth, she now seemed an old and wisened soul.

What was the purpose of these places they'd found in the Fourth? The space of emptiness, the cloud of darkness? Most likely they were simply places that existed, and each individual soul made of their experiences there what they would. Whether for their detriment or improvement was completely up to each individual.

The end of physical life also brought the end of any overarching establishment trying to force ways of living onto its people. True, there were those who tried, like the ones at the pyramids. Yet, in the vastness of the universe, one could at least get away from all that bullshit to simply exist.

For Tashon, that was enough to call the Fourth some sort of heaven. He closed his eyes and slept as Ishlea carried him on toward his destination.

Chapter 33

"Where the hell are my boys?" Leona stood on top of Cowley's wall, watching the headlights get closer.

Pole, Naut, Healer and Carnivore stood nearby, along with dozens of others. All were armed with with pistols, AK-47s and even a few 50-caliber rifles. Anything to protect their town. Both entrances were guarded by more town soldiers with guns, and the ground inside the town was filled with dozens of others willing to die for their town. Leona hoped they wouldn't have to.

Pole shook her head. "I don't know, but those trucks will be here in a minute. Two, at most."

"Listen up," Leona called. "We try talking first. If we can, I want this resolved without bloodshed." She looked around, gauging everyone's willingness to obey her command. "Okay," she said, looking to a man a dozen feet down. "Flip the lights."

The man hit a button, flooding the door and the dozen yards of road leading to it in blinding light. As planned, Pole and Naut crouched down, hiding themselves. Those coming didn't trust either, and having Pole join the conversation would only complicate things.

A hush filled the crowd as the trucks neared, the only sound a gentle wind on the rolling of tires on cracking asphalt. The trucks stopped in a single line and a woman stood up from the bed of the lead vehicle. A wisp of dark hair peaked out of her red beanie and an AK-47 hung from her shoulder.

She lifted a hand and waved. "Hello, Mayor Gaines."

"What can we do for you... what's your name?"

"Astrid," the woman said. "And I think it's more what we can do for you."

"Oh," Leona said, lacing as much sincerity into her words as possible. "You're here to help? Are you offering our town your services?"

Astrid smiled. "We are, Mayor. We are."

Leona nodded thoughtfully. "We could always use more hands. What services are you offering?"

"Pest control," someone yelled from behind Astrid.

"Quiet," Astrid said. "Mayor Gaines, have you heard of fakes?"

Leona had decided beforehand how to discuss the topic. "No. Is it dangerous? Is that why you've got an army at our doorstep?"

Astrid smiled, her eyes sparkling. "We're looking out for you and your town, Mayor Gaines. These fakes look like people, but they're not. And, yes, they are dangerous."

Leona nodded thoughtfully. "I see. I haven't heard about them, but thank you for the warning. What's dangerous about them?"

"We have reason to believe these fakes are to blame for what's happening to our planet."

Leona believed whatever was happening was most likely the fault of humanity, or at least part of humanity. She kept the thought to herself. "That's a harsh accusation, Astrid. So what're you doing? Spreading the word on these fakes? Killing any you find?"

"Essentially, yes," Astrid responded. "We've made it our duty. Our calling."

"Huh." Leona clicked her tongue. "If these fakes are to blame for our dying Earth, wouldn't it make sense to keep them alive? Maybe they could tell us how to fix it."

Astrid shook her head, her calm demeanor fading, if only slightly. "They aren't human, Mayor. We don't even know if they're alive, strictly speaking. They wouldn't respond to such questioning the way a human would."

Leona raised an eyebrow. "You've tried, then?"

"I don't follow," Astrid said.

"You say it's impossible to get such answers from them, so I presume you know from experience."

Astrid opened her mouth, then closed it.

A man stood up next to her, pointed a pistol in the air and fired. "All right, cut the bullshit, Gaines. We know you have Pole and that hot fake in the suit. And rumors say you got others, too. Let us search the town and take any fakes you got, and we'll let you be."

Leona's face hardened. "And if we don't comply?"

"We have the means to take them by force," the man said. "With no thought for the safety of your town or its people."

"You're crazed fanatics," Leona said. "On a mission you don't even understand. Innocent until proven guilty. Cowley stands behind that, even for those who might not be human."

"You admit to harboring fakes?" The man sneered.

"I admit to protecting humanoid beings whose origins we don't understand," Leona said. "But they are very real." The man pointed his gun at Leona.

Then a young man on the wall, named Gentry, raised his hands. "Wait," he yelled. "Wait. See that woman in uniform?" He pointed at Carnivore. "She's a fake. The other soldier, too."

"Gentry!" Leona said. "That's enough."

Before the boy could respond, someone fired from the Cowley wall, striking Astrid's shoulder. Gunfire erupted from both sides.

All plans and strategy Leona and her town had discussed went out the window. Most of them had never seen an actual battle, and each was taken over by the natural instinct to survive. Men and women jumped from truck beds, swung truck doors open and rained bullet after bullet at Cowley's defenses.

Those atop the wall valiantly returned fire, ducking and rising at random to avoid injury. Pole jumped to her feet, a pistol in each hand. Each shot she took connected with an enemy head, quickly taking out six enemies. She dropped again, pulling Leona down with her.

"What the hell are you doing, Mayor?"

"Huh?" Leona said.

"You're standing there like a damn statue," Pole said. "Fight or get down. We can't lose our mayor."

Leona blinked. Had she really been frozen in the heat of battle? She looked at her hip—her gun was still holstered. Ten yards down the wall, half a man's head exploded and his body fell to the ground. Her people screamed in anger, pain and fear. And she had just stood there like an idiot. Two more bodies collapsed simultaneously, then the entire wall shook. Leona's mind caught up with the threat she was in and she pulled her gun out as she rose to her feet.

The trucks were now side by side, forming a line parallel to that of the wall. The Cowley guards outside the door were all dead, their bodies crushed into the ground by tires. The enemy guarded themselves behind the trucks, peaking in and out of sight as their muzzles flashed with bursts of light.

Guns continued to fire. Someone among the enemies yelled a command, and in unison the trucks sped forward and slammed into the wall. It shook more this time, and Leona nearly fell to the enemy soldiers below. Some did fall, their bodies splattered apart by bullets before even hitting the ground.

"Rifles and AKs," Leona yelled. "Aim for the engines and drivers!"

Shots thudded into cars and glass as those with pistols continued to shoot at those on the ground, though hitting their targets grew harder. They hid behind open doors, peaking out only briefly to take their shots.

But the Cowley soldiers adopted the same strategy, quickly transitioning from standing to crouching, crouching to standing.

The trucks slowed their slamming barrage, becoming more deliberate. The wall shook more with each hit.

"Don't we have anything bigger?" Pole asked Leona over the pounding barrage of battle.

"What?"

"Bigger weapons," Pole said as she fired off a round.

"Grenades, maybe," Leona said. "But they'd be at the station."

"Damn it." Pole looked around. "And where the hell is Naut and those two soldiers? We could use their skills right now."

She wasn't wrong, Leona knew. The wall shook again as metal scraped against metal, then the enemy cheered.

Leona turned around and looked down. A truck burst into her town, knocking her people to the ground. Two more vehicles sped in right behind, and stopped.

"Fire!"

The trucks were barraged with bullets by every gun in Cowley. Tires popped tires, glass cracked and metal dented.

"Where are the rest of them?" Leona turned around and saw the other seven trucks, stuffed with soldiers, driving away as fast as they could. "Away from the trucks! Everyone! Get away from the trucks!"

A few ran immediately, but others stood still, obviously confused.

"Bombs!" Leona yelled.

This shocked most of them free, and they sprinted from the vehicles as the first truck exploded. The wall shook, but held still. Someone yelled at her to hold on to something. She squatted and wrapped her arm around an exposed two-by-four.

The last two trucks exploded, one right after the other. Leona's face smashed into sharp wood as the wall fell away from town, then stopped at a steep angle.

Screams and scattered footsteps followed, then silence. Leona forced her breaths to slow as she wiped blood from her face. She was alive, and she had a town to lead. Leaning against what had been the walkway of the wall, she made her way to the nearest ladder and climbed to the ground.

Her people ran frantically, putting out fires and pulling those who might still be alive to safety. Ignoring the pain in her head, Leona helped Pole carry an injured man away from the burning wreckage.

They placed him on the dirt, blood soaking his pants.

"Where's he bleeding from?" Leona asked.

Pole pulled a knife from her pocket and sliced through the fabric. But by the time they found the source of the bleeding, he was gone.

"Damn it," Leona said.

A voice called her name from the broken entrance. "Here come your boys."

Leona stood and turned. They rode in with two empty horses. Madame President was gone, and Avet was draped over Claw's back. Leona ran to them as Bennet jumped from his mount and the two lowered Avet to the ground.

"Avet, hey, Avet." Leona crouched over her son, stroking his hair.

Avet's eyes fluttered open, then closed again. "Mom."

"What happened?" she asked, keeping her eyes on Avet.

Bennet squeezed his mom's shoulder. "Mountain lion. The bleeding's stopped."

She nodded and wiped a tear from her cheek.

Bennet stood up. "Mom?"

"Yeah?"

"Where's Cylindra?"

***

Cylindra awoke to the sound of shouting. As she rubbed sleep from her eyes, she realized it was her family shouting her name.

She sat up in her hole. "Out here!"

Her mother ran outside, her face bruised and scratched. She collapsed by Cylindra's side and hugger her. "Why are you out here?"

"I needed to be close to her," Cylindra said.

Leona nodded. "You're closer to the Earth than any of us."

Cylindra pulled away and blinked back the tears. She looked up, and saw the smoke in the sky. "What happened?"

Leona shook her head. "They broke through the wall in their trucks. Then three of the trucks blew up."

Cylindra swallowed hard. "Car bombing?"

Leona nodded.

"How many?"

"We lost eighteen right away, from the bombs and gunshots," Leona said. "We have another twenty in critical condition."

"What about us?" Cylindra asked.

"We're all okay," Leona said. "Avet's hurt, but he'll be okay."

"What happened?"

"He was on recon and a mountain lion attacked him."

"What?" Cylindra said.

"Mountain lion attacked him, bit down on his shoulder."

A laugh burst from Cylindra's lungs, and continued rolling out of her.

Leona tried to stop her, but the boisterous laughter took her over as well and soon mother and daughter were short of breath, wiping tears from their eyes.

"But *why* is that so funny?" Leona asked.

Cylindra giggled again, then took a deep breath. "We just had a war for our town with *guns* and *bombs*, and Avet gets laid down by a mountain lion. I'm not happy he's hurt, but the way it happened seems *good* to me. An animal, fighting for survival. Earth, she's not done yet."

***

Avet lay on his mom's couch, gripping a pillow tight, his mind pulled back in time.

He found himself back in Los Angeles, wandering alone, separated from his troop during a small skirmish with the enemy.

No, no. Not here. Why am I back here?

But there he remained, no matter how much he questioned it. Broken homes lined both sides of the street as he walked in the blazing sunshine. Again, he tried to radio his troop. No response. At least he could use the sun and his compass to get back to base camp. He turned a corner and soon made his way out of the suburbs into the city. Buildings with shattered windows and sagging roofs surrounded him. Then voices echoed from both sides. A language he didn't understand. Not Spanish. He knew enough of that to get by. Mandarin, maybe? Whatever it was, the voices sounded aggressive. He walked faster.

Maybe I can change it this time.

The voices got louder and angrier. Someone yelled for help. A child, he was certain. He stopped and listened. They called for help again, from the building to his right. It was definitely a child.

He pulled out his pistol and his flashlight, then went inside. Light leaked in from the windows. Screaming and the sound of clanking metal rang from farther inside. Cautiously, back against the wall, he advanced. Light leaked from under a door down a hallway. He walked to it and stopped, listening.

Three distinct voices speaking... Mandarin. He was certain. A younger voice cried, begging for help in English. Anger surged through Avet. What the hell were they doing to a kid in there?

No, holster your gun!

He swung the door open. Three men stood over a boy strapped facedown to a table. The men screamed at Avet, telling him to leave.

Do it! Leave!

He fired three shots, dropping three bodies, then holstered his gun.

Too late, you damn idiot.

He ran to the boy. A large gash down his back split his skin open, and blood was leaking out. But it was halfway stitched. Avet took a closer look at the men he'd just killed. They were wearing medical gloves.

"They were helping him," Avet whispered.

He quickly searched the floor for needle and stitching thread, but by the time he'd found it the boy had bled out. Avet dropped to the floor, sobbing. He'd just killed four innocent people.

But when he opened his eyes, Claw was there, smiling and watching over him. He fell back to sleep, this time without dreams.

When he opened his eyes, Doctor Ronsie was sitting on the coffee table, a metal box with a handle next to her. Nearly eighty years old, she'd been taking care of the Gaines family since before Avet was born. She swiped her thinning white hair out of her face and smiled.

"How are you?" she asked.

Avet pushed himself up with his good arm. "Fine. It hurts, though."

"Obviously."

She opened the box. Buttons lined the bottom of the lid, each labeled according to its purpose.

"Damn," Avet said. "When did you upgrade?"

Doctor Ronsie smiled. "When my wife died. I used her life insurance money."

Avet nodded and started unwrapping his shoulder.

Doctor Ronsie gently smacked his hand away. "Stop it. That's my job."

Avet mumbled an apology and dropped his hand into his lap.

"Thank you." She pushed a button on the box twice.

It whirred and then a mechanical voice said, "Dispensing gauze times two." Two shrink-wrapped squares of antibiotic gauze slid out vertically. Doctor Ronsie pulled them out, set them on the table, and then pressed another button. "Dispensing bandages." A tightly wound role of crisp white bandages popped out and rolled onto the table.

"Now we can get that off." Doctor Ronsie leaned forward and carefully unwrapped Avet's shoulder. "A mountain lion, huh?"

Avet nodded. "Yeah. Just took a nibble on my shoulder."

Doctor Ronsie dropped the bloodied T-shirt bandage on the floor. "Damn. More than nibble."

Avet looked down. Two deep gashes, separated by a few smaller ones, formed a row from the middle of his collarbone to the outside edge of his shoulder. And based on the pain, the same pattern was repeated on the backside of his shoulder.

He leaned in, examining the exposed flesh. "You have some new equipment that is better than stitches, right?"

Doctor Ronsie smiled and shook her head. "My wife's insurance wasn't that good. Only big corporations can afford that type of nanotech, anyway. Not a soul in the state owns that."

"Get it done, then." Avet closed his eyes.

Doctor Ronsie retrieved a needle and thread from the box and went to work. Avet ignored the pain as best he could. It was better than getting shot, but not by much. He could twitch and whine about the pain, but it wouldn't help. If anything, it would drag out the process. Besides, Doctor Ronsie moved quickly. She set the needle and thread down, pressed gauze against the gashes on front and back, then wrapped it up.

"Thanks, Doctor."

"Of course." She closed the box and stood up. "If the pain gets worse or you get a fever, let me know. The antibiotics on the gauze should be strong enough, but an infection could still develop."

Avet nodded. "Copy that, Doctor."

***

Ling floated above Cowley. His town, his home. Smoldering and broken because he'd decided to harbor the soldiers. The fakes, as those idiots called them. He didn't regret helping the soldiers, not at all. But a sadness had sunk deep into his essence. In small part, because of the pain his town was now suffering. In larger part, because humanity, after everything, still let fear, doubt and ignorance result pointless violence.

For that reason, he found he was at peace with his death. Instead of spending his time keeping his town safe from idiots like those, he could focus on discovering what the universe had to offer. And, more intriguingly, what the universe *was* and what it all meant. With his passing from Earth to...wherever he was, his attachment to that place and what happened faded far quicker than he would've expected. What happened down there had no real impact on his own essence, no matter how sad or wrong it may be.

Besides, he trusted Leona and Avet to take care of things down there.

Somewhat lighter, deciding not to question or regret his decision, he turned from Cowley and journeyed into his new life.

***

Bennet sat on the cracked steps outside town hall, staring at the broken and burnt shells that used to be vehicles. He wiped sweat from his face as others worked to repair the wall. He'd just finished his shift and sat as he slowly sipped his water rations.

Thankfully, or perhaps surprisingly, they lost far fewer people than they could have. But their town had still been attacked. Small, peaceful Cowley targeted by self-justified zealots.

Bennet stood up and started walking. The world had gone crazy, and he'd decided it was his turn to bring some of his own crazy to Cowley. Heart pounding with nerves yet fully committed to his course of action, he made his way toward his mom's house.

Dark clouds hung in the distance, heralding a blizzard. Winter would be upon them before they knew it, and he hoped they were ready. It was likely they'd lose more to the cold than they had in the battle. And freezing to death sounded far more excruciating than death by bullet.

He walked on. The wind picked up and small white flakes fell from the sky. By the time he made it home, the edge of the blizzard was whipping around Cowley.

He walked inside. "First blizzard is coming in," he said.

Claw saw on the couch, Avet's head resting in his lap. Cylindra and his mom sat on the floor, arms on the coffee table. Gella stood in the kitchen doorway, leaning against the frame. He smiled at her, and her eyes lit up as she smiled back.

"Used to love the first blizzard," Cylindra mumbled. "Now it's terrifying."

But Bennet didn't hear her. He walked by all them, straight to Gella. With a deep breath and a smile, he wrapped an arm around her waist and pulled her in for a deep, long kiss.

Claw whistled loudly, earning a groan and a gentle swat from Avet.

Bennet let go, smiled again, and dropped to one knee. Then his mind went blank. He knew everyone was staring at him, waiting for some grand endearments of his love for Gella. But only two words formed. "Marry me?" he croaked. Then he remembered a third word. "Please?"

Chapter 34

Madame President stood in a small box with Healer, Carnivore, Naut and a little girl in a ballerina dress. Save for one glass side, the rest of the box was black. The five have stood side by side, staring out of their little prison.

Two people, far larger than any of the five, talked in a narrow room that stretched left and right, out of sight. Lights flickered lazily on the ceiling. One of the towering humans had long, braided hair, thick glasses and wore a purple robe. The other looked exactly the same. As far Madame President could tell, both were men.

Every few feet was a concrete slab that reached the waists of the tall humans. The tops were at a slight angle, a tangle of wires protruding from a hole in the high end. The two talked loudly, as if the five in the box weren't present. And perhaps they weren't. At least not from their perspective.

"What are we going to do?"

"I don't know. That wasn't supposed to happen."

"I know. That's why I'm asking *what the hell are we going to do*?"

"I don't know. We need to do something."

"I know that, too. And it still doesn't answer my question."

"Then why don't you answer your damn question?"

"Maybe send the medic back?"

"That won't fix anything long term."

"It won't. But we should've left them there. They could've saved that town."

"That only would've brought five more armies down on Cowley. You saw what happened in Matlacha. Those violent idiots almost figured out where our assets are coming from. Almost found us."

"I know. But people died."

"We're trying to stop the world from dying."

"It's dying because of us. Because of who we work for."

"And they're trying to stop it too. All of us are."

"By hiding? Why not take responsibility? Show what technological advances we've made. Someone out there might be able to help."

"Or they rain hellfire on us for killing the planet."

"Isn't it worth the risk? What if we die, but someone out there saves the planet?"

"We'll be dead."

"You seem okay that people in Cowley died. And in Lovell. And anywhere else, as long as it's not here."

"Even if I agreed with you, Doctor won't let that happen. We'd both be dead before we got the chance. You want to die trying to take responsibility? Go ahead. I'll stay alive, and try to save the planet."

Silence. Madame President looked at the others, and the others looked back. There was an awareness between them, a connection that Madame President didn't understand. And the box that contained them seemed familiar. But where was she? Who was she?

The two tall humans talked of Cowley. Wasn't that the place she'd just been? Or was it just a dream? Or a story? She opened her mouth to ask her fellow prisoners, but no words came out. She couldn't speak. She had the feeling she wasn't even supposed to be aware of what was happening around her.

A loud vibrating echoed through the room. Each of the identical humans pulled out a screen and stared at it.

"No. He can't do that."

"We advised against it. We can't let them do it."

"But he's the doctor."

"But we can't let him."

"You'll fail at trying to stop him, then die."

Silence.

"You know you will."

"I know. Then what can we do?"

Both looked directly at the box. Madame President felt uncomfortable under their gaze, as if the eyes looking at her knew more about her than she did.

"Hope."

"What?"

"Hope. With what the bosses are planning, they'll need hope. And that's all we can give, really."

"The girl, then?"

"Yes, the girl."

"Call one of them in."

"What number are we on?"

A shrug. "Does it really matter at this point?"

One pressed a button on the wall. "Send in Hedrie, please."

A speaker on the wall crackled. "Who?"

"Number thirty-four."

"Sending thirty-four."

The button was released.

"They're not supposed to know we've named them."

"Does it really matter at this point?"

The two smiled at each other. A door opened somewhere, then footsteps rang through the hallway. A young boy appeared wearing a loose gray jumpsuit.

"You ready, Hedrie?"

The boy nodded. The two helped him onto a concrete slab and he leaned back. As his head lowered, the wires lengthened, squirming up to his neck. They stabbed into the skin with a hiss, and the boy lay down as if asleep.

"Hope?"

"Hope."

"The girl?"

"The girl."

Both typed quickly on their screens. The box around Madame President buzzed and shook. She looked at the others for signs of knowledge or even fear, but only saw her own confusion reflected back at her. Then a white glow appeared around the girl in ballerina clothes, and she disappeared. Five had become four, and Madame President found herself longing to be free of that place.

Wherever that place was.

Chapter 35

Tashon watched the Fourth fly by through half-open eyes. The energy boost he'd gotten from the fruit was fading, and he knew his body was slowly dying too. He tried to push the fear away, but at times it was all he could do not to scream.

It wasn't death he feared. No, that fear had long since passed. What he feared was not finishing his journey before he died. Or, even worse, discovering his journey had no purpose.

For most of his time in the Fourth, he'd been able to keep those thoughts at bay, reminding himself of the undeniable pull he'd felt the first time he heard the cry for help. But as he faded, so did the will to be optimistic. Eventually, his eyes closed and he fell into a blissful, dreamless sleep.

He awoke as his body slammed to the ground, air exploding from his lungs. Gasping and coughing, he rolled to his feet. Ishlea and Jonstin were faced away, screaming words he couldn't make out. Between their forms he caught a glimpse of another being. Something about it was familiar, but through blurry vision he only saw a few flailing, string-like limbs.

The being spoke in an unfamiliar language, then flung its limbs at Ishlea and Jonstin. The two dodged away, and Tashon watched helplessly as its attack became increasingly aggressive.

***

Jonstin feared they'd find them again, even though Ishlea had blown them all away. He knew the grudge they held against him for leaving the fight at the pyramids wouldn't disappear. And now, one of the most violent of his former army had somehow found them. He remembered her from his many 'rescue missions' as they attempted to bring those who fought at the pyramids.

His hulking, blocky form launched stringy tentacles at him and Ishlea, faster and faster.

"Damn." Jonstin spun out from under a whipping string, but the end slapped his shoulder. It sent a deep coldness into his essence. For a moment, he fell back into a memory of his dad, pounding a fist into his mother's face.

He shook it off quickly, dodging another barrage. The being screeched and turned all of her attention to Jonstin. Strings pierced through Jonstin's form, then wrapped around after exiting and pierced him again. He fiercely tried to free himself, but it was of no use. With each stab, his will to fight was sucked from him. He yelled at Ishlea to grab Tashon and flee.

Ishlea responded by speeding toward the enemy, swirling wisps of light spreading out from her form. One by one, she latched onto the enemy tentacles. She pulled and twisted, but Jonstin remained trapped.

"It's okay," Jonstin said. "Leave me and take Tashon!"

***

Ishlea ignored Jonstin. She released the strings of her enemy and charged directly at her. Ishlea slammed into her, the glow around her momentarily transferring to the enemy as they flew through the air. The enemy released Jonstin as they came to a stop, then the light flooded back into Ishlea. The two pulled apart.

Ishlea paused and stared. Was her light changing her enemy? She'd felt as if it had been considering leaving them alone as the light seeped further into it. Could she use her light to convince this assailant to cease its attack?

With a burst of new light, Ishlea wrapped lines and strings around the other form, encircling her in light. She pushed the light against her, then into her. At first, the being relaxed, as if comforted by Ishlea's light. But the deeper that light pierced, the more fear and hatred Ishlea encountered. Flashes of violent and bloody scenes burst into Ishlea's mind as she saw her enemy's life. The life of a zealous soldier, always fighting for a 'justified' cause. Along with a fear that all the fighting and killing would amount to nothing.

Ishlea focused on that fear, pushing her light toward it, confident that she could convince this being to leave. She weaved the light in and out of the fear, exuding a feeling that she hoped indicated that the fear would leave if she simply decided to stop fighting.

It fought back with fear and darkness, refusing the light that Ishlea offered. When she'd last fought, it was her fuligin mass, the darkness and anger of her past, that had destroyed the enemy. But now all she had was light. But how could she fill with light that which only wanted darkness?

She couldn't, and she wasn't sure she had enough darkness of her own to hurt or destroy her enemy. Or if she even wanted to destroy her. There was only one option.

She pulled her light out, but kept her adversary wrapped in it. Her dark strings whipped out in all directions but were unable to pierce the cocoon of light. A cocoon Ishlea knew she couldn't hold for long. She pulled herself away, stretching the light strings and tightening the cocoon. Then she spun, slowly at first, then faster and faster until everything around her was nothing but a wall of light.

She dropped the cocoon, and her enemy sailed out of sight.

Jonstin sped toward her. *"Thank you."*

"Yeah," she said.

"She'll find us again," Jonstin said.

"I know. But I couldn't destroy her."

Ishlea picked up Tashon and they continued on.

Chapter 36

Bennet and Gella sat side by side in town hall. They ate a breakfast of expired food bars at an old wood table, one that would probably have to be turned into firewood before the winter was over. Swift wind blew falling snow across the white landscape. Three feet of snow and counting. It would be a hard winter, but at least the blizzard would deter any more attacks against the town.

Before the storm had gotten too severe, the entire town had moved into the building, along with all the supplies, freezers, and generators possible. Sticking out the winter as a town seemed like the best option. Even if it was in the oldest building in town.

Bennet looked at the stained gray carpets and peeling yellow paint. Just a few months ago, the town council was trying to determine how much money should be allotted to fixing the place up. Bennet shook his head. Now, town budgets and carpet maintenance seemed pointless. Maybe it always had been pointless. Bureaucrat to-do lists made to distract them from the atrocities of the modern day government.

"So where's my ring?" Gella asked.

Bennet smiled. "I have a Sharpie in my pocket."

"We could use my mom's ring," Gella said.

"You still have it?"

Gella shrugged. "In a way. We'd just need to dig up her grave to get it."

Bennet tossed his head back and laughed. "We'll use the Sharpie for now." He reached into his pocket and pulled out the marker. "Ground will be too frozen to dig for a while."

Gella jumped to her feet and ran to the window. "Hey, Ben."

Bennet set the pen down and walked to the window. "What?"

"Do you see that? In the clouds?"

A pinkish form hovered in the distance, then disappeared, then reappeared. Noticing the two staring out the window, others joined in their observation.

The form floated closer and closer, then shot into the sky, too high to see.

"What was that?"

"Something else from the sky?"

"Well, it was in the sky."

"Shut up. Like those damn planes that ruined everything?"

The speculations ran rampant. Bennet and Gella didn't speak. They clasped hands and stared out the window, waiting. Something about the shape felt familiar. Like a person he'd known, or imagined he'd known.

Avet appeared at Bennet's side. "It's her," he said.

Before Bennet could ask what his brother meant, the glowing pink body appeared right outside town hall. It was the ballerina girl they'd seen in Lovell, hovering ten feet above the snow, surrounded by a crisp, airy light.

She descended, the snow flying slowly up around her as her feet touched the ground.

"Another fake," a man said.

"What do we do?"

"Let her in," Avet said.

"How do we know she's safe?" another asked.

"She just a girl," a woman said. "Let her in."

"She's not just a girl," the man retorted. "She just flew through a blizzard to get here."

Muttered agreements.

"She's good," Avet said. "We let her in."

"She is," Bennet said. "We've met her."

Leona climbed on top of a chair. "The soldiers were of great help to our town. We let her in."

The ballerina walked slowly to the door of town hall, then knocked.

"Bennet," Leona said.

"Yes, ma'am." He walked to the door and swung it open. "Welcome back," he said to the girl.

She looked up at him and smiled. He stepped back and welcomed her in with a sweep of his arm. The crowd muttered hellos. The little children excitedly ran to her. None of them had made a new friend in months.

"I like your dress," a girl said.

"I like your white hair," a boy said.

"Yeah, you're pretty," said another, then ran away, giggling.

She nodded and smiled.

Leona walked to her and crouched down to her level. "What's your name, ballerina?"

The girl smiled.

"We couldn't get her to speak in Lovell, either," Bennet said.

The ballerina's fingers twitched violently, followed by her lips and tongue. When the twitching stopped, she stood up straight and opened her mouth. "I come with a warning, and a message of hope."

Bennet raised his eyebrows. Was this the same girl?

Leona pointed to the chair she'd been standing on. "Hop up there, Ballerina. Tell us what you have to say."

"She's just a kid," someone hollered.

"She's cut from the same cloth as Madame President and the others," Leona said. "We're going to listen to what she has to tell us."

The girl climbed onto the chair and spoke in a calming, singsong voice. "Those who sent the planes. They're sending more. Their goal is to reverse the damage they've done, but it won't work. It will make things worse. Prepare for the worst."

Pole pushed to the front of the crowd. "Who is it? Tell us and maybe we can stop them. Hold them accountable."

The girl gave Pole a blank stare. "I'm just a messenger. That's all they told me."

Bennet sighed and shook his head. They were already prepared for the worst. "How should we prepare?" Bennet asked.

"Be prepared to stay indoors. For a *long* time," she said.

"Wait." A man pushed past Pole, standing a foot from the girl. "You have to know more. Who the *hell* are they? Don't give a bullshit answer."

"I do not know."

The man moved as if to grab her, but she flickered away, then reappeared near the children. She reached into her pocket and pulled out a toy tree.

"Tree!" a young boy squealed.

She set it on the floor, then pulled tree after tree out of her pocket, laying each on the floor. As the miniature forest grew, the children began playing among the toy trees. They carefully stepped over them, placing each foot on the ground, spinning and stepping as though dancing in a forest.

The ballerina joined them. Her skirt twirled out as she spun, sending an invisible warmth that spread out and into everyone. The warmth swirled around Bennet, a moving blanket of comfort and peace. He smiled at the feeling, but also at the pure and innocent joy of the playing children.

"They're our hope," he whispered.

The adults slowly scattered around the rooms of town hall, leaving the children to their play.

***

Avet sat up on his sleeping mat, stretching his aching shoulder. It felt like it might be infected, but he knew they were low on antibiotics already and didn't want take any for himself unless he had to.

He looked down at Claw, asleep and snoring. Claw had always wanted to adopt a child, had insisted Avet would be a great father. For the first time, Avet saw the same vision Claw did. Watching the children play carelessly showed him a side of humanity that he'd since forgotten: purity.

Not purity in the sense of perfect, but the purity of naturalness. He'd been through hell over and over and had let it suck his original nature away, a nature of calm, peace and wonder. Could he return to that state? After all he'd done, was that even likely?

Images flashed through his mind. All the lives he'd taken—directly and indirectly. The child dying in his arms after he killed the doctors who were trying to save him. He looked back at Claw. Maybe he should tell him about the boy. Maybe in the telling of it he could get rid of some of the stain it'd left on his mind. But not now. No, he wouldn't wake Claw for that.

With a sigh and another stretch of his shoulder, Avet stood up. He stepped over a few other sleeping bodies, then opened a door and walked into the lobby. A few other sleepless souls sat or paced back and forth. Some alone and silent, others whispering in groups of two or three.

Gella and Cylindra stood side by side, silently staring out a window. Avet squeezed between them and leaned on the windowsill. Cylindra rested her head on his good shoulder and Gella stared at a string wrapped around her left ring finger.

"Pick a date yet?" Avet asked.

"I don't even know what date it is," Gella said. "The sooner, the better."

"Can't wait to be with him, huh?" Avet said.

Cylindra elbowed his ribs.

"Ow!"

"No," Gella said. "So we can do it before one of us dies."

Avet glanced at her then looked back out the window. The wind had stopped, but a gentle snow continued to fall. The top inch of a sedan peaked above the pile of white powder.

A sharp pain stabbed Avet's shoulder and he winced.

"Hey, you okay?" Cylindra asked.

Avet nodded. "Yeah, good. Shoulder's just sore still. What about tomorrow?"

"What?"

"Gella, why not get married tomorrow?"

Gella laughed. "And honeymoon where? The entire town is stuck in this building."

Avet kept his gaze focused outside. "Like you said. Life is short. And I've never seen Ben happier."

Gella smiled. "Of course he is. He's with me."

Avet laughed, then turned to look at her. "Seriously, Gella. The world is literally dying, but with you my brother is the happiest he's ever been."

Gella nodded. "Thank you, Avet. But really, how would we do a wedding now, with all this shit?"

"I think," Cylindra said, "shitty times are the best times for weddings."

"Maybe you're right," Gella said.

Avet agreed, but for the first time he noticed a painful loneliness in his sister's eyes. She didn't have anyone besides her family. And he knew she loved them, but everyone needed someone. Didn't they?

Gella and Cylindra left. Avet blew out a breath and gripped his shoulder. Something wasn't right. He'd have to swallow his pride and have a doctor look at it.

Soon, he thought. *Don't want to wake her up.* But he could wake up Claw, now that there was a wedding to plan. Planning weddings wasn't something Claw exactly enjoyed, but it was something he was good at. *I should tell him about my shoulder,* he thought. He shook his head. No, his shoulder could wait. It was time to get things ready for his brother's wedding.

***

"Tomorrow?" Leona asked. "You're getting married *tomorrow*?"

Bennet wrapped his arm around Gella and nodded. "Why the hell not? We could all die any minute."

Leona looked out the window of her office, taking in the white, lifeless Earth. "But that's always been true," she said.

"But now it's more *real*," Bennet said.

Leona looked back to her son. "I get that. But you don't get married because you're afraid you'll die soon. You do it for love and commitment."

"We are," Gella said. "We really are. We're just doing is so soon because we want to be married before anything can happen."

Leona smiled. She knew they loved each other and that they'd be good together. "Okay. Don't expect anything fancy."

Gella and Bennet laughed softly.

Leona wrapped an arm around each of them and pulled them in for a hug. The world was falling apart. Life was harder than it had ever been. Still, she didn't want it to end. If she could, she'd make it last forever.

She let go. "I love both of you."

"I love you, Mom."

"Love you too."

Leona smiled as the two left her office, leaving the door open. She barely got the chance to breathe before Clawman walked in.

"Hey," she said with a smile. "How's the wedding planning?"

"I don't know why Avet volunteers me for this stuff." Claw shook his head. "It's a gay stereotype, you know. And I don't like it."

"But you are good at it," Leona said.

Claw shrugged. "Yeah. At least this one was easy. No invites to send out. No gift registry. Bennet and Gella insisted we stick to the daily rations. They don't want to waste anything."

"Makes sense," Leona said. "So what've you been doing?"

"Making sure we have enough chairs."

Leona stared at him. "That's it?"

"Basically, yeah."

"Who's performing the ceremony?" Leona asked.

Claw smiled. "Mother Goose and Mother Hen are arm wrestling for it."

"Who?"

"Right, sorry," Claw said. "The two reverend moms."

"Reverend Mothers," Leona corrected, then laughed. "Of course they would."

"You know what's funny about weddings?"

Leona shook her head.

"None of you have ever talked about church or religion. Not more than just philosophizing, at least. But then two people get married and you get a preacher to do it. You could just as well use a judge. Or probably the mayor."

"I don't want to officiate the wedding," Leona said. "But you've got a point. Interesting how tradition lasts, isn't it?"

Claw shrugged.

"No, think about it. We're using a religious leader out of tradition. And sure, if the world was still normal it wouldn't surprise me if Bennet and Gella had someone non-traditional marry them. Why do you think they decided to stick with tradition?"

"Tradition can be good, I guess," Claw said.

Leona nodded. "Right. I think, in times of intense struggle, tradition can ground us. Bring a sense of safety and community."

"But tradition's held humanity back, too. Traditionally, marriage was only between a man and a woman. Look what that did to the mental state of millions who didn't fit that mold."

"That's true, Claw. Very true. But a marriage between two people, regardless of gender, is a tradition that I think brings a sense of hope for the future. I think that's really why they chose to get married."

Claw raised his eyebrows. "They're getting married to give the town hope?"

"Yes," Leona said. "And themselves."

Claw took a deep breath and blew it out. "All right, then. See you at the wedding."

"Yeah. Thanks, Claw."

He walked out slowly, stopped at the door as if he wanted to say something else, then left.

Leona smiled. Her son, getting married. *Yes,* she thought. *The world's gone to shit. But I still want to live in it.*

Chapter 37

Tashon existed, yet was aware of nothing but that simple fact. He drifted through a river of other existences, each a drop of water in the vast cosmos. He knew not his name, neither his history. Whether he was, or had been, human, plant, animal or stone. Each moment was the only moment, and each moment was every moment. And in all of those moments, each drop of water was wholly connected. Not one was alone or independent.

All he knew was a contented peace in that connection. Flowing in the river of existence as a part of existence itself. Nothing else mattered, yet every drop mattered. He was none of them, yet all of them. On he went, knowing each moment as the only moment, as all moments.

Then a new moment burst into his consciousness. A screeching, terrified cry burst into the river and split the ground beneath the water in two. The water poured out, drop separating from drop. Tashon slowly returned to conscious awareness, and opened his eyes.

With a dry, cracking voice he said, "We're here."

"Yeah, I see it," Jonstin said.

Ishlea set Tashon on the ground, and the three looked into the third dimension. Below, a planet hung in the blackness, dying and crying in terrified pain.

"Jonstin," Tashon choked the words out. "Is that Earth?"

Jonstin's form trembled. *"It is."*

***

His planet, dying. Even when he lived on the Ship of Nations, and after that on Aethera, Jonstin had always considered Earth to be his home. He stared at the grayness of the continents. At the lack of electricity. Here and there people starved, fought and died. Then in other places, hope seemed stronger. Groups of people banded together, doing their best to survive.

But as far as Jonstin could tell, it was a losing battle. There was no way humanity would survive this. And how did Tashon expect to do anything about it?

"Earth is crying?" Jonstin asked.

Tashon nodded softly, too exhausted and starved to show surprise or despair.

"You need to get down there," Ishlea said. "Before you die."

Tashon nodded again, closed his eyes and lay down. Then he popped out of the Fourth, dropping to the Third in a small town covered in deep snow.

"*I hope someone will help him,*" Ishlea said.

"*Me too.*"

"*You think he can do anything to help Earth?*"

"*I don't think anyone can,*" Jonstin said.

***

"I now pronounce you husband and wife," Reverend Yinsey said. "You may now kiss your bride."

Bennet wrapped an arm around Gella's waist and pulled her in, pressing his lips against hers. The large meeting room erupted in cheers. The newly married couple clasped hands as they walked down the aisle, flaunting their wedding outfits of jeans and matching T-shirts. Elated and laughing, they pushed the back door open and stumbled into the lobby.

Gella gasped as the door swung shut behind them.

"What? You just realize who you married?" Bennet asked.

Gella pointed at the window. "Look."

In the falling snow at the bottom of the steps a young man crouched on all fours, stark naked and shivering. Bennet ran forward and stumbled into the frigid wind. He moved swiftly yet carefully down the steps and stopped at the naked man's side.

"Can you stand?" Bennet asked.

He showed no indication that he'd heard Bennet, or was even aware of his presence.

Bennet crouched down and wrapped his arms around his waist. "Oh, shit."

The young man was starved, nothing but skin and bones. Bennet lifted him up, cradling him in his arms like an infant. He turned and hustled back up the steps. The door swung open for him as he neared it, and arms pulled the shivering body away from him as he ran inside.

"Who is he?"

"Is he dead?"

"Is he human?"

Questions swirled around until Leona told everyone to be quiet and step back so that Doctor Ronsie could examine the newcomer.

"Put him down, gently." Doctor Ronsie knelt by the skeletal body, taking every possible vital sign. "Alive. Barely alive."

"Can we save him?" Leona asked.

Doctor Ronsie nodded. "Someone grab my med box. Quickly!"

A teen boy sprinted away.

Doctor Ronsie leaned into to the vacant face. "Can you hear me?"

He gasped and coughed, but said nothing.

The doctor picked her head up. "Is the ballerina around?"

Still in her pink dress, the ballerina leaped over the crowd and floated to the ground next to the doctor.

"Is he like you?" Doctor Ronsie asked.

The ballerina touched his forehead, then his chest. She looked at the doctor and shook her head.

"Human, then," Doctor Ronsie said.

The boy returned with her med box. She opened it, pressed buttons and retrieved multiple items. A portable IV pump, along with water and vitamins. She dumped these into the pump, which would drip the liquid into the young man's body the same as if it had been suspended above him. Then she got an alcohol swab and a needle. She stuck him in his vein on the first try and quickly connected it to the pump.

"How long 'til we know if he's okay?" Bennet asked.

"He'll be okay," Doctor Ronsie said. "But until he can talk to us? No idea. I'd say at least a day."

"Put him in my office," Leona said. "I want someone keeping an eye on him at all times. I want to trust him, but we don't know who he is."

Bennet picked up the limp body as Gella grabbed the med box. They followed Leona to her office and placed it near the far wall, behind the desk.

"Memorable honeymoon," Leona said.

Bennet smiled and shook his head. "I just hope we have plenty of years left to remember it."

"Shut up," Gella said. "We'll have plenty of time."

"You will," Leona said.

Bennet nodded and swallowed a sob. "Okay," he said. "Okay."

Gella grabbed his hand. "Let's go start that honeymoon."

Bennet smiled nervously. "Yeah, sounds great."

They turned and rushed from the office.

***

Avet stood outside town hall at the top of the stairs, soaking in the first rays of the morning sun. The clouds were gone, and the snow finally ceased falling. He took a deep breath and blew it out, watching the white cloud his breath made in the cold air.

His shoulder still ached, and sweat lined his forehead despite the cold. But he'd deal with that later. Doctor Ronsie was working on the naked man.

Avet shook his head at that thought. Who the hell was he? Where did he come from? According to the ballerina, he was human. And everyone seemed to readily accept that fact. True, Doctor Ronsie agreed after a quick examination. Also true that he hadn't flickered in and out of sight like the soldiers did.

The ballerina popped into the air next to him, then reached out and grabbed his hand. The gesture made him realize, human or not human, it didn't matter. What mattered was whether the unconscious newcomer would be good for their town, or not.

He closed his eyes for a few breaths, a soft smile on his lips. When he opened them, ships were on the horizon.

"Damn it." He let go of the girl's hand and ran inside. "Hey! The ships are back."

Chaos erupted. People yelled or cried. Some went silent, cowering in corners or under desks. Others ran to the windows, staring in wide-eyed terror as they took in the sight of the ships that had killed their planet.

"Shit."

"We're all dead."

"Hell, hell, hell."

The ships grew nearer, their shapes coming into clear focus. This time, it wasn't a purple dust that spilled from them, but small, glowing spheres. They came in every color, and floated down with the grace of snowflakes. Each one that landed melted a circle of snow a few inches across, then stopped glowing.

Avet looked for the ballerina. She walked through the crowd as if floating, then hopped onto a chair. She let out one crisp note, and everyone went silent, staring at her.

"You can survive this." She started flickering. "But...ing to g...gerous...lo...care...." She flickered once more, and disappeared.

The End

ACKNOWLEDGEMENTS

Thank you to the divine, in whatever form they may exist. Thank you to my beautiful wife and best friend, Meaghan. Thanks to my parents, and all my wonderful family. Thanks to Luke Dylan Ramsey; this series would not be what it is without his aid and insight. Thank you to Carol Powell and Josh Allen, the two best writing teachers I could have ever asked for. Many thanks to Dave Lane (aka Lane Diamond) of Evolved Publishing for believing in this series as much as I do. Thank you to my editor, Becky Stephens, and to Cindy Fan for providing the phenomenal cover art. And lastly, thank you, reader, for taking the time to read this book. I hope you join me again as this journey continues.

ABOUT THE AUTHOR

Author J.S. Sherwood has a passion for stories that show the existence of peace and beauty even in the darkest of times. He spent many years teaching English at the junior high, high school, and college levels, and now brings that love of great writing to bear in his own books.

When he isn't reading or writing, he's spending time with his wife, five kids, and two dogs in Arizona. Most likely they're outside, soaking up the fresh air and sunshine.

For more, please visit J.S. Sherwood online at:
Website: www.WorldsByJSSherwood.com
Goodreads: J.S. Sherwood
Facebook: @js.sherwood.7
Twitter: @SciFiSherwood

WHAT'S NEXT?

J.S. Sherwood is hard at work on the rest of the "This Foreign Universe" series, through Book 9. Please stay tuned to developments and plans by subscribing to our newsletter at the link below.

www.EvolvedPub.com/Newsletter

MORE FROM EVOLVED PUBLISHING

We offer great books across multiple genres, featuring high-quality editing (which we believe is second-to-none) and fantastic covers.

As a hybrid small press, your support as loyal readers is so important to us, and we have strived, with tireless dedication and sheer determination, to deliver on the promise of our motto:
QUALITY IS PRIORITY #1!

Please check out all of our great books, which you can find at this link:
www.EvolvedPub.com/Catalog/

Thank you!

CPSIA information can be obtained
at www.ICGtesting.com
Printed in the USA
BVHW031519120223
658285BV00006B/1320